SHADOWS REEL

C.J. Box is the author of twenty-two Joe
Pickett novels, five stand-alone novels, and a
story collection. He has won Edgar, Anthony,
Macavity, Gumshoe, and Barry Awards, as
well as the French Prix Calibre .38, and has
been a *Los Angeles Times* Book Prize finalist. A
Wyoming native, Box has also worked on a
ranch and as a small-town newspaper reporter
and editor. He lives outside Cheyenne with
his family. His books have been translated into
twenty-seven languages.

Follow him on @cjboxauthor and cjbox.net

BY C.J. BOX

THE JOE PICKETT NOVELS

Open Season

Savage Run

Winterkill

Trophy Hunt

Out of Range

In Plain Sight

Free Fire

Blood Trail

Below Zero

Nowhere to Run

Cold Wind

Force of Nature

Breaking Point

Stone Cold

Endangered

Off the Grid

Vicious Circle

The Disappeared

Wolf Pack

Long Range

Dark Sky

THE STAND-ALONE NOVELS

Blue Heaven

Three Weeks to Say Goodbye

SHORT FICTION

Shots Fired: Stories from Joe Pickett Country

THE CASSIE DEWELL NOVELS

Back of Beyond

The Highway

Badlands

Paradise Valley

The Bitterroots

Treasure State

SHADOWS REEL

C.J. BOX

HEAD of ZEUS

An Aries Book

First published in the UK in 2022 by Head of Zeus Ltd
This paperback edition first published in 2022 by Head of Zeus Ltd,
part of Bloomsbury Publishing Plc

Published by arrangement with G. P. Putnam's Sons, an imprint of
Penguin Publishing, a division of Penguin Random House LLC

9 7 5 3 1 2 4 6 8

A catalogue record for this book is available from the British Library.

ISBN (PB): 9781803283944
ISBN (E): 9781803283906

Section photograph by Philip Bird LRPS CPAGB / Shutterstock.com

Printed and bound in Great Britian by
CPI Group (UK) Ltd, Croydon, CR0 4YY

Head of Zeus Ltd
5–8 Hardwick Street
London EC1R 4RG

WWW.HEADOFZEUS.COM

For Laurie,

always

Turning and turning in the widening gyre
The falcon cannot hear the falconer;
Things fall apart; the centre cannot hold;
Mere anarchy is loosed upon the world.

—William Butler Yeats,
"The Second Coming"

WEDNESDAY, NOVEMBER 23

The blood-dimmed tide is loosed, and everywhere The ceremony of innocence is drowned.

—William Butler Yeats, "The Second Coming"

CHAPTER ONE

The Moose That Wasn't

LORNE TRUMLEY HAD CALLED DISPATCH TO REPORT A DEAD moose on his ranch. Since it was two weeks after the close of moose-hunting season in the Bighorn Mountains of Wyoming, Joe Pickett had responded.

He slowed down and then stopped his green Ford F-150 pickup in front of the closed barbed-wire gate. Engine running, he limped out and approached it, all the while keeping his eye on several Black Angus cattle who had poked their heads out of a seven-foot stand of willows to stare dumbly at him. Even though he was moving slower than usual, Joe was able to open the gate, drive through, and close it again before the spark of a bovine thought—*We can run out on the road!*—slowly worked its way through the cows' brains. By the time they'd realize their escape was possible, it would be too late.

He grunted as he dropped the iron loop over the top of the gatepost and levered it closed. Most of the muscles in his body still hurt, and he had stitches in his back and thighs from an encounter with a wolverine.

He wished old Lorne Trumley would replace the ancient wire gate and install a cattle guard at the entrance to his place. It was unlikely, though. Lorne was in his eighties, and like a lot of longtime local ranchers, he only fixed things for good after they'd been repaired so many times there was nothing left of them. And the three-strand gate still worked, sort of.

Joe winced as he pulled himself back into the cab. His Labrador, Daisy, scooted toward him on the front seat and placed her heavy head on his lap, as if offering sympathy for his infirmities.

He patted Daisy's head and eased down the worn two-track road that would take him to Lorne's home.

"Thanks, old girl," he said to her.

As he drove by, the cattle finally leaped to action and charged past him toward the closed gate. Yup, too late.

Lorne Trumley's Crazy Z-Bar Ranch was a fourth-generation holding spread over lush, unique landscape six miles west of the town of Winchester. It was largely a glacial river bottom, and the north branch of the Twelve Sleep River did a series of lazy S-curves through it, providing a version of a natural irrigation ditch. Trumley raised cattle and grew hay, and because of the river branch there was plenty of water, which was a rarity in the valley. The water sustained thick, tall stands of willow and knotty brush that divided the ranch land as if by windrows. It was a geothermal area as well, with warm-water seeps and heated quicksand that steamed in the winter.

The name of the ranch had nothing to do with the ownership or history of the place. "Crazy Z-Bar" was just a description of the brand used on its cattle: the letter Z tilted forty-five degrees to the left over a single line.

Joe knew from experience that the Crazy Z-Bar was a good place not to get stuck. The first time he'd come out to talk to Trumley about a change in hunting regulations, he'd mired his pickup in quicksand and had to walk the rest of the way to the house. After delivering a lecture about the big-game biologists in Joe's agency knowing absolutely nothing about anything and any change in the hunting seasons would be foolish as hell, the rancher had followed Joe back to his pickup in a tractor and pulled him out.

It was a cool day and the sky was close. The summits of the Bighorn Mountains were shrouded with cloud cover. Joe looked at the digital temperature display on his dashboard: forty-two degrees.

FOR JOE, IT FELT GOOD to go back to work that morning after lolling around his house for too many days. It felt right to him to pull on his red uniform shirt and pin on his badge and J. PICKETT, GAME WARDEN nameplate. It even felt right to buckle on his holster and .40 Glock semiauto.

Marybeth had told him a strange story that morning. He pushed it to the back of his mind for now.

WHILE RECOVERING, he'd used part of his time to thoroughly clean out his pickup. He'd done a lot of the things he'd always promised to do when he "had the time." He'd repaired his equipment and repacked his extra clothing. His weapons were all cleaned and oiled, and the console box of maps, ticket books, notebooks, and agency bulletins had all been organized and replaced. He'd vacuumed Daisy's dog hair off his bench seat and power-washed the floor mats.

It was as if he were driving a new pickup, he thought. He wondered how long it would last.

ALTHOUGH HE HAD the business about the moose to take care of first, Joe looked forward to seeing all of his girls together in their house for Thanksgiving. It would be strange, since the family had their history and memories in another state-owned home that had been burned to the ground and not at the newer, much nicer residence on the bank of the Twelve Sleep River. It was unfair to his girls, he thought, that there were now more rooms and more space than there'd ever been when the three of them were growing up.

Although Sheridan stopped by often—not often enough for her mother—April and Lucy had been to the new place infrequently, and separately, depending on their schedules. This wasn't really their home—it was the place where their parents now lived.

With Lucy bringing a friend along and the added presence of Liv Romanowski and her baby daughter, Kestrel, Marybeth was organizing a fairly large Thanksgiving meal and weekend. No doubt, she'd already determined who got which room to avoid conflict and how the seating at the table would be assigned. Joe's job, he knew, was simply to be available.

He was good at that.

Joe hoped Liv would have news about Nate Romanowski, her husband and Joe's longtime friend. Nate was away, following the trail of an outlaw falconer named Axel Soledad, who had beaten up Liv, threatened baby Kestrel, and stolen Nate's falcons. Nate had left in a black rage and Joe hoped he could recover his Air Force without leaving a body count. But Joe knew Nate all too well, and he feared for what could happen.

WITH SO MUCH on his mind that morning, he was grateful for the distraction when Lorne shambled out of his old house and waved hello. Joe pulled into the overgrown ranch yard and parked next to a muddy ATV bristling with irrigation shovels strapped down by bungee cords. The butt end of a lever-action carbine poked out of a leather saddle scabbard.

"Hey, Joe," Lorne said.

"Hey, Lorne."

Trumley looked like a piece of jerky that happened to be

wearing an oversized flannel shirt, a Carhartt vest, and baggy jeans cinched by a belt with a rodeo buckle so ancient and smoothed off, the engraving had vanished. His short-brimmed cowboy hat was stained and battered and it gave his appearance a comical framing.

He raised his arm and pointed vaguely over Joe's shoulder. "That way," he said. "Just look for the birds."

"When did you find the moose?" Joe asked.

"This morning. I was looking for a couple of missing heifers and I seen it across the swamp. It isn't very far from the edge of my property." He pronounced it *prop-ity*.

"Did you hear any shots?"

"I don't hear much of nothin' these days."

"Is it a bull or a cow? Could you tell?"

"I don't know. I just know it was black like a moose. Too dark for an elk and not one of my cows."

Joe asked, "Can I get there in my truck?"

"If you try, you'll get stuck again, would be my guess."

"Can I borrow your Ranger?" Joe asked, chinning toward the ATV. He had one back at his game warden station, but it would take a few hours to drive there, load it on a trailer, and return.

"Be careful with it," Trumley cautioned. "My other one's broke down."

Joe nodded.

"Just follow my tracks through the meadow and you *should* be okay."

———

JUST LOOK FOR THE BIRDS, Trumley had said. Joe understood. Predatory birds like ravens and crows were always the first on the scene of a carcass. Birds of prey, like eagles and falcons, would show up next. Larger predators would follow their lead, and scuttling armies of insects would later mop up.

Daisy loped alongside the ATV as he drove in Trumley's tracks across the meadow, through ditches, and via openings in the hedgerow brush. Several of the openings would have been too narrow for his pickup, and on either side of the high ground where Trumley had traveled was soft mud and hidden swamp. Daisy liked to splash through it, and she gave chase—for half a minute—to a pair of mallards she'd flushed.

Before leaving the ranch, Joe had secured his necropsy kit in the bed of the Ranger, plus his twelve-gauge Remington Wingmaster shotgun, which was primarily for safety if the poachers were still about. He'd also thrown in a heavy chain and nylon towrope.

After photographing the scene and looking for evidence like spent brass casings or boot prints, he would likely have to drag the carcass out behind the ATV to perform the necropsy and find out how it had been killed. If the animal had been shot, he'd attempt to locate the bullet. More often than not, the projectile would be located beneath the skin of the hide on the opposite side of the entry wound.

Moose season had closed. It was a special permit area, so he knew from experience that it was unlikely a moose hunter with a legitimate license had been involved in the poaching incident. The violator—if there was one—was probably an elk hunter who'd chosen the wrong species, or an out-and-out outlaw who wanted to kill a moose out of season. Which made his blood boil.

EVEN BEFORE HE SAW the birds gathering near a stand of thick willows up ahead, he caught the whiff of what smelled like burned pork. Daisy noticed it, too, and out of the corner of his eye he saw her stop and raise her snout in the air.

Joe rounded a knot of brush and saw a high-grass swamp between him and the birds. It was as far as Trumley had traveled that morning—the ATV tracks stopped short before attempting to cross the bog.

As Trumley had described, a dark and heavy form was on the ground beneath an overhang of thick brush on the other side of the swamp beyond the clearing. Parts of it appeared to be smoldering and wisps of steam or smoke rose from the upper part. Despite that, ravens covered it and fought off newcomers to the scene. Several let out shrill cries.

He stopped the ATV at the swamp edge and dug his binoculars out of his gear bag. Although the idling engine made his field of vision tremble, he zoomed in on the form and sharpened the focus.

The first thing he noticed made him draw a sharp intake of breath.

The body was black and charred and curled up beneath the overhang. Two rows of white teeth, human teeth, appeared bright and almost electrified from the lower part of the skull. The lips were either burned away or eaten off by the ravens.

An arm stuck out from the body as if reaching out for help that didn't come. Three of the five fingers had already been cleaned of flesh to the bone by the ravens. A fire-blackened silver wristwatch hung loosely from the carpal joints.

Joe felt his stomach clench and his body go cold.

It wasn't a moose that Lorne Trumley had found on the edge of his property.

CHAPTER TWO

Joe and the Body

"WHAT DO YOU MEAN, *BURNED*?" SHERIFF SCOTT TIBBS ASKED Joe as they drove Trumley's Ranger from the ranch house on the same ATV tracks Joe had used earlier.

"I mean burned," Joe said over the sound of the engine. In order to hear each other, each man had to lean toward the other.

"Like he stepped in that thermal water?" Tibbs asked. "I heard there were hot springs out here."

"There are," Joe said. "But no, like he caught on fire."

"Well, I'll be a son of a bitch," Tibbs said, reaching up to clamp his hat tight on his head. "This I got to see."

IT WAS AN HOUR after Joe had discovered the body and called Tibbs directly on his cell phone. Tibbs had driven his own Twelve Sleep County Sheriff's Department SUV to the Trumley ranch, followed by Deputy Ryan Steck and rookie officer Tom Bass. Joe had left Steck and Bass to mill around in the ranch yard with Trumley because the Ranger was the only vehicle they could use to access the crime scene. Forensics tech Gary Norwood was also on his way from town, as well as another deputy, who'd been ordered to tow a trailer with two additional ATVs chained on its bed.

Tibbs had been the sheriff for only a few months, after being talked out of retirement in Buffalo by the local county commissioners. He was portly and folksy with a thick white mustache, and jowls that trembled with the vibration of the Ranger. He still wasn't settled into his new job, and since he had started, events had come at him like water from a fire hose. First the mayhem in the Bighorn Mountains, and now this. Joe felt sorry for him, because there was no way Tibbs had had the time yet to get his bearings in the new county. Locals were already starting to question his competence and ability.

Joe was also well aware that most of the trouble Tibbs had encountered involved . . . Joe. He guessed that Tibbs had probably cringed when he saw who was calling, and Joe couldn't really blame him.

"Do you know who the victim is?" Tibbs asked. "Is he local? You know a hell of a lot more people around here than I do."

"I don't even know if it's a he," Joe replied. "I didn't get close enough to identify him or her."

"You didn't touch the body or tramp around the location, did you?"

"I didn't even cross the swamp. I called you as soon as I found it."

"That was the right decision," Tibbs said. "I know you have a reputation for inserting yourself into sheriff's department business where a game warden doesn't belong."

"Who told you that?" Joe asked.

"It's well known."

Joe didn't think it was the right time and occasion to defend himself, so he bit his tongue. Since he'd been assigned to the Saddlestring District nearly twenty years before, there had been exactly one good sheriff who'd done his job well: Mike Reed. He'd also been Joe's friend. All the other county sheriffs had been corrupt, incompetent, or both. The last one, Brendan Kapelow, had falsified his résumé and vanished when the lie was discovered. So *of course* Joe had involved himself in investigations even though he often wasn't wanted.

Tibbs shouted, "You described the body as 'still smoldering' when you found it."

"Yup."

"How long has it been there, do you think?"

"I don't know, but I'd guess just a few hours. The birds were just getting started."

"Are you sure he's deceased?" Tibbs asked.

"Has to be," Joe said. "There was absolutely no movement."

Despite his answer, though, the question felt like a knife thrust into his belly. He hadn't even considered that the person could still be alive. The body was burned beyond recognition, being fed on by predator birds, but still, the thought of him leaving a suffering human being was sickening. He wished he had checked on the victim before calling Tibbs, even though Tibbs would have chided him for contaminating the scene.

"I remember reading an article about how some people spontaneously combust," Tibbs said. "Do you believe something like that can actually happen? You're walking along minding your own business and then *poof,* you realize you're on fire?"

"I don't know," Joe said. He was still reeling from the fact that Tibbs had even *assumed* Joe was the kind of man to leave a victim to die. He prayed he hadn't screwed up like that.

"Maybe it's an accident of some kind," Tibbs said. "Or a suicide."

Joe didn't respond.

Tibbs craned around to look into the bed of the Ranger.

"I just wanted to make sure I brought the evidence bag," he said. "I'm kind of out of practice, you know. You'd think after the number of bodies we found a while back up in the mountains, I'd be more on my game. Do you leave a pile of dead men everywhere you go?"

"I do not," Joe said defensively.

"Could have fooled me," Tibbs said.

Joe wheeled through the opening in the willows and braked to a stop in the place he'd parked before. The body was still where he'd spotted it and it appeared to be in the same position. The biggest difference was that two bald eagles had scared away the ravens from the torso and they looked up and stared at the arrival of Joe and the sheriff with cool disdain in their unblinking eyes.

Tibbs swung out and fired his service handgun twice into the air.

"*Now git, you birds!*" he shouted.

The eagles rose with ungainly flaps of their huge wings and they struggled above the height of the willows. One of them had a long red strip of flesh in its hooked beak. The other issued a piercing *Skree*.

THE SHERIFF'S RADIO squawked to life and Deputy Steck's voice came through clearly. "Boss, is everything all right out there? We heard the shots."

"Everything's fine," Tibbs reported back. "I was just chasing off some birds." Then Tibbs reconsidered. He said, "No, it's not *all* fine. We've got a situation."

Tibbs holstered his weapon while shaking his head. "Good thing you didn't find it tomorrow," he told Joe. "There wouldn't be much of a body left."

Joe agreed, although he was still unsettled by the possibility—however remote—that the person could have still been breathing when he'd left.

"Can we get across that swamp?" Tibbs asked.

"We can try."

The sheriff started to lumber back to the four-wheeler, but stopped short and stared down at something near his feet.

"There's something strange here in the grass," he said. "Like chunks of food."

Joe flushed. "That's where I threw up."

"Oh."

"HOLD ON," Joe said as he clicked the four-wheel-drive toggle on the dashboard and jammed his boot on the accelerator. The ATV jerked forward and plumes of muddy water shot up from the tires on both sides. Tibbs clutched the handhold over his head on the frame of the Ranger and turned toward Joe so he wouldn't get splashed in the face.

Joe felt the four-wheeler slip to the side until the treads gripped, and he kept it floored as they bucked through the swamp. He hoped his momentum would carry them across before he got bogged down. Dirty water covered the plastic windshield and the wipers couldn't keep up to clear it, so Joe leaned out of the cab to make sure they were headed in the right direction. Not until they were twenty feet from the victim did the treads really dig in, and they lurched up onto dry ground.

The burned-meat smell was much stronger now and Joe could see that the eagles had done some real damage to the victim's face and underbelly. He felt like getting sick again, but he swallowed hard and clamped his jaws together to try to stave it off.

"Damn, you were right," Tibbs said with awe as he took in the scene. He surveyed the brush and grass beneath them. "Nothing else looks like it caught on fire around here. Just this poor thing. What in the hell happened?"

"Don't know," Joe said as he removed his Stetson and slid a fly-fishing buff over his nose and mouth.

"Maybe lightning?" Tibbs speculated.

"In November?" Joe asked.

"Good point."

Tibbs pulled on a pair of black nitrile gloves and approached the body. He held his breath and reached down to touch the victim's throat.

"Dead for sure," he said. He looked up at Joe. "Been dead for a while, I'd say. At least a few hours, like you thought. The body is cooling off, but rigor mortis hasn't yet set in."

Joe closed his eyes and sighed with relief. He hadn't left a person to die.

"Our victim is definitely a man," Tibbs said while turning the head to its other side. The victim's face was not completely burned and he wore an inch of gray beard that had not caught fire. A single light blue eye was open and filmed over. Joe noted that the stripped finger bones of the man's outstretched hand were broken, but not detached. That seemed incongruous to the state of the body.

Although Joe couldn't yet place him, there was something familiar about the victim.

"Know him?" Tibbs asked.

"I think so. It'll come to me."

"When it does, please notify your local sheriff," Tibbs said. Then: "What was he doing out here that got him burned up? I don't see any signs of an accelerant. Who knows—maybe he was welding somewhere, and he had an accident?"

They were rhetorical questions Joe couldn't answer.

"How did he break his fingers?" Joe asked.

"Maybe he fell after he climbed the fence," Tibbs offered.

"Maybe." But the theory didn't jibe with what Joe could see.

"Was he out here hunting?" Tibbs asked as he groaned his way to full height.

Joe looked around for a hunting rifle or any other evidence to suggest why the victim was located there. The man appeared to be wearing slippers or light shoes, not hunting boots. But it was difficult to tell exactly what his footwear consisted of because they were burned and had melted into the skin of his feet.

The *prop-ity* line was marked by a taut four-strand barbed-wire fence mounted to T-posts just behind the brush where the body was curled up. Trumley, Joe knew, was a stickler for a good tight fence. On the other side was an ancient overgrown two-track road. He could see that the grass in the ruts was pressed down.

Joe said, "Look at that top strand of wire."

Tibbs did so and saw bits of burned clothing and skin hanging from the barbs.

Joe said, "I'm thinking he either climbed the fence and died here or he got tossed over it from the other side."

Tibbs grunted, apparently agreeing with the theory. "Don't touch anything," he said.

"You don't need to tell me that. There was a vehicle on that road," Joe said. "The tire tracks look fresh."

"I see that," Tibbs said. "I'll get Norwood to climb the fence and take a good look at that road. We might be able to find a tread pattern.

"But who would do such a thing?" he asked. "And why?"

"Maybe they thought the predators would clean it up before anyone found the body," Joe said. "Like you said, it wouldn't take very long. It's lucky for us that Lorne just happened to come this way this morning. Otherwise, that body could have been there for the entire winter before anyone noticed it, if they ever did."

"Which suggests some planning," Tibbs said.

He shook his head and moaned. "This is quite a bit worse than I thought it would be."

"Yup."

"Do you think we should question the rancher?"

"Can't hurt," Joe said. "But I'd be surprised he has anything to do with this. If Lorne wanted to hide a body on his own ranch, I'd guess he would find a better place to put it. And he wouldn't call it in."

Tibbs indicated his agreement, but he had a very sour look on his face. Although Joe didn't know him well yet, he surmised that Sheriff Tibbs would much rather make quips during town council meetings and ride in his SUV during the Fourth of July parade than investigate another murder. Not to mention his not-very-secret affair with Ruthanne Hubbard, the sexy and twice-divorced dispatcher.

Joe told Tibbs he would take the Ranger back to the ranch house and turn it over to his deputies so they could join him at the crime scene. He didn't know how long it would take Norwood and the other deputy to arrive with the ATVs.

"What, and just leave me here?" Tibbs asked with alarm.

"Somebody needs to stay and keep the predators away," Joe said. "Besides, you made it real clear this is sheriff's department business. I don't want to get in your way."

Tibbs narrowed his eyes. "Fine. Just call me when you think of the victim's name, even though by then we'll probably know anyway."

Joe nodded and climbed into the Ranger and started it up.

"Tell my guys to hurry," Tibbs said as he dug into his evidence bag for a thick roll of crime scene tape to mark the perimeter of the scene.

"Will do," Joe said.

"This place was described to me as sleepy by your county commissioners," Tibbs said, gesturing around him with the roll of tape to include the entire county.

"Bait and switch," Joe responded.

Then he did a three-point turn and rocketed back through the swamp toward the ranch house. The farther he got from the burned body, the less likely he'd get sick again. But he had no real doubt that the sight and smell of the burned man would stay with him for a long time.

JOE WAS HALFWAY back to the ranch headquarters when Tibbs called.

"Do you know a guy named Bert Kizer?" Tibbs asked.

Then it hit Joe, where he'd seen the victim before. It had been on the Twelve Sleep River. The dead man was rowing a drift boat at the time while two visiting fly fishermen casted streamers toward the banks.

"He's wearing a metal dog tag on a chain around his neck," Tibbs said. "One of those cheap ones. It says: 'Bert Kizer, A-positive.' I guess that means his blood type."

Joe said, "He's a local fishing guide. He's been around this valley for a long time—longer than me. He used to own an outfitting company, but it went belly-up, so now he hires on with other outfits when they need an extra hand. He's a free-lance rent-a-guide. I'm pretty sure he's divorced and lives alone in a shack not all that far from here."

"Do you know much more about him than that?" Tibbs asked.

"Like what?"

"Does he have enemies who could do this to him? Is he in-volved in something that might get him killed?"

"I really don't know much about him," Joe said. "I've seen him on the river a few times when I was fishing. He just nodded and kept rowing. I wouldn't say he was a gregarious guy. Which is unusual, because most guides are real talkers."

"Is there someone we can talk to who might be able to shed a little more light on the situation? Does Kizer have friends or acquaintances we can interview?" Tibbs asked.

"That sounds like a job for the sheriff's department," Joe said. He terminated the call.

"JUST FOLLOW THE TRACKS," Joe said to Deputy Steck, who had climbed behind the wheel of the ATV.

"Why do you get to drive?" Deputy Bass asked Steck.

"Because I'm not the rookie," Steck said.

Joe stifled a smile. Bass was young and fresh-faced with a slight mustache. His uniform was starched and pressed. He looked overeager, and Joe wondered how he'd react when he saw and smelled the victim.

They roared off.

"I told you there was something out there," Trumley said to Joe. "I just wish it would have been a damned moose after all."

Joe turned to him. "Doesn't Bert Kizer live around here?"

"Just up the county road in a shitty little shack. Why do you ask?"

CHAPTER THREE

Bert's Dog

Joe pulled off the road and waved at Norwood and the deputy as they went by, hauling the ATVs to the ranch. He continued on toward the county road. Daisy was curled up in the passenger seat after leaving muddy prints all over the cab. His clean new truck had lasted exactly half a day, he thought.

He could hear Tibbs requesting an ambulance for the body over the mutual aid channel on his radio. Ruthanne, the dispatcher, asked him if everything was all right with him, and Tibbs was terse in his response and deflected the question. He was still playing it coy when it came to their personal relationship, Joe thought. But it was a small town and Tibbs was a public official. Word would eventually get to Mrs. Tibbs, and all hell could break loose.

He hesitated at the junction on the county road. Then

instead of turning right toward the highway and back to Saddlestring, he turned left.

BERT KIZER'S SMALL HOME was two miles from the ranch turnoff and was tucked into an alcove of mature river cottonwoods still blazing yellow and red with fall colors. The visual feast surrounding it made Kizer's place look even more faded and drab than it already was. The structure was a simple ranch-style bungalow covered by unpainted siding. Yellow leaves blanketed the gray roof and covered the small unkempt lawn in the front. A twenty-year-old Dodge Power Wagon was parked on the side of the house. On the other side was a low-profile ClackaCraft drift boat on a trailer covered by a tarp. Next to the drift boat was an NRS river raft. Tools of Bert's trade.

Joe parked in the ditch on the side of the road. He didn't want to drive to the house on the two-track that led to it because he feared driving over and obscuring any recent tire tracks.

He knew he shouldn't go to the scene there before the sheriff and his team arrived, but he had to be sure. This, he thought, was the kind of thing that had gotten him into trouble in the past. Not that it would stop him now.

He walked the sixty yards from his pickup to the house over a carpet of just-fallen yellow leaves. The cool morning made his joints stiff and he limped as he walked from both his recent injuries and the bullet wound in his leg from the year before. It took longer to recover from injuries than it used to, he'd found. It was annoying.

There were no sounds coming from inside, and he noted that the front door was open a crack. Kizer had obviously not taken his truck anywhere. So he was either inside, or . . .

"Bert, are you in there?" Joe called out. "It's Joe Pickett, the game warden." He wanted to give the man plenty of notice that he was trespassing. The last thing he wanted to see play out was for Kizer to step outside his home with a shotgun. Wyoming's Castle Doctrine would render it a justified shooting.

Joe placed his hand on his Glock as he got closer. He called out several more times, and the only response from the shack was when a dog peered at him from around the corner of it. The dog was some kind of mixed breed, tall and willowy with mottled coloring, a long snout, and piercing hazel eyes. It trembled and looked scared and ready to bolt away at any second. Joe didn't feel threatened.

That's when he smelled it: gasoline.

He mounted the wooden porch and called out again. There was no response.

Drawing his weapon, Joe stood to the side of the door. He glanced at the dog to see it had taken a couple of steps toward him, but it was still too wary to come any closer. Then he leaned over and pushed the door all the way open and peered inside.

Although he didn't know Bert Kizer's housekeeping regimen, it was obvious the interior had been wrecked. Side tables and lamps were overturned and a board-and-block bookshelf had been ransacked. A single hardwood chair had been repositioned from the table to stand alone in the middle of the living room. Strips of duct tape hung from the arms and legs.

The facing wall was filled with cheaply framed photos and most of them were askew. There was a younger Bert with a fine 5×5 bull elk, Bert offering a thick twenty-two-inch rainbow trout to the photographer, Bert holding up the severed head of a pronghorn. Two older black-and-white photos showed Bert as a child. In one, he sat on the back of a horse. In the other, he stood thigh-high next to a man with haunted eyes wearing a U.S. Army uniform. His father?

The dining room table was empty except for a long-billed cap that looked as if it had been tossed there haphazardly. A jacket hung from the top of one of the chairs.

On the kitchen counter next to the table were assorted hand tools: a hacksaw, a hammer, pliers, and a DeWalt twenty-volt hand drill armed with a dark-stained bit. Joe knew the drill because he had one exactly like it himself.

Joe didn't go inside because he recognized the scene for what it was and he didn't want to disturb it. The chair, the tape, the tools. Someone had been bound to the chair and tortured.

FEELING QUEASY AGAIN, Joe backed away from the door and stepped off the porch. The dog backpedaled farther away with Joe's every step.

In the distance, Daisy barked at the dog from inside the cab. Daisy didn't like Joe paying attention to any other dogs except Tube, their half-Corgi, half-Labrador at home. The scared dog loped away, and Joe called after it.

When it stopped at his voice, Joe said, "You know what went down here, don't you? You saw it all. I wish you could talk."

The dog simply stared back.

Joe walked around the side of the house to the fenced back-yard.

This was where it had happened.

Two dented gasoline cans lay on their sides. In the middle of the yard was burned grass and blackened leaves.

Joe dug for his cell phone and called Tibbs. The sheriff answered after one ring.

"I'm at Bert Kizer's place up the road. It looks like he was tortured here and dumped where you are. I can't tell if he was alive or dead when they set him on fire."

"Oh my God," Tibbs said. He sounded stunned.

"Don't worry, I didn't go inside," Joe said. "And this is just my working theory after about five minutes of looking around. But the house looks to be a wreck inside and they didn't clean up after themselves. I'm guessing Norwood can find prints and DNA in there."

"Shit, this is awful," Tibbs said.

"I'll stay on the scene until you get here," Joe said.

"Don't let anyone go inside until we do."

Joe punched off. Tibbs was a master of stating the obvious.

TWENTY MINUTES LATER, Sheriff Tibbs paced in the front yard with his cell phone pressed to his face. He'd seen what Joe had seen and he looked harried. Joe understood. The first hour at a newly discovered crime scene was often the most crucial, and that was when every small procedure or decision that later turned out to be clumsy or wrong could be amplified by a sharp defense attorney to imply the investigation had been botched from the beginning. That was why Tibbs was already requesting assistance from the adjoining Shell County Sheriff's Department as well the Wyoming Division of Criminal Investigation (DCI). He was covering his butt, and Joe thought it was smart and the correct way to go.

While Tibbs paced and talked, forensics technician Gary Norwood arrived. He looked almost as harried as the sheriff. They'd all parked out on the county road behind Joe's pickup.

Norwood was in his mid-thirties and was shared by three northern Wyoming counties. He was gangly and balding and Joe noticed he'd taken to wearing glasses full-time. He was already wearing white scrubs and his face mask was pulled down below his chin.

"Processing two crime scenes at once isn't optimal," Norwood complained to Joe.

"Did you get an impression of the tire tracks back at the scene?"

Norwood nodded. "Brand-new, they looked like. Sharp clean edges on the tread."

"Those same tracks might be out on the road to this place," Joe said, pointing.

"Great. I'll get to those as soon as I can."

"That kind of narrows it down to new vehicles in the area—or a new set of tires," Joe said.

There were fewer than a half-dozen shops that sold new tires around there, Joe knew. And only two auto dealerships.

"Correct," Norwood said as he pulled on a pair of puffy white paper booties. "I told the sheriff."

"Any more physical evidence around the body?"

"Not that I could determine. I got called over here before I could do a thorough examination, but I'm pretty sure the body was tossed over the fence by the evidence we located on the top strand. Tossed over like a sack of potatoes, is my guess."

"So he was already gone?" Joe couldn't shake his earlier fears.

Norwood shrugged. "Either that, or he wasn't in any condition to put up much of a struggle.

"I'll do a quick prelim here before I go back," he said. "The real work starts later. I've got to find what I can find outside before the weather changes in both locations."

"You've got a busy day ahead," Joe said.

"No shit. A busy day and night," Norwood said as he handed Joe a pair of booties and Tyvek gloves. "How about you take some notes to save me time?"

Joe glanced at Sheriff Tibbs. The man's back was turned. He knew Tibbs wouldn't approve.

"I'll follow you and stay out of your way," Joe said.

HE SHADOWED NORWOOD, entering the home with his digital recorder in one hand and his cell phone in the other. Joe chose to record Norwood's own words rather than interpret them into his notebook, so he wouldn't misunderstand anything.

Norwood carried his forensics bag and had a Canon EOS digital SLR camera hanging from his neck.

"From the outset, the room is in disarray . . ." Norwood said as he described the scene Joe had observed earlier. He detailed the tools on the kitchen counter and the chair with the tape on it.

"A substance that looks like partially coagulated blood is on the drill bit," Norwood stated as he leaned over and narrowed his eyes at the tool.

"There's also blood stains on the floor around the chair itself and what looks to be arterial spray on the ceiling."

Joe looked up. He'd missed that. The blood spray looked as if a painter had flung his brush through the air over his head.

Norwood raised his camera and shot dozens of photos in rapid succession while slowly turning 360 degrees. Joe stayed behind him so he wouldn't be in any of the shots.

"There might be latent prints on the tools and other surfaces," Norwood said. "I don't observe any footprints on the floor or any obvious hair or fiber evidence, but that will involve further testing . . ."

He went on for the record.

While Norwood talked, Joe took a closer look around the room and took photos on his cell phone camera. A pile of books was on the floor where the cheap shelving had been pulled down from the wall. Kizer was apparently not a reader of novels except for the Lord of the Rings trilogy, which looked decades old. He recognized the titles of several classic fly-fishing and fly-tying manuals. And he noted well-thumbed World War II history paperbacks: *The Longest Day* by Cornelius Ryan, *Band of*

Brothers by Stephen Ambrose, and *Beyond Band of Brothers* by Major Dick Winters, as well as T. A. Larson's *History of Wyoming*.

"It appears the subject was bound by duct tape to the chair and tortured using common hand tools," Norwood said. "Probably his own." Then: "I wonder what they wanted from a fishing guide?"

It was a question Joe had been asking himself. He had no answer. Judging by Kizer's possessions, it didn't appear that he had much money. Fishing guides rarely did.

Joe followed Norwood with his recorder through the small kitchen toward the back screen door. Norwood carefully stepped around to the side of it and Joe did the same.

"I observe blood spatter on the linoleum leading out through the back door to the yard," Norwood said as they followed it. He paused before pushing the screen door open.

"There's a dirty frypan on the stove and a half-eaten plate of scrambled eggs and bacon on the counter. My initial observation from what I can see is that the victim was having his breakfast when the perpetrators struck."

AFTER PHOTOGRAPHING and describing what he saw in the backyard, and making a note to check for prints on the steel surfaces of the empty gasoline cans, Norwood turned and summed up his observations. Joe held the recorder out so the tech's words could be heard clearly.

"Although this is extremely preliminary and could be contradicted by further examination of the evidence, it appears that the subject was interrupted during breakfast and then was bound and tortured by at least one individual, then dragged or led out to the backyard and burned by an accelerant. My preliminary guess is that the crime occurred in the early-morning hours, as indicated by the uneaten breakfast, as well as the partial but not complete coagulation stage of the droplet rim desiccation. It is not fully separated and dry yet.

"It also appears," he continued, "that the victim was transported from the scene after the crime to rancher Lorne Trumley's adjoining property and tossed over the fence, which is three and a half feet tall. That suggests the perpetrator was either a very strong man or, more likely, it was two or more individuals, because the victim was at least a hundred and sixty pounds, maybe one seventy.

"There is a lot of additional crime scene investigation needed to complete before offering up anything more definitive."

He looked up at Joe and said, "Okay, you can turn it off."

Joe did. Then he popped out the digital card and handed it to Norwood.

"Thank you," Norwood said, dropping it into the breast pocket of his coveralls.

"There is a lot of physical evidence here," Joe said. "Why leave the house like this? Why not clean it up or burn it down?"

"I was asking myself the same question," Norwood said.

"Maybe they didn't get the chance," Joe speculated. "Maybe Lorne found that body too soon? Or something interrupted their plans to come back and get rid of the evidence?"

"Beats me at this point," Norwood said. "But there's a lot here. More than there usually is, I mean. Tire tracks, torture tools, plenty of surfaces where we might be able to pull a print. At least I hope so."

Joe nodded.

Norwood leaned closer to Joe and whispered, "Do you think Tibbs is up to this?"

"I was wondering the same thing," Joe replied.

As he said it, Sheriff Tibbs rounded the corner of the house, trailed by Deputies Steck and Bass. He still looked distressed, and his mood was further blackened when he saw Joe standing next to Norwood on the back porch.

"Joe, we've got this," Tibbs said through tightly clenched teeth.

"You bet," Joe said. "Just doing what I could to help Gary out."

"You've helped out plenty," Tibbs said flatly. Steck and Bass exchanged amused grins.

"You can be on your way now," Tibbs said to Joe.

As he walked around the house to the front and tossed the booties and gloves into the bed of his truck, Joe heard Tibbs groan and say, "I hope this here thing doesn't ruin my Thanksgiving."

DAISY WAS UP and alert in the cab with her front paws on the window ledge and her nose pressed against the driver's-side glass when Joe got to the pickup. She was agitated and he turned and followed her line of sight over his shoulder.

The dog he'd seen earlier lurked just inside the stand of trees on Kizer's property. He assumed it was Bert's dog because it had stayed around even with all of the sudden commotion. The animal gazed at him with those disturbing, mesmerizing eyes.

Joe called to it.

"Come on, boy," he said, not knowing if the dog was male or female. Then: "Come on, girl. I'll take you home and feed you. Daisy here won't do anything but lick you to death."

The hound started to come, then stopped.

"Come on, we don't want to leave you here."

The animal seemed to be considering it for a moment, but then Norwood walked out through the front door in his baggy white coveralls and let the door slam behind him. The dog jumped at the sight and sound, and wheeling around, it loped away into the underbrush.

"Poor thing," Joe said to Daisy as he climbed in and shut the door. "I think that dog had a really rough day."

Joe needed to get home as quickly as he could. He knew Marybeth would be anxious to tell him about her own very strange day.

CHAPTER FOUR

Marybeth Pickett

EARLIER THAT MORNING, MARYBETH HAD SWUNG HER MINI-van into the library parking lot before dawn and aimed it for her reserved DIRECTOR space. As she'd made the turn, her headlights had revealed movement near the outside of the entrance foyer. Someone was there on a cold Wyoming November morning three hours before the building was to open.

She stopped before pulling into her space. There were no other cars in the small parking lot, and she hit the button to lock all of the doors in the van—they responded with a solid thunk—while she reversed slowly and turned the wheel to the right. Her lights swept across the skeletal line of bushes on the side of the ancient red-brick library exterior and she tapped the brakes when they flooded the entrance area.

A man was bent down in front of the glass door with his back to her. When the beams hit him, he glanced quickly over his shoulder, winced at the brightness, and stuck out his palm to shadow his eyes and face.

He was old, tall, and disheveled with a white shock of hair sticking out on each side of his head beneath a baseball cap. He had light-colored eyes and a long nose and he moved stiffly in a stooped-over way that betrayed his age. He was wearing a thick green fleece coat with a patch of some kind—maybe a faded rainbow trout—on his shoulder. She couldn't see his face clearly because the cap had a long brim and he kept it tilted down so his features were in shadow.

He scuttled away around the other corner of the building.

And he was gone.

MARYBETH SAT in her idling car for a moment while her heart raced and a shiver rippled through her body. Something about the man—his stare or the way he'd retreated so quickly—unnerved her. She opened her purse on the passenger seat and found both her phone and the canister of pepper spray Joe insisted she carry with her. As usual, she'd left her five-shot hammerless LadySmith .38 at home. For once she wished she hadn't.

Marybeth slid her side window down a few inches, listening for the sound of a car starting up in the dark. But she heard nothing. Was he on foot?

There were not many homeless people in Saddlestring. Transients came through in the summer months looking for a more hospitable location, but rarely in the winter. She was very aware of them, because as the director of the county library, she knew that her building was like a magnet for those who had no place else to go. Transients used the restrooms, the couches, and the computers. No one had ever vandalized the interior or harassed her patrons, but she did have to call the sheriff on one middle-aged woman who insisted on wheeling her shopping cart full of possessions inside with her three days in a row. When Marybeth had followed up with Sheriff Tibbs, he told her they'd driven the woman to a halfway house in Casper, a hundred and thirty miles away.

She looked around to see if she could see the man again. Hopefully, she thought, she'd catch a glimpse of him under a streetlight, doing his best to get away. What worried her was the possibility that he had simply ducked around the corner of the library and was lurking in the bushes or in the stairwell that led to the basement storage area.

Marybeth tapped out 911 on her phone but hesitated to hit the call button. The county library was a public building, after all. The man hadn't been trespassing or attempting to break in, as far as she could discern. Patrons were encouraged to return books at all hours via a slot in the building. Maybe he had overdue books and he didn't want to return them in person and pay a fine? There were plenty of other scenarios she could think of.

She wasn't a jumpy woman and she didn't want to be characterized as one. Her husband was in law enforcement, and the dispatcher at the county building was notorious for gossiping about the calls she received. That the director of the county library had called the cops to check out a man returning a library book after hours would certainly make the rounds and portray her as foolish.

So instead, she called Joe.

"What's up, babe?"

"Probably nothing."

She could envision him on the other end getting ready to go to work. He was likely pulling on his red uniform shirt with the pronghorn patch on its sleeve or packing his lunch. Daisy would be trembling with anticipation near the front door.

Although he was still limping from his injuries in the mountains the month before and he'd yet to have all of his stitches removed, Joe was nothing if not conscientious. Annoyingly so. It drove him crazy when he was not doing his job in the field, especially during the last weeks of the big-game hunting seasons. It drove her crazy that he wouldn't stay home to recuperate and rest, like their doctor had ordered.

It was especially maddening now, she thought, since their fortunes had changed almost overnight. A lot had happened within the past month. Joe had been injured and had nearly lost his life up in the mountains. The trauma of the experience still affected her. The community itself was still in shock from the violent incidents that had taken place and the familiar people involved, and so was Marybeth. She couldn't get Joe to talk about it yet.

Also unsaid between them was the strangest thing of all— the possibility that, for the first time in their married lives, they were . . . wealthy?

Maybe.

———

She told Joe about the man she'd seen and what he appeared to have been doing.

"Was he sleeping there, do you think?"

"I don't think so."

"But you can't see where he went?"

"No."

"You're sure you didn't recognize him?"

"I'm sure."

"Make sure you check your mirrors so he doesn't sneak up behind you in the dark."

That sent another chill through her and she quickly confirmed that there was nobody behind her van.

"Stay put," Joe said. "I'll be there in twelve minutes and check things out."

Joe knew exactly how long it took to drive from their state-owned game warden home on the bank of the Twelve Sleep River to the library.

"Really, you don't need to do that," she said. "I'm still on edge, I think. Now I feel kind of silly for calling you."

"What are you doing there so early, anyway?" he asked. She could tell from the background noises that he'd shut the front door of their house and was making his way across the yard toward his pickup.

"I left you a note on the refrigerator," she said. "I wanted to get an early start. I was hoping to knock off after lunch today so

I could get home and start cooking, since April will be back tonight and Lucy's coming tomorrow."

"Oh, I missed the note," he said.

Of course he had. She referred to it as his "man-scan," the glance that often missed obvious things right in front of him. Two nights before, he'd searched the house for twenty minutes for the reading glasses that dangled from the front of his shirt. Earlier that week, he'd remarked on how he liked the "new" lamp in their living room that she'd placed there four months before.

It was especially irksome because she knew that when he was out in the field investigating a crime, he could see everything quite clearly.

It was on the cusp of Thanksgiving break and their three daughters were coming home for the holiday. The youngest, Lucy, was a sophomore at the University of Wyoming in Laramie. She was bringing with her an international student from Hong Kong whom she'd befriended. When Lucy had learned her friend had nowhere to go over the break, she'd invited her along. That was Lucy.

Twenty-two-year-old April had graduated from Northwest Community College in Powell with a law enforcement degree and was working for a Western-wear store. Their oldest daughter, Sheridan, was twenty-four and local, so she wouldn't be sleeping at the house with them for the holiday. Sheridan worked for their friends Nate and Liv Romanowski, owners of Yarak,

Inc., a bird abatement company. Like Nate, Sheridan was a falconer. She'd been in the middle of the trouble in the mountains with Joe and Nate, and Marybeth had still not come to grips with what could have happened to all of them.

Marybeth heard Joe shut the door of his pickup and start the motor.

"Really, you don't have to come into town," she said.

"I'm on my way."

"I'll tell you what," she said, "I'll get out and make my way to the front door and stay on the line with you. If I see anything strange, I'll report it and you'll hear it as it happens."

"That's crazy," Joe said. "Just sit tight."

She ignored him, got out, hooked the strap of her purse over her shoulder, and walked toward the library with the phone in one hand and the pepper spray in the other.

There was no movement from the corner of the building or the spindly bushes.

"I'm nearly there," she said.

"Turn around and go back to your car and lock your doors."

"I'm twenty feet from the door."

"Do you have your weapon available?" Joe asked.

"It's at home in the cupboard, as usual."

Joe groaned. "This is why I bought it for you."

"I know. I have pepper spray." Then: "Ten feet."

She saw the package on the step near the base of the door. It was about a foot by a foot and a half in size and probably four inches thick, messily wrapped in brown paper with the edges taped down.

Written on it in quivering black marker was: *For the 12 Sleep County Library Collection.*

Marybeth sighed audibly as the tension melted out of her. She quickly dismissed her ludicrous worst-case scenario—that it was a bomb.

"It's okay," she told Joe. "Somebody dropped off a package at the front door, is all. It happens all the time. Turn around and go get some breakfast."

He paused for a few seconds. "Are you sure?"

"I'm sure."

"Get inside and lock the door. Then I'll turn around."

"Okay."

She swiped her keycard in the lock, opened the door, and pushed the package into the vestibule with her foot. It was surprisingly heavy, but she could tell by experience that it was a large thick book of some kind. That it had even occurred to her that the package might be a bomb was unnerving to her. It was a glimpse into how fragile and conspiratorial her mental state still was.

"I'm in," she said to Joe as she turned and locked the door behind her.

"What's in the package?"

"I'll let you know later," she said. "I'm not worried about it. People clean out their houses and they don't know what to do with their books, so they 'donate' them to the library. Occasionally, there's even something of value, but most of the used books get pulped or put into our book sale."

"They do this anonymously?"

"Sometimes."

"You're sure you're okay?"

"I'm fine," she said. "Just a little embarrassed, is all. I'm glad I didn't call the sheriff. Go home now."

He said he would.

Before she hit the master lights to illuminate the stacks of the old Carnegie library, she raised her eyes and looked outside through the glass door.

On the corner of the next block, the man who'd left the package stood partly illuminated by the blue glow of an overhead streetlight. He raised his hand tentatively and waved.

She read a message in his wave that might or might not be true. To her, the wave said, *It's your problem now.*

Then he turned and walked off into the dark.

AFTER SHE'D MADE a cup of strong coffee in the Keurig machine, Marybeth turned to the package in the middle of her desk and took a photo of it—just in case.

As she pulled on a pair of latex gloves from the archive department, she wondered if her precautions were even necessary. But she'd learned over the years from working closely with Joe and other law enforcement personnel that it was better to be methodical when it came to studying unknown objects. The parcel could turn out to be important in some way. The circumstances in which the mystery man had left it there suggested that he placed value on it. Fingerprints or DNA on the wrapping could even help identify him.

Marybeth used an X-Acto knife to carefully slice through the tape—she didn't want to tear the paper if she could avoid it. She recognized the rough brown wrap as that of a grocery bag from Valley Foods, the local grocery store. Meaning the man who left it was likely from the area.

She peeled back the paper on the top until she could see that inside was, indeed, a very thick book. Not a book, exactly, but a very odd leather-bound binder.

The front cover was wrapped in dark red leather held in place by a heavy silver square, with an X in the middle made of silver as well. A large round medallion was in the center of the X, featuring a full-bodied eagle on a platform, its wings spread and its balled talons curled up as if showing off its biceps. The silver was tarnished with age.

Heavy silver rivets in the shape of four-leaf clovers attached the silver work to the leather. They also separated a series of heavy numbers on the bottom of the cover:

$$1 * 9 * 3 * 7$$

Marybeth frowned not only at the date but at the font. It was Gothic Germanic, popular in Germany in the 1920s, '30s, and '40s.

It wasn't a binder, after all. It was a photo album.

And when she leaned over it to get a closer look, she saw the Nazi swastikas carved into the silver of the X.

Then she opened it and gasped and thought, *It's your problem now.*

CHAPTER FIVE

Marybeth and the Nazis

Marybeth spent the rest of the morning studying each thick page, by turns mystified, enthralled, and enraged.

The binder appeared to be authentic. It had a musty odor, but it was in excellent condition overall. The pages were filled with hundreds of original black-and-white images either glued to the paper or mounted by small corner pockets. There were very few handwritten captions, but it wasn't long before she realized what she was looking at.

In chronological order, the album memorialized a year in the life of a Nazi government official named Julius Streicher. Marybeth had never heard of him before. The first page of the album was titled simply:

DAS

JAHR

1937

The Year 1937.

In all, there were over one hundred and seventy-five pages. Some contained a single image, and others as many as six.

The first large photo was of a portly bald man with a slight toothbrush-style mustache gazing off at something while posing with his fists tucked into his waist. His chest was thrust out and his chin was raised haughtily and he wore a uniform with an iron cross pinned to the breast pocket. Behind him was the top of a flagpole. The pose suggested that this was a man to be admired.

The second photo chilled her to the bone. A black-leather-clad Streicher reached out for the hand of an obviously delighted Adolf Hitler. An airplane on a runway provided the background. In the foreground, two uniformed soldiers smiled on while one raised his hand in a Hitler salute. A young blond girl with braided hair trailed Streicher, carrying a bouquet of flowers.

The hand-lettered caption read: *Der Führer und Gauleiter Streicher auf dem Flugplatz in Nürnberg.*

She knew enough German to know that it said Streicher was greeting "the Leader" on an airfield in Nuremberg. She had to look up *Gauleiter* and found it was the term for the governor of a regional branch of the Nazi Party.

Julius Streicher, she determined, was no mere party functionary. In many of the photos, he posed with men who were somewhat familiar to her from the twentieth-century history classes she'd taken in college. Methodically, she looked them up as she proceeded, matching the faces with those of top Nazi officials.

Here was Streicher with Heinrich Himmler. Himmler had the face and bearing of a mousy accountant or professor, she thought, the kind of weakling who had been bullied by larger, fitter men his entire life and now reveled in his circumstances: black-clad, medals on his chest, a swastika armband, flunkies tailing behind him to accommodate his every wish.

Himmler, she knew, in addition to overseeing the Gestapo and Waffen-SS, was considered to be the chief architect of the Holocaust. His Einsatzgruppen shock troops had built the ex-termination camps that killed six million Jews and a half mil-lion others. He'd been a believer in occultism and had inserted pagan symbols and rituals into the structure of the secret police. He'd died by suicide in 1945.

And there he was, right in front of her. Standing next to a glowing Julius Streicher.

As she paged through the album with a growing sense of dread, she alternated between the photos and her computer to try to fill in the unknowns and translate the meager captions. One in particular stopped her in her tracks.

It was of six men standing outside in a knot at what looked to be a street parade or march. They seemed to be sharing a hilarious joke.

All six, she confirmed from her research, had been there from the beginning of the Nazi Party. They'd fought in World War I, later participated with Hitler in the failed Beer Hall Putsch in 1923, and were the first on the scene after the Reichstag fire in Berlin that launched the party into power.

In the photo, from left to right, were Adolf Hitler, Rudolf

Hess, Hermann Göring, Streicher, Joseph Goebbels, and Himmler.

Hess was dark and almost handsome, but something looked off about him, she thought. He'd been the Deputy Führer as well as a close friend and confidant of Hitler, and while in prison with Hitler had served as an assistant in the writing of *Mein Kampf*. Hess had served as a kind of vice president with a twist—he'd attended ceremonies and funerals on behalf of Hitler, but also signed most of the regime's legislation and edicts, including the Nuremberg Laws of 1935, which stripped Jews of their rights.

In 1941, unbeknownst to Hitler or the party, Hess made a secret flight to Scotland to try to end the war, and was promptly arrested. Hitler wanted nothing more to do with him. Later, he was returned to Germany for the Nuremberg trials and sentenced to life in Berlin's Spandau Prison. He hanged himself in 1987 at the age of ninety-three.

Hermann Göring, obese, with fat gargoyle features, looked jolly and mischievous in the photo, as if he were about to tell another joke. She recognized him, but still looked him up to fill the gaps of her knowledge.

Göring had been wounded in the Beer Hall Putsch, and in the hospital developed a morphine addiction that he maintained for the rest of his life. He'd created the Gestapo and been named commander in chief of the Luftwaffe. He was fond of elaborate uniforms he designed for himself and considered himself Hitler's successor, even though he was the least anti-Semitic in the

Nazi government. That hadn't stopped him from acquiring a massive collection of stolen art primarily from Jewish families. He'd died by suicide in 1946 just prior to his sentencing at the Nuremberg trials.

Joseph Goebbels stood next to Göring like a hatchet-faced ferret.

She sat back and shook her head. All of the men in the photograph looked remarkably like weak men playacting. Like members of a third-tier men's club devoted to dressing up in silly uniforms and singing drinking songs. But the more she read about them, the more it was clear they were evil, depraved, mentally ill monsters.

Goebbels had been Reich Minister of Propaganda, and had molded and shaped Hitler's message for the masses through brilliant public relations efforts that legitimized the outlaw regime. He once wrote, "Adolf Hitler, I love you because you are both great and simple at the same time. What one calls a genius."

Goebbels had actually been named in Hitler's will as the man to succeed him, and after Hitler had committed suicide in his Berlin bunker, he'd held the job of chancellor for exactly one day. Then he and his wife poisoned all six of their children before killing themselves.

How, she wondered, had this photo album found its way halfway around the world to Saddlestring, Wyoming?

And who was Julius Streicher? That was the one she'd never heard of.

———

MARYBETH HAD BEEN so consumed by her research that she hadn't heard Evelyn Hughes, the front desk librarian, come in, until she asked, "What is that?"

Marybeth looked up, alarmed. It felt like she'd been caught doing something improper, probably because the things she'd learned made her feel dirty.

"It's apparently a gift to the library," she said. "Someone left it on the front step this morning."

"Do you know who it was?"

"He didn't want to be seen."

Marybeth described the man as best she could and asked Evelyn if he sounded familiar to her, if maybe he'd tried to donate the album at the front desk and been rebuffed.

Evelyn frowned. "Is it another ranch history?" They got a lot of those.

"Far from it," Marybeth said. "Come take a look."

Evelyn approached cautiously. She was a jumpy woman and she loved conspiracy theories. The album was still open to the photo of the Nazi leaders.

Evelyn recoiled and stepped back. "I don't want to see it," she said.

"I'm guessing it may be a valuable historical item, although I'm still trying to figure it out. Where did it come from? Who left it?"

"I don't care."

"Aren't you curious at all?"

"No. I don't want to touch it and I don't want to see it."

"That's not the best attitude for a head librarian," Marybeth said.

"It is for me," Evelyn snapped. She bolted through the open door and closed it tightly behind her.

MARYBETH TURNED BACK to the album:

A tour of Streicher visiting the twelve "Adolf Hitler Schools" across Germany. Apparently, they were boarding schools set up specifically to train future generations of Nazi leaders.

There he was "speaking to the men of the press about the struggle."

There were many photos of adoring women and children fawning over Streicher, and several particularly disturbing images of him pawing very young girls dressed in taffeta, holding flowers, and gazing upon him in awe. She could not fathom the significance of the photos of him posing with a little dog on a world globe.

There were farmers holding pigs like babies in their arms, offering them to Streicher for his admiration.

The theme of the album was hagiographic—an attempt to portray Streicher as a man much admired by his subjects. There were dozens of photos of him kissing babies, signing autographs, and walking through throngs of worshippers. In several, his very presence seemed to part the crowd like Moses parting the sea.

He seemed inordinately fond of surrounding himself with large-eyed children—mostly girls—and little dogs.

Marybeth almost laughed at the series of images of a shirtless Streicher using a shovel to break ground on a new parade location. He was flaccid, white, and fat, his trousers hitched up nearly to his armpits to disguise his belly and flabby torso. She could tell by the strained look on his face that he was holding in his gut to the point of nearly injuring himself.

The photographers had obviously been instructed to show their subject in the most flattering way possible. He was, she thought, keenly aware of the camera at all times.

Many of the photos were of his apparently official duties, such as greeting foreign officials, marching with "Hungarian Youth" in Nuremberg, touring a new museum display called *Terror-Revolt-Death: The Bolshevik Revolution*. Meeting with Italian officials as well as "Members of the All-Russian Fascist Party."

There were dozens of photos of obviously choreographed Nuremberg rallies where the crowds looked both robotic and rapturous at the same time.

Although the album was not fully captioned, Marybeth spent a good deal of time reading and translating the displays on the wall behind Streicher as he spoke to a packed crowd in what looked like a new museum.

The collection was titled *The Eternal Jew*.

Some of Streicher's speech had been transcribed by hand:

"If the Jew came to power and influence again from the inside or outside in the land of Stusch, then our heroes at the Feldherrnhalle will have died in vain . . ."

Written on a display of grotesque hook-nosed caricatures of

what were obviously supposed to be Jews were the words *Their rituals correspond to their depraved Talmud morals . . .*

MARYBETH HATED THIS MAN.

So who was he?

A search of his name made her hate him even more.

Julius Streicher had been the publisher of a sensationalistic and low-brow weekly tabloid newspaper called *Der Stürmer*, meaning "The Stormer" or "Attacker" or "Striker." He was also one of Hitler's very few intimate friends. Streicher had declared in 1922 that his destiny was to serve Hitler. His name was mentioned in *Mein Kampf.*

Der Stürmer was a virulently anti-Semitic publication founded in 1923, a publication so popular with the German public that it made Streicher a multimillionaire. Hitler had called it his favorite newspaper, although it was so over-the-top that other Nazi Party leaders had refused to give it any official sanction or endorsement. In fact, it was removed from Berlin during the 1936 Olympics so visitors from around the world would never see it.

Der Stürmer featured salacious drawings of hook-nosed Jews eating babies, Jewish ritual murder, the sexual violation of German women by Jewish men. Its motto was printed on the bottom of the front page of every issue: *Die Juden sind unser Unglück*, or "The Jews are our misfortune."

Its peak circulation had been six hundred thousand paid subscribers in 1937—a fact that startled Marybeth. It confirmed for her that the German people had been along for the ride Hitler was taking them on. It disproved the revisionist history she'd been taught that the average German citizen at the time was unaware of the anti-Semitism of their leadership.

She read on.

Streicher was so crude and anti-Semitic that he'd even repulsed some other top Nazis. Although Himmler tolerated him and the publication because he shared Streicher's hatred, Goebbels fretted that if *Der Stürmer* was seen by outsiders, it would reveal something about the Nazi regime that he preferred to keep under wraps. Göring hated Streicher (although he happily posed with him in photos) and forbade *Der Stürmer* from being sold or circulated within the Luftwaffe.

Hitler, however, was loyal to his friend and installed him as the governor of Franconia. Streicher was known by the populace as either the "King of Nuremberg" or the "Beast of Franconia." In 1938, he ordered that the Grand Synagogue of Nuremberg be destroyed.

Hitler stated, "Streicher is reproached for his *Stürmer*. The truth is the opposite of what people say: He idealized the Jew. The Jew is baser, fiercer, and more diabolical than Streicher depicted him. One must never forget the services rendered by the *Stürmer*. Now that the Jews are known for what they are, nobody any longer thinks that Streicher libeled them."

Streicher was loyal to Hitler until the end. Prior to his death by hanging after the Nuremberg trials, he used his last words to praise *Der Führer* and declared his eternal devotion.

———

MARYBETH SHUDDERED as she turned over the last page of the album and closed its heavy back cover. She felt soiled. The album was a prolonged, personal glimpse into the mind and ego of a monster. She imagined Streicher selecting each photograph and directing where he wanted it placed on the page. She imagined him to be very pleased with the result.

If there was a narrative to how the photos were displayed and what they revealed, it was a celebration of Streicher as a historic and important figure of a nation that, unbeknownst to him at the time, was at its aspirational peak. Streicher rode the bloody crest of Nazi history before it washed over the European continent the very next year, when Germany invaded Poland in September 1939.

She thought about how often political opponents in contemporary America accused each other of being Nazis. It had become a cliché. But in this album in front of her was the real thing, and it was unspeakable.

SHE SLIPPED HER PHONE out of her handbag and called Joe again.

"Joe, you won't believe what that guy dropped off at the library this morning."

"Let me guess—another ranch history?"

"Not even close."

"Try me," he said.

"It's a photo album from Nazi Germany. It belonged to a man named Julius Streicher, who may have been one of the worst people ever to walk on the earth."

"I don't think I've ever heard of him. Is it authentic?"

"It seems so. It kind of creeps me out."

She could hear road sounds from his phone.

"Where are you?" she asked.

"On my way to Winchester. I got a call from a rancher up there who thinks a wounded moose died in his field. I'm going to check it out."

Joe had inordinately warm feelings toward moose, she knew. He got angry when they were poached out of season and especially if their carcasses were left to rot.

"Are you feeling up to it?" she asked.

"Sure," he said. He didn't sound convincing, but he obviously didn't want to discuss it any further. "Do you know who left it at the library?"

"No clue. There's nothing inside to indicate who owned it. Except Julius Streicher, of course. I saved the paper it was wrapped in."

"That was smart," Joe said. Then: "Do you think it's valuable?"

"I would guess so."

"Can you donate it to a museum or something?"

"Probably," she said. "Some archive out there might want it. I'm still wondering how it wound up here after eighty-some years. I think I'm going to do some investigating of my own. But in the meantime I don't know what to do with it." She paused. "I think I'll bring it home tonight."

"Really?"

"Yes. I don't want to lock it up for the long weekend here. I'm not really sure why I'm thinking that, but for some reason it feels like the correct thing to do."

"I've learned over the years to trust your judgment," he said. Which meant, she knew, that he had no idea what she was thinking or why. But he was kind that way.

He asked, "Are you still planning on knocking off early?"

"Yes, even though I wasted most of the morning going through this terrible thing."

"Let me know if you need anything from the store," he said. "I'll be coming back through town this afternoon, I'm sure."

"Okay, sweetie."

"Here's my turnoff," Joe said. "I'll call you on my way back."

"Love you."

"Love you."

AN HOUR LATER, Marybeth had lugged the album to her van in a Twelve Sleep County Library tote. It was heavy and the tote handles dug into her fingers. She placed the album on the floor of her back seat along with another tote filled with romance novels. As usual, their neighbor Lola Lowry had asked Marybeth to deliver her weekly assortment of titles. Because she had asked so nicely months before and she was their only close neighbor, Marybeth had agreed to drop off the books on the way home.

She tried to shake off the pall that had enveloped her from when she'd first opened the binder. It was almost as if the album itself radiated a kind of dark, almost seductive power over her psyche—that she'd made some kind of personal connection with the evil mind of a man she'd never heard of, but who had invited her in. She hoped the spell would break.

And she questioned why she had felt the need to keep it with her instead of leaving it at the library. Why had she decided to take it home, where her returning daughters would soon gather?

CHAPTER SIX

László and Viktór

THE SCENE IN THE LIBRARY PARKING LOT WAS VIEWED WITH interest by two brothers parked half a block away in a rented SUV. The vehicle was splashed with mud. Two pairs of industrial blood-spattered and sooty Tyvek coveralls were wadded up and stuffed into a trash bag in the back seat of the vehicle. Their plan was to dispose of the soiled clothing in an incinerator—if they could find one in this sleepy place.

László Kovács, the driver, was tall and thick and still as physically imposing as he'd been when he was an Olympic wrestler. He had a shaved head, a square face that looked like a balled-up fist, heavy brows, and a deep voice. His big ears stuck straight out from his head. He moved with purpose and grace and was surprisingly quick.

Viktór was dark and lean and wore black plastic glasses with thick lenses that were crooked on his V-shaped face. His features were much softer than his brother's. He was older than László by a few years, but neither of them had any questions about who was in charge. Unlike László, Viktór had only been to America twice in his life: once to New York City and once to Disney World.

"See that?" László asked in Hungarian.

"She's got it," Viktór responded. "What else would she have in that bag?"

"Who is she?"

László lifted a pair of binoculars from his lap and focused them on the license plate of the van, then read out the numbers. His brother scrawled them on the back of the rental car receipt envelope.

"Are we going to follow her?" Viktór asked.

"Oh, hold it," László said, this time in barely accented English. "When she pulled out, I can see that the space is reserved for the director of the library. So she's the boss of that place."

The van exited the parking lot and turned onto the street toward the men in the SUV.

"Get down," László ordered.

As both men rolled to their sides on the seat, they bumped heads while doing so. They didn't sit back up until they clearly heard the van pass by.

"You have a hard head," Viktór said with a grimace. He took off his baseball cap and rubbed his scalp through his hair.

"Get your phone out," László said. "Find out the name of the library director. Then look up her address."

"Now? I'm hungry and tired and I want to eat."

"We eat when we're done."

"I want to eat now. This jet lag has thrown off my internal clock."

László stared straight ahead with his jaw clamped. He was angry with his brother.

"We discussed this," he said. "We want to get in and get out of this place. People will notice us the longer we are here. You can get plenty of sleep on the plane home."

Victór moaned.

"We have to believe in why we're here," László said. "Never forget that."

CHAPTER SEVEN

Nate Romanowski

NATE DROVE SOUTH ON I-25 TOWARD DENVER IN SILENCE, except for the sizzling of his tires on the highway wet from snow. His five-shot .454 Casull revolver sat in a coil of its shoulder holster within easy reach on the passenger seat. He had revenge on his mind and violence in his heart.

In falconry terms, he was entering the mental state of *yarak*, where his complete focus was on the hunt. Despite his hours on the road, everything was coming together. His eyesight seemed sharper, his hearing had improved, his instincts were on high alert, and his jaw was clamped tight.

Physically, he didn't feel like he was there yet. Since marrying Liv and having a daughter, he hadn't regained the lethal edge he'd once had. He hadn't quite gone soft, but his life and outlook had been redirected. His new life as an on-the-grid husband, father, and small-business owner was much more fulfilling and rewarding than he'd ever imagined. But he knew he needed to temporarily step aside from all of that and invite his old self back in.

Because the man he was hunting was just as skilled as Nate had ever been, not to mention younger and more ruthless.

AFTER CROSSING the Wyoming border into Colorado before dusk, he stopped for coffee and gasoline in the small town of Wellington. Large snowflakes drifted down, briefly illuminated by pole lights bordering the convenience store and fuel stop. He could hear the drone of the interstate to the east.

While he filled the tank of his specially retrofitted panel van, Nate checked his phone and dialed up a website called Blood Feathers, which was a falconer's term for nascent raptor feathers that were still growing. It was a crudely constructed site that hadn't been updated in years, and it was used primarily by master and apprentice falconers who were out of the mainstream but still wanted to communicate with like-minded practitioners. The falconers on the site were a motley crew of outlaws, ex-cons, survivalists, and former military. A few had even served as elite special operators in the same small unit to which Nate had belonged. They weren't friends exactly, and he'd never met most of the people who posted on the site. Falconers tended not to congregate, lest they lose the all-consuming and necessary concentration on their partnership with their birds. But they were like-minded for good or ill.

Nate scrolled down through the crude graphics on the site

until he found the log-in box for a special portal called Bal-Chatri, named for an especially effective trap for capturing wild raptors. The offshoot access was heavily encrypted, and he keyed in a series of passwords until it gave him entry. Then he scrolled down through the message threads.

Ninety percent of the content on Bal-Chatri pertained to best practices, tips, and interactions between falconers. There were forums on the qualities of individual species, and debates about the ethics of using wild raptors for commercial bird abatement enterprises. The other ten percent of the content fell into the category of "political."

This part of Bal-Chatri was devoted to unofficial and civilian-generated special ops.

The outlaw falconers who populated Bal-Chatri were almost all anti–government regulation, libertarian, pro–Second Amendment types who simply wanted to leave others alone and be left alone themselves. They railed against bureaucrats and politicians and social justice warriors of all stripes who would, if given the chance, impose their mores and wills upon them. Nate's own sympathies tended in that direction, but he rarely participated in the discussions. Even very well-known and experienced falconers throughout the world couldn't access the special portal. It was available only through special invitation.

What was of value to him via Bel-Chatri wasn't the politics or even the collective knowledge of fellow falconers. It was the geographic dispersal of the members and the fact that although they were largely antisocial loners, they all shared an unwritten code. Bal-Chatri was used to call out violations of that code so members could work together to expose and expel falconers who broke it.

Honorable falconers didn't steal or injure birds from other falconers; honorable falconers never trespassed on hunting territory used by others; honorable falconers looked out for the best interests of others; honorable falconers never snitched regarding federal wildlife regulation violations; honorable falconers never engaged in practices that would damage the reputation of falconry; honorable falconers were permitted to capture and sell birds despite domestic and international prohibitions—but only to other honorable falconers.

The man Nate was hunting had broken every single one of those tenets, plus he'd physically attacked his wife and threatened his baby. His name was Axel Soledad.

Nate's legitimate bird abatement business depended solely on his inventory of wild falcons, each of which he'd worked with for hundreds of hours until each raptor was fine-tuned. He'd flown each bird—peregrines, red-tails, prairie falcons, a gyrfalcon, kestrels, and Harris hawks—to develop their particular specialties and to enhance their hardwired skills. His Air Force had been practically wiped out. The three birds that weren't stolen had been killed and left at the mews. None had escaped.

Not only was his Air Force captive in the vehicle of an outlaw, but his means to make a living and to support his family had been dashed—and that very family had been attacked. Retribution would come.

After Nate had posted an account of it all, the forum had exploded with rage. Many on the site had their own stories to tell about Axel Soledad. Although considered charismatic and a very experienced falconer in his own right, Soledad went against everything the Bal-Chatri community of falconers believed.

The members on the site not only wanted to see Nate recover his birds, they wanted Soledad disappeared by whatever means necessary. Nate didn't disagree.

So the network looking out for Axel Soledad had been established. One member who called himself "Geronimo Jones" posted he'd seen Soledad and two other associates in downtown Denver. He'd provided Nate with a cell phone number to call once he got there.

Geronimo Jones. Nate already liked him.

SINCE IT WAS RUSH HOUR, the traffic had started to build once Nate drove south past Fort Collins. The Front Range was booming, and there were housing developments on both sides of the highway where open fields had been just a few years before. Economic and cultural refugees from California, Illinois, New York, New Jersey, and other states had recently contributed to an influx of population in Colorado. Nate barely knew the state anymore, even though he'd once lived there in his youth.

Denver had transformed from a large Middle American cow town to a high-tech hipster haven. The Rocky Mountains to the west were still out there, he knew. It was just that the ambient light from the Denver area glowed so brightly ahead of him that the mountains and the stars were washed out by it.

Colorado drivers had gotten worse, not better, than Nate

remembered. Many were no doubt newcomers, based on the way they rudely and carelessly weaved through traffic on the highway in the snowfall. He saw a Prius spin out ahead of him and plunge into the median and a Honda Civic do a loop-de-loop across three lanes of traffic and come to a stop backward in the borrow ditch, as if the concept of winter driving was a shocking and unexpected phenomenon.

"Idiots," he hissed.

AFTER ENTERING the northern suburb of Broomfield, Nate eased to the side of the highway and stopped. Speeding cars whizzed by and covered the side of his van with angry slaps of slush. He punched in the cell phone number from the forum on Blood Feathers.

It was answered after two rings.

"Yeah." The voice was a deep bass. So deep it almost sounded electronically distorted. Nate's antennae went up.

"Is this Geronimo Jones?"

"Yeah."

"This is Nate Romanowski." Unlike Geronimo Jones, Nate used his real name on the site. He did so because he knew that within the outlaw falconry community, his name meant something.

"Seriously? That Nate Romanowski? For real?"

"Yes."

"Well, fuck."

"You said you knew where I could find Axel Soledad."

"Yeah."

"I'm in Denver now. Or pretty close, anyway."

"You're here now?"

Nate was getting annoyed. "Are you going to help me find him or not?"

There was a long pause. Then: "I'll text you the address where to meet me. It's downtown."

"Tonight?"

"Yeah. But keep your head on a swivel when you get down here. There's a ruckus going on. Dudes in the street going at it."

Geronimo Jones punched off and Nate found himself looking at his cell phone as if for a further explanation. Then a text appeared.

It read:

Palomino Lounge, 2211 Corona Street. Speer Blvd. Exit off I-25.

Nate looked behind him for insane drivers, and seeing none, he eased back out onto the interstate.

NATE ROMANOWSKI WAS tall and rangy with a blond ponytail he'd recently considered cutting off because not only was he in his mid-forties, but his daughter, Kestrel, liked to tug on it. He had big hands and a stillness about him that unnerved people. So did his smile, which had often been described as cruel.

As instructed, he took the Speer Boulevard exit and drove

over a wide overpass into the heart of downtown Denver. The Ball Arena where the Nuggets played, as well as a darkened amusement park, were to his right as he descended. In the distance was the undulating profile of Empower Field at Mile High Stadium, home of the Denver Broncos.

Tall buildings seemed to move in on him from both sides and press against him as he cruised. It was a canyon of brick, glass, and steel. He was reminded of how long it had been since he'd been in a city—any city—of any size. The Denver metro population was 2.9 million people and growing, nearly five times the entire population of the state of Wyoming.

Hundreds of windows from the floors of hip condos provided snapshots into the lives of the people inside. They flashed by too quickly for him to see any of the tenants in detail, although he got the impression by the glow in the windows that most of the people were simply watching television. The buildings stood where a ramshackle warehouse district had once been, he recalled.

He'd looked up Corona Street on his phone, but he was confused by the blizzard of one-way streets and restricted turning lanes as he neared the glass-and-steel Colorado Convention Center. The wet blacktop reflected overhead lights and business signs and when he looked ahead he saw pedestrians crossing quickly without waiting for green light permissions to do so. The pedestrians looked odd to him. They were furtive in movement and bundled up for much harsher weather than it was tonight. Plus, they were out late. He wondered if a sporting event had just concluded. Denver wasn't known as a city that never slept—but perhaps that had changed, too.

Two blocks in front of him on Speer, he saw a fountain of sparks shoot up from the pavement. In the yellow light of the display, he could see more people knotted together in the middle of the street. They, too, were misshapen due to heavy clothing. Fireworks in November? he thought.

Nate hit his brakes when he saw movement through his wet-streaked passenger window just outside his van, and he narrowly missed running into a black-clad man wearing a balaclava and carrying an oversized skateboard. The man whom he'd nearly hit saw Nate at the last second as well and he turned in anger and slammed the skateboard down onto the hood of the vehicle, then darted across the street before Nate could react.

From the direction in which the man had come, a cop in heavy body armor appeared and gestured for Nate to stop. Nate did, and powered the passenger-side window down as the officer approached his vehicle. Nate saw the cop veer to check out his license plate, then he filled the open window and leaned inside. Nate caught a whiff of pepper spray from the cop's uniform.

"You nearly hit that asshole," the cop said. "You need to turn your car around and go back where you came from, you hear me? This is not the place for a cowboy from Wyoming."

"What's going on, anyway?" Nate said, bristling at the officer's tone.

"If you can't tell, we're having a little disturbance tonight. Now, I need you to turn around and go back."

The cop, who wore a helmet and a clear plastic face shield, looked not only agitated but aggressive, Nate thought. He could see the man's wide eyes, flushed face, and bristly ginger mustache through the breath-fog of the plexiglass face shield.

"Or I'll sure as hell take you in," the officer continued.

Nate suddenly recalled that his weapon was in plain sight on the passenger seat if the cop decided to look down. Had he covered it with a jacket? He wasn't sure. Nate kept his hands on the steering wheel and didn't look down at the gun to give it away.

Although he remained still, Nate wanted to smack himself in the forehead with the heel of his hand for being so stupid as to drive through downtown Denver with a firearm in his car in plain sight. He'd lived too long in rural Wyoming, where firearms were as ubiquitous as ballcaps. They were in every car and truck and backpack and saddlebag. Guns were left in the open in unlocked vehicles on Main Street in Saddlestring. But this wasn't Saddlestring, and he'd have to realign his thinking.

"Can I make a U-turn right here?" he asked.

"What in the hell do you think?" the cop yelled. "Turn around like I told you."

"Then please step aside," Nate said.

As the cop took a few steps back, Nate saw his name badge. COLLINS.

But instead of cranking the wheel and going back toward the overpass, Nate pressed on the accelerator and blasted forward. He glanced at his rearview mirror and saw the officer threatening him and waving his free hand. The other hand was on the grip of his sidearm.

Nate leaned forward as he drove, just in case the officer fired a shot at him through the back window. Stranger things had happened, he knew.

He was in luck that the light turned green on the next block and he didn't have to blow through a red light on his way into the steel-and-glass guts of downtown Denver.

As he did, he glanced over to see that, yes, he'd concealed his weapon under a down vest. Which was probably a reason to arrest him on its own.

THERE WAS A small-scale riot going on. Knots of black-clad people, most wearing helmets or masks, appeared in his headlights at street corners and from the mouths of alleys. Some of them shouted at him as he drove by and Nate heard a rock or other projectile clang against the side of his panel van.

He gritted his teeth and kept going.

Red and blue wigwag lights from a phalanx of law enforcement cruisers lit up the white marble of the Colorado State Capitol Building as he passed it, and he could see tendrils of smoke or tear gas floating under streetlights from the direction he'd seen the fireworks. He caught a glimpse of three or four men smashing the plate-glass window of a darkened cannabis emporium with a fire extinguisher. He drove on by.

Sheets of plywood covered the front of most of the retail businesses, although a few plate-glass windows had been spared. Graffiti was scrawled on the plywood and exteriors. He didn't read the text and didn't care to. Every hundred yards or so, someone had spray-painted a capital A with the lines of the letter extending past an encompassing circle.

Antifa.

The Capitol Hill neighborhood was compact, and in just a few minutes he was through it. The residential streets to the east of the dome were stately and Midwestern-looking, made of brick and likely described as "leafy" in the spring and summer.

He took a right on Corona Street, and a little finish-line flag chirped on the map app on his phone. He saw an off-street strip mall with several squat structures on it surrounded by homes. Only one place appeared to be open. It was marked with an ancient red neon PALOMINO LOUNGE sign out front. Five older-model cars were parked in the small lot.

Nate didn't park in the lot because he didn't like the look of it. There was one entrance and one egress, and the cars were all nosed against the front of the Palomino itself. There was a series of old-growth cottonwoods near the sidewalk before reaching the street. To make a fast escape, you'd have to reverse from a spot in the lot, do a three-point turn to carefully avoid crashing into one of the trees, and head for the exit. It would make for a messy maneuver.

Instead, he parked on the street half a block away from the lounge. He wedged his van between a Subaru with CO-EXIST stickers on the rear bumper and a rattletrap red Jeep Cherokee.

He drew out his phone and found the text thread with Geronimo Jones and tapped out: I'm here.

Then Nate slid out of the driver's seat and crab-walked into the back of the van. He located a toggle switch on the interior panel and turned it on. Because there were no side windows to the van and the back ones were covered by shades, no one outside could see in.

He pulled on the shoulder holster with the .454 and buckled it on and covered the rig by zipping his down vest over it. He slipped an eight-inch Buck knife into the top of his left lace-up boot. He strapped a 9mm semiautomatic Sig Sauer P365 pocket pistol on his right ankle and concealed them both by rolling down the cuffs of his jeans. A stubby canister of bear spray—a favorite tool of his friend Joe's—went into the right pocket of his vest.

Although he wanted to put his trust in Geronimo Jones, he had no illusions. "Geronimo Jones" could be Axel Soledad's alias, or the name being used by one of Soledad's accomplices to lure him in.

Before going out and clicking off the light, he looked around. Empty cages stood stacked and secured against the interior walls on both sides of the van. A bulging duffel bag of clothes and gear was shoved against the inside of the back doors.

His phone lit up as he exited through the driver's door into the street.

It read: Come on in.

NATE THREADED HIS WAY through the parked cars in front of the Palomino Lounge. The bar was from another era, before Denver was gentrified. It was square and plain, and the neon COORS sign in the window was so old it looked new again. It was a neighborhood bar.

The front door was faced with dented metal and the handle was a well-worn horseshoe welded to the frame.

He pulled it open and slid inside. He knew better than to stride right in. Instead, he kept his back to the wall on the side of the door until he could assess the situation.

The Palomino was dark and close inside. Except for a lighted shadow box containing a John Elway–signed football on the wall, he could have been stepping into a portal that took him to "Denver, 1976."

There was an unused pool table lit by a hanging lamp, its green felt ripped by errant cue tips. Black-and-white photos of downtown Denver in the 1930s decorated the walls.

The backbar was carved wood and inappropriately ornate and had no doubt come from somewhere else.

Five customers sat with their backs to him at the bar. They'd been hunched over bottles of light beer, but four of the five swiveled on their stools to check him out. A shaggy-headed man narrowed his eyes as he looked him over. He didn't offer a greeting.

Next to the shaggy-headed man was an overweight woman in an oversized sweatshirt with a graphic of Santa Claus on the front of it. She had tight silver coils of curls and appeared to be with a skinny dark man next to her wearing horn-rimmed glasses and a pencil-thin mustache. A lone drinker who appeared to be in his sixties sat at the left end of the bar, trying to keep his head from dropping to the surface of it.

Moving lazily in front of this group of four was a gaunt bald man with narrow eyes and a beak of a nose. The bartender. He seemed content to stay near his customers and wasn't eager to look up and challenge Nate's entrance. The bartender kept his hands low beneath the bar. Nate guessed he had a baseball bat or other weapon down there within easy reach.

There was a large gap between those customers and a menacing-looking man, who sat by himself to the right. The man had a mass of dreads that cascaded down his back and partially obscured his wide mahogany face. He wore a bulky tactical jacket with dozens of pockets and heavy combat boots. A green tactical bag sat on the floor near his feet.

Why were the patrons so suspicious? Nate got his answer when he read the lips of the bartender, who whispered to the older couple, "No black bloc."

He was assuring them that Nate wasn't dressed like the rioters outside, so he probably wasn't one of them. With that, the customers turned their backs on him again.

Nate drew out his phone and found the text thread.

Geronimo Jones?

He watched as the Black man slid his big paw into the side pocket of his coat and pulled out his phone and read the screen. Then he looked up and their eyes met.

Nate took the stool next to the man and turned so that his back was to the others.

Before he could speak, the man said, "Follow me." Then to the bartender: "I'll be back. Don't take my beer."

NATE THOUGHT THE MAN didn't fit in with either the neighborhood or this particular bar. Just like Nate didn't.

He followed Jones down a narrow hallway past the restrooms. The man was built like a linebacker, with wide shoulders, a thick neck, and a huge woolly head. He had so much thick coiled hair it was almost a helmet. His gait was graceful, smooth as silk. Nate was taller, but he was outweighed by twenty or thirty pounds.

Jones darted left into a room with a sign that read STAFF ONLY.

When Nate turned the corner, he was greeted by the unblinking maw of a three-eyed monster aimed squarely at his face.

"Close the door behind you," Jones said softly. Nate did as he was told.

He'd heard of the particular weapon before but had never seen one in person: a Charles Daly Honcho triple-barrel twelve-gauge shotgun. It was slightly over twenty-five inches from the pistol grip to the three muzzles, and it had therefore been fairly easy to conceal beneath the baggy parka Jones wore. It was an overwhelming shotgun, and at close range Nate knew that a blast from it could cut him in half. The weapon was perfect for close-in urban combat or home defense.

"I need to know that you're who you say you are," Jones said.

"I'm your worst nightmare if you don't take that shotgun out of my face."

"Show me what I'm looking for," Jones said. "You're not the only white boy with a ponytail, you know."

Nate slowly reached up and unzipped his vest and opened it. He peeled back the left side until Jones could clearly see the grip of his .454 Casull revolver.

A slow grin came over Jones's face and he lowered the shotgun. He opened his coat and slipped it into an inside sleeve, muzzle-first.

"You're Romanowski, all right," Jones said. "A fellow bigbore enthusiast, just like I heard about."

"And you go by Geronimo Jones. What's your real name?"

"Geronimo Jones. It's on my birth certificate."

Nate accepted that. Then he looked around. The storeroom was cluttered and smelled of sour beer. Empty kegs were stacked to the ceiling, and dusty liquor bottles lined the shelves.

"How is it you have access to this room?" Nate asked. He noted that the man's military-style coat had JONES stenciled over one breast pocket and BLM stenciled over the other.

Nate knew that in this instance, "BLM" didn't stand for Bureau of Land Management.

"I keep the riffraff out," Jones said. "You probably saw those crackers out on the street. Did you see all the graffiti and boarded-up windows downtown on your way here?"

"I did."

"They know not to come in here," he said. "I've had words with them." When he said it, he patted his shotgun through his coat.

"The owner pays you for protection, then," Nate said.

"That's one way to look at it. The other way is that he wants to keep his customers safe. They're a bunch of soft old mouthbreathers, but they're harmless enough. I've gotten to like them."

"Do they like you?"

"They love me," Jones said. "This is a dangerous neighborhood because we're a few blocks from the capitol. Didn't used to be, but it is now."

"I don't care about Denver's problems. I'm here for Axel Soledad," Nate said. "You said you've seen him around."

Jones nodded slowly. He said, "You want a beer? It's on me."

THEY SAT NEXT to each other at the end of the bar and spoke softly. They stopped when one of the customers got up to leave or a new one came in. When that happened, Jones watched the proceedings carefully. He was alert to any time the door opened, and Nate could sense him tense up. The only time Jones got off his stool was to escort the older couple outside to their car and to make sure they got out of the parking lot okay.

When he returned, Nate asked, "How long ago did you put eyes on him?"

"This afternoon. An hour before it got dark. I saw a big SUV with dark windows go down an alley a block from the capitol. Something about that car made me suspicious. It was just a feeling, but the car was moving real slow and cautious. Most folks know not to come to this neighborhood that time of day, especially when the word came out there was going to be street action tonight. So it didn't fit.

"I was on foot," Jones said. Then: "I have a place across the street. I stay there when I'm not out with my falcons west of town in the mountains. I got a place out there, too. Anyway, I saw this SUV creeping around. I climbed a ladder to get to the roof of this building so I could see it better."

Jones drew his phone out and tapped in a password and punched up the photo app. He swiped through the photos until he found the one he wanted, then used his big fingers to zoom it out. He handed his phone to Nate.

The shot was out of focus because it had been taken at a great distance. The SUV was parked in the alley with the back hatch open. Two men wearing black clothing and motorcycle helmets were at the rear bumper, reaching inside the car. A third man stood to the side, directing them.

Axel Soledad was unmistakable in the image. He was tall and imposing, with a hatchet-like nose and a week's growth of dark beard on his face. His head was shaved and reflected the ambient light.

"That's him," Nate said. "What were they doing?"

"Do you want to see for yourself?"

Nate indicated that he did.

"Back soon," Jones called out to the bartender.

CHAPTER EIGHT

April Pickett

WHEN SHE HEARD TIRES GRIND ON THE GRAVEL OUTSIDE THEIR home, Marybeth closed the photo album with a thud and lowered the screen on her laptop. A quick glance at the digital clock on the microwave induced immediate panic.

She'd been so engrossed in her research that she'd let herself become completely sidetracked.

Her list of Thanksgiving to-dos had barely been addressed. The horses needed to be fed, the beds in the two guest rooms needed new sheets, the bathrooms needed fresh towels, the turkey needed to be brined, pies had to be baked . . . on and on. And yet she'd opened the album again when she got home from the store and once again had been swept away. She'd deliberately let herself get behind schedule.

After a trip to the grocery store, where she'd had to navigate through dozens of other Thanksgiving shoppers, she'd completely filled the back of the van and headed home.

Her only stop was a quick one to check on Lola Lowry and deliver her bag of books. Lola lived in a double-wide trailer on a small parcel of land en route to their home on the river. Despite her provocative name, which amused Marybeth and Joe to no end, Lola was an eighty-two-year-old widow, who, being the last person alive in her family, had inherited the land and the trailer from her deceased uncle, who had used it as a hunting lodge on his annual trips from Michigan.

Lola was feisty and independent, and except for a cat, she lived alone. She was fond of those romance books and Marybeth used the weekly visits to check on her in general. Lola was still very sharp, although she thought the couple down the road near the river were named "Pridgett."

When Marybeth arrived, Lola was drinking Dixie cups of peppermint schnapps and watching her soaps on television. Before leaving, Marybeth invited the woman to Thanksgiving dinner with them, and although Lola demurred at first, she agreed to come if no one minded that she left early.

Which meant they had to plan for an additional seat at the table, even though Marybeth doubted that Lola ate much.

But after unpacking the groceries in her kitchen, Marybeth felt the photo album pulling at her. She assured herself that she'd devote only a few minutes to it. That had been three hours before.

Only the arrival of the vehicle outside broke her trance.

———

SHE PUSHED THE ALBUM and laptop to the side of the dining room table and tossed a spare apron over the top of them so neither could be seen. The subject matter of the materials was too disturbing to be viewed without context. The album exuded a malignant evil. If it was able to penetrate and infect her, no doubt it would have the same effect on others.

Nevertheless, she couldn't wait to show it to Joe, tell him what she'd learned about the original owner, and what she was starting to discover about how it might have found its way to rural Wyoming. She was obsessed with it.

But when she parted the kitchen curtains she noticed that the headlights in the drive weren't from Joe's pickup. They were narrower and the beams were less focused from the headlamps.

Someone was coming, and she didn't recognize who it was.

ALTHOUGH THERE WAS a small wooden sign out on the county road indicating the turnoff through the timber to the Saddlestring District Game Warden Station—which was what their house was officially called, since it was owned by the state agency—it was always interesting and sometimes alarming to see who showed up after dusk.

Since it was in the latter part of the big-game seasons, it could be hunters arriving to turn themselves in for violations or to report others for transgressions. Occasionally, local landowners who couldn't contact Joe by either cell phone or via the dispatcher would simply show up to report trespassers or make their case against changing regulations or opener dates.

The Pickett house had always been quasi-public. Only in larger communities like Cheyenne, Casper, Jackson, or Lander were there dedicated office buildings for Game and Fish personnel.

Marybeth was used to handling situations on the fly, and when people showed up, she no longer had the added worry about their daughters in the house. Not that being completely alone was that much better. But there was no doubt having a woman open the door instead of the game warden himself sometimes defused tense situations.

As agreed between them long ago, she snatched her cell phone from the counter and texted Joe.

Someone coming down the road.

Seconds after she sent it, she saw the word balloon go active on her screen as Joe typed out his reply.

On my way.

Marybeth smoothed her pants with the palms of her hands and strode through the kitchen into the dining room. She checked to make sure the front door was bolted—it was—and the twenty-gauge pump-action shotgun was leaning upright in the corner near the door. Joe had insisted on it, and it was times like these when she remembered it was there and she was grateful. No hunter or fisherman had ever showed up and threatened her, but over the years she'd had to deal with inebriated men who wanted to come in and wait for Joe. She wouldn't let them.

She paused at the door and leaned into the peephole. The lens distorted what she could see.

An older-model Toyota Tundra with dealer plate tags drove up to the front gate and stopped. She couldn't yet see who was driving or how many men were inside.

Not until the driver's door opened and the dome light came on. Then Marybeth cried out, threw back the bolt, and stepped outside.

A tall, flinty-looking female swung out of the cab and her cowboy boots dropped to the gravel. She stepped away from the open door and stretched. The light from inside the cab illuminated the side of her angular face and one almond-shaped eye. Her hair was dirty blond, streaked with pink and violet highlights.

"April," Marybeth said. "I didn't expect you until much later tonight."

"I figured I'd just drive straight through from Montana."

"Why didn't you call me?"

"My cell phone died," April said. "I forgot to bring my charger."

That was not unusual when it came to April, Marybeth thought but didn't say. April operated in her own universe and Marybeth knew how much that distressed Joe. One of his daughters driving alone at night without a working cell phone would make him crazy. But this was April, after all. She could be a tough customer.

"Well, come on in," Marybeth said, stepping aside. "Do you need any help with your things?"

"Nope," April said, reaching into the bed of her pickup for a duffel bag. "This is all I've got. Except for my new dog. Can I let him come in?"

"You got a dog?"

"I got a dog."

That's when Marybeth saw the massive head of a jowly bull mastiff rise from the front seat and almost fill the passenger side of the windshield. Twin ropes of drool strung down from the sides of its mouth.

"Goodness, April."

"He's a sweetie. His name is LeDoux. You know, like Chris LeDoux."

April called him out and LeDoux lumbered across the seat and dropped heavily to the ground beside her.

"I got a new truck, too," she said. "I mean, an old truck that's new to me. Pretty sweet, huh?"

"It is."

"Do you know there's a cow moose blocking your road? I thought she wasn't going to let me get by."

"She does that every night," Marybeth said. "Especially to your dad."

"It's weird coming home to a place I never lived before."

"Come into the light," Marybeth said. "Let me see you."

"I haven't changed."

But she had.

Marybeth quickly texted the news to Joe, who replied:

> Don't let her drink all of my beer.

After April claimed the larger of the two guest rooms and justified it by saying she "got there first," Marybeth offered her a glass of wine if she'd help her in the kitchen.

"I'll help, but I'd go for a beer instead," April said as she ducked out to the garage to her dad's refrigerator and grabbed a stubby bottle of Coors as if she'd done it dozens of times before. Which, Marybeth thought, she probably had in their other home.

April had grown at least two inches in the last few months, Marybeth thought, as she mentally did the calculation while they stood next to each other at the counter making deviled eggs. April was now taller than her, and her high-heeled cowboy boots made the disparity even more obvious. As did the fact that April jokingly referred to Marybeth as "my little mama."

April wore cowgirl jeans with faux rhinestones on the back pockets, a tight white tank top under an open snap-button shirt, and a collection of bangle bracelets that clicked as she worked. Her expression had always been hard, but now it was harder: more angles, a downturned mouth, and a flinty look in her eye.

April looked more and more, Marybeth thought, like her birth mother, Jeannie Keeley. She wasn't as hard—few could be—but she came off as tough and no-nonsense, and Marybeth knew that she unfortunately attracted a certain kind of man.

Like her ex-boyfriend, the rodeo star Dallas Cates, who was in the last years of his sentence at the Wyoming State Penitentiary in Rawlins.

"This is a nice place," April said as she pulled at her beer and looked around. "Is the river just outside? I couldn't see very much in the dark."

"It is. Your dad loves the fact that he can grab his fly rod and walk to the water. He told me his lifelong goal was to someday live in a place where he didn't have to break down his fly rod and put it in a case every time he was done casting. I never knew that before he mentioned it a few months ago."

"What else hasn't he told you?" April asked with a devilish gleam in her eye.

"Always the instigator," Marybeth said. "That hasn't changed."

MARYBETH OUTLINED THE LOGISTICS of the Thanksgiving weekend. Lucy was scheduled to show up the next day with her new friend from college, and Sheridan could show up at any time, but wouldn't sleep over because she was staying at Nate and Liv Romanowski's place eight miles away.

"Lucy is bringing a friend?" April asked with an eye roll. "How Lucy is that?"

"Very Lucy." Their youngest was by far the most social of the girls and the quickest to make friends.

"How's it working out for Sheridan to work for Nate?" April asked. The question surprised Marybeth because she assumed

April and Sheridan were in regular communication. Apparently, she'd assumed wrong.

"It's going very well from what I can tell," Marybeth said. "Despite much more drama than I'd like."

She knew April was well aware of the situation that had occurred weeks before in the mountains and the fact that Sheridan had ended up in the middle of it. The murder plot against the high-tech executive had made national news and there were conspiracy theories online about what really had happened.

"Nate's away right now, though," Marybeth continued. "That's why Sheridan is staying with Liv and the baby at their house."

"Will he be here for Thanksgiving dinner?"

"Doubtful, from what I understand."

"Where is he?"

"He's trying to track down a man who beat up Liv and stole his falcons."

After a moment's shock, April said, "That won't end well," with a ghoulish delight Marybeth found uncomfortable. But that was April. She believed in rough justice.

"We'll fill you in on all of that later," Marybeth said. "Or you can ask Liv herself. She's bringing desserts. And she's bringing Kestrel, their toddler. She's fourteen months old and growing up in front of our eyes."

"I'm glad you have a baby around to keep you occupied," April said.

As before, the statement was more than a little provocative.

All the girls knew Marybeth couldn't wait to be a grandmother. Marybeth didn't take the bait.

"So how are things going at the store in Montana?" she asked.

After graduating from Northwest Community College, April had taken a job in Cody at the Western-wear retailer she'd worked for in Saddlestring. Within two months, she'd been offered a promotion to manage an outlet in Bozeman and had moved north across the border.

"First let me get another beer," April said. "It's been a long day."

"EVERYTHING'S GOING FINE at the store, but it's not what I want to do for the rest of my life," April said as she resumed her post next to Marybeth at the counter and began mashing hard egg yolks into a bowl. "The work's okay, but being the manager of employees is no fun. Personnel management is a bitch. We can't keep people very long. We train them and then they realize they actually have to work, so they start whining. I swear," she said, "I really can't stand being around most of the people my age. They're just pussies."

"April," Marybeth cautioned.

"Sorry, but it's true. They want days off after they've worked there for a week. I'm not kidding. And I'm just lucky I don't have to drug test the associates or we'd have nobody to work."

"I understand."

She did. Marybeth headed the hiring committee at the library, and of the seven millennials they'd brought on, only one remained, and he had already exhausted all of his sick leave and vacation time for the year.

"Anyway, it isn't going to be my career. I'll do it until I can find something else. Something I can really dig into, you know?"

"Like what?" Marybeth asked.

"Well, you know how I always wanted to punish pukes?"

"You mean criminals?"

"Yeah. But I don't want to be a cop. Cops give me the creeps."

"Your dad is law enforcement."

"Yeah, but he's different. He's out there with the deer and elk all day, you know? He's not busting kids for speeding or possessing weed."

Marybeth bit her tongue and didn't argue. It was rare when April was so open with her. She didn't want to derail the conversation.

April took another long drink and said, "So I was in the process of getting my name changed when this, um, opportunity came up."

Marybeth froze, her knife blade an inch from another hard-boiled egg.

"What name change?" she asked.

"Yeah. I'm getting it changed from April Keeley to April Keeley Pickett. Didn't I tell you about that?"

"No, somehow you forgot," Marybeth said, trying to keep the sarcasm out of her tone.

"Well, I am. I think it's better, don't you?"

Marybeth nodded. Her eyes misted suddenly. "Of course I like it. And so will your dad."

"I'll try not to get my name in the news and embarrass you," April said. "Unlike Dad."

Marybeth started to turn to hug her, when April laughed and stepped away. "Be careful with that knife," she said. "Don't gut me, Mom."

"I WAS DOING the name change paperwork with this lawyer in Bozeman," April continued, "when she mentioned that her investigator might be looking for some help. I said I was interested. Who doesn't want to be a PI?"

Me, Marybeth thought but didn't say. *Nobody I know. And hopefully not my daughter.*

"Anyway, I did an interview with the PI at her firm and I really liked her. I think she liked me. I mentioned my name change and somehow she'd heard of Dad and that probably helped. So who knows? I may be able to do something with a little excitement in it, you know? More exciting than fitting cowboy boots on tourists, for sure."

"So you might be working for a firm made up of women?"

"Crazy, huh?"

"When will you know?" Marybeth asked.

"Maybe next week," April said. "She said she might want to do a second interview. The job would start after the first of the year."

"Interesting."

"I've been looking at what I would need to do," April said. "You have to get a PI license from the state, and probably a concealed carry permit. I need to figure all that out. But at first I think I'll be doing a lot of boring things like answering the phone, filing, that kind of crap. But compared to retail, I think I can gut that out for a while."

AFTER THE DEVILED EGGS were made and covered with plastic and stored in the refrigerator, Marybeth poured herself a second glass of wine. Next on her list was to mix the brine and pour it into a brining bag with the turkey. She'd reserved an entire shelf of the fridge for it.

Despite her initial reaction, she was proud of April. Her most troubled and difficult daughter was turning into her own woman. She wasn't asking to move back home, and as far as Marybeth knew she hadn't taken up with another loser like Dallas Cates. April was charting her own path and taking responsibility for her future. No wonder she didn't like working with people her age who didn't have the same outlook and determination.

Marybeth's phone chimed twice and she checked it. There were texts from both Sheridan and Joe. Sheridan said she was on her way there with Liv and Kestrel. Joe asked if there was anything he needed to pick up in town.

Great, Marybeth answered Sheridan.

You might want to get more beer, she texted Joe. And peppermint schnapps for Lola.

———

MARYBETH TOLD APRIL that Sheridan and her dad were on their way to the house, when April sat down at the kitchen table and twisted off the top of another beer.

"Cool," she said. "I can't wait to see them. I'm sure I can still take Sheridan."

"Take" meaning wrestle her to the ground. Marybeth smiled at that.

April casually flipped over the spare apron on the table to reveal Marybeth's laptop and the leather-bound photo album.

"What's this?" April asked, sliding the album across to her and opening it.

Marybeth felt a pang of guilt she couldn't explain.

April furrowed her brow as she turned the pages. "Fucking Nazis," she said.

"April . . ."

CHAPTER NINE

Geronimo Jones

GERONIMO JONES LED NATE ON FOOT THROUGH PASSAGES AND alleyways in the direction of the capitol building. Geronimo knew the nuances of the neighborhood and they ducked through gaps in fences and under wire ostensibly protecting commercial parking lots.

Nate was on high alert and he could feel the power of *yarak* envelop him as he walked. Despite the layer of city sounds that provided a distracting soundtrack, his eyesight improved in the dark, his ears perked up at every sound, and his nostrils flared at strange odors. He kept his vest unzipped so he could reach up and draw his weapon smoothly without snagging the hammer on the nylon material.

Although Geronimo Jones seemed to be who he said he was, Nate was still cautious. Antifa was out there on the streets and Geronimo displayed his BLM allegiance literally on his coat.

Weren't most of the urban riots across the nation described as "BLM/antifa protests"?

Nate had never encountered Axel Soledad in person, but knew through Sheridan Pickett's research that Soledad was a leader in the antifa movement, even though the group claimed not to have leaders. Soledad had spoken at rallies, written incendiary posts on the dark web, and traveled to Europe to liaise with well-established antifa chapters. His role in the movement was a mystery, though. And so was how he came to embrace the ideology.

Soledad, like Nate fifteen years before him, had been a member of the Five, an elite special operator unit associated with the U.S. Air Force. Few people knew the group existed, and they deliberately kept it that way. "The Five" was a derivation of their official designation, which was Mark V. The unit deployed to international locations in secret, accomplished its covert mission, and returned without fanfare. They were informally known within the unit as the Peregrines, after the fastest species known to man.

Being a member of the Five affected different operators in different ways. The intensity of the missions led some to crack up, others to drink or take drugs, and some, like Nate, to become thoroughly disillusioned with their commander.

Something had happened to Soledad to turn him. Nate didn't know what it was, and Soledad, at least publicly, had never explained it. But he'd gone from being the tip of the covert spear for American interests to a man who wanted to burn the country down. And steal falcons from fellow falconers along the way.

Soledad's current allies and associates were murky, but they were no doubt international. There were no clear lines between Soledad, antifa chapters across the nation, other anarchists, and offshoots of BLM. For all Nate knew, Geronimo Jones was a pal of Soledad's.

Was he being led into a trap?

After a few minutes at the bar, Nate had confirmed that Geronimo was, in fact, a master falconer. He spoke knowledgeably of the avocation and he knew as much about hunting with gyrfalcons in particular as anyone Nate had ever met. But was his allegiance to falconry, BLM, or antifa? Or some combination of all three?

Nate told himself he had no choice but to trust the man until he had reason not to. So he followed.

"You know why I want Axel Soledad," Nate said to Geronimo. "You read my post and responded. What beef do you have with him?"

"Yeah," Geronimo said. "Poaching on a man's territory, stealing his birds, and threatening his family is about as bad as you can get. I can see why you're after him."

"So answer my question," Nate said.

Geronimo said, "You've got your reasons. I've got mine. Let's leave it at that for now."

"As long as we find him," Nate said.

"We're on the same page here," Geronimo said. "You would be invited to the cookout."

Nate had no idea what that meant other than it sounded like he'd be included in whatever Geronimo was up to.

———

THE BUILDINGS GOT TALLER as they got closer to the capitol. Nate assumed by their uninspired architecture they were government buildings.

Through an opening onto the street, a small knot of protesters moved under a streetlight. Nate and Geronimo kept themselves in shadow and watched the group pass. Nate saw they were all in black clothing and they wore motorcycle helmets with the shields down. Two of the group held their glowing phones out in front of them.

Nate whispered to Geronimo, "Why do they dress like that?"

"There are closed-circuit cameras everywhere, not to mention that everyone on the street has a phone camera and all the cops have body cams. If they mask up and dress alike, it's impossible for the cops to identify individuals who do bad shit and get caught on video."

"Are they packing?"

"Rarely, but sometimes. They'd rather kick ass with boots and clubs and they like to use their skateboards as weapons. It keeps them out of jail and it doesn't give the media reasons not to love them."

"You know a lot about antifa," Nate said.

"I've only scratched the surface, nature boy."

"What's the street action all about?" Nate asked.

Gernomio shrugged. "What do you got?"

"Why don't the cops just round them up?"

"The cops have learned it's useless, even though they could

do it in one night. There's not that many of them, maybe fifty or so. But we've got a progressive DA that cuts them all loose without charges. These yahoos are back on the street hours after they're arrested. They get arrested, get released, and do it all over again. Rinse and repeat. It makes it seem like there are more of them, but there aren't."

"There's no law enforcement?"

"Hey—I've been pulled over thirteen times for Driving While Black. And you just have to look at me to know some of these cops are just begging for a reason to light me up."

"But they let you go?" Nate asked.

"They do now. All they have to see is this," he said, pointing to the BLM stencil on his jacket. "Get-out-of-jail-free patch, is what it is. It's the word from on high."

"I don't understand," Nate said.

"And I don't have time to explain right now, my man."

THEY APPROACHED THE LOCATION Geronimo had scouted through a long narrow opening between two buildings. Nate didn't like the situation they were in at all. It would be too easy to trap them in the pathway by blocking both ends. The only way out would be to scale the brick walls.

He felt a wave of relief wash over him when they emerged into the dark alley. He looked over his shoulder through a space between the buildings and could see the top of the Palomino Lounge in the distance. That's where Geronimo had seen and photographed Axel Soledad's SUV.

"This is it," Geronimo said. "I scoped it out after Soledad left, to find out what they were doing here."

Geronimo drew out his cell phone and punched up the flashlight app.

"Check this out," he said.

Against the wall of one of the buildings was a large pile of something covered by a blue tarpaulin. The corners of the tarp were held down by rocks.

Nate watched as Geronimo kicked the two nearest rocks aside. He leaned down and grasped the corner of the plastic and whipped it back to reveal a big pile of primitive ordnance: loose bricks, three-foot lengths of one-inch steel rebar, dented aluminum baseball bats, sledgehammers, crowbars, cases of commercial fireworks, and a few single-blade axes.

"So that's what they unloaded," Nate said. "Is it to fight the police?"

Geronimo nodded while he used his phone to call up another app.

"The exact location of the cache was posted on a secret geocache site tonight at eighteen hundred hours. Everybody out here on the street can find it if they need it."

"How?"

"We have our ways," he said. Then: "Encrypted software and message boards. It just looks like chaos out there, and sometimes it is. Other times, it's very, very organized. These weapons were left here tonight to mess up the police in case things get out of hand."

Nate nodded. "So Soledad is equipping them."

"He's equipping someone, for sure," Geronimo said cryptically.

Nate knew there was much more to the story, but he was distracted by the figure of a man darting across the mouth of the alleyway. He'd been silhouetted by the ambient streetlight beyond.

"What?" Geronimo asked.

Nate gestured to the opening as another figure ran across it. Then two more. The group of protesters they'd seen earlier had turned around and come back.

Geronimo doused his flashlight and whispered, "Looks like we've got us some antifa assholes."

NATE AND GERONIMO stood their ground shoulder to shoulder. It was too dark to see clearly, but they could make out that the four visitors were approaching them as quietly as they could along the left wall. One of their boots crunched on a piece of glass as they got close.

Then a bright light came on and bathed Nate and Geronimo. Nate lifted his left arm to shield his eyes. He kept his right hand free and ready to reach up for his weapon. The light swept across him and settled on Geronimo.

"Hey, man, what are you doing?" the man with the flashlight asked. His voice was muffled behind an opaque face shield and a bandana mask.

"Checkin' out this treasure here," Geronimo said.

"That's cool. What's with the mountain man? Is he with you?"

"He's with me," Geronimo said.

Nate noted that Geronimo's vernacular had suddenly become "street." He found that telling.

"Are you in touch with your brothers?" the first antifa asked. "Are they on their way?"

The first antifa, apparently the spokesman of the four, also lapsed into a faux "street" cadence.

"They're on their way," Geronimo said.

Nate's eyes adjusted slightly and he could see better with the throwback light from the flashlight. Four of them, all right. They wore black bloc: shielded helmets, face coverings, heavy boots. One of them held a length of rebar alongside his thigh. Two held oversized skateboards much like the one the rioter had used to hit Nate's van. The last man wore a rucksack that bulged with commercial fireworks. He could see the snouts of aerial explosive devices sticking out from beneath the top flap of the pack.

They inched closer along the wall.

Nate said, "Not another step."

As he said it, he envisioned a scenario where, in one controlled motion, he drew his revolver and cocked it at the same time, moved into a shooting stance, and took them out one by one with four rapid center-mass shots. That would leave him one live round to spare.

But, he conceded, he was getting ahead of himself.

"Who is this guy?" the first antifa asked Geronimo. The tone of his question betrayed his sudden alarm.

"Friend of mine," Geronimo said. "If I was you, I'd back the fuck up."

The four of them froze, unsure of what to do. Their spokesman wasn't giving them any direction.

"Is he with you?" Antifa One asked. "I mean, is he *with* you?"

"I already told you he was," Geronimo said. "That's all you need to know."

"Do any of you know Axel Soledad?" Nate asked quietly. He could tell by the way the four shuffled and looked around that they knew something.

"Speak up," Nate said. "Don't be shy. I need answers and I'm in a hurry."

Finally, Antifa Two said, "Hey, man. We don't talk about him."

"Until now," Nate said.

"We're just gonna back out of here now," Antifa Two said. Then: "Right, Tristan?"

Tristan was apparently Antifa One.

"Shut up, Robbie," Tristan said.

"Tristan and Robbie," Nate echoed. "Couple of country-club names. Why am I not surprised? Shouldn't you boys be playing video games in your parents' basement?"

Nate was on them before they could react or go for their weapons. He kneed Robbie hard and doubled him over while smashing Tristan in the throat with his left elbow. As both men went down, he drew his heavy revolver and hit Antifa Three so hard on the side of his helmet that it cracked open like an egg. Antifa Four jumped back and cocked his skateboard over his shoulder like a baseball bat.

As the first three writhed in the gravel, Nate raised the gun and placed the front sight squarely in the middle of the man's face shield. He cocked it.

"Don't you know better than to bring a skateboard to a gunfight?" Nate asked.

Antifa Four wheeled and dropped his skateboard. He ran down the alley in a panic and into the street without looking, narrowly avoiding being hit by a yellow taxi that slammed on its brakes. Then he was gone.

Nate returned to the squirming pile of antifa and chose Antifa Three, whose face had been revealed when his helmet was split open. Nate kneeled down and pressed the huge muzzle of his revolver into the soft skin of the man's cheek. He reached down with his other hand and gripped his left ear.

Antifa Three had a pudgy white face with the texture of tapioca pudding, a wispy blond mustache, bright green eyes, and an antifa *A* symbol tattooed on the side of his neck. He looked terrified.

"So we've got Tristan and Robbie," Nate hissed. "What's your name?"

"Please, I don't wanna—"

Nate twisted hard on the ear and the man screamed out.

"No screaming," Nate said. "Someone might hear you. I asked your name."

"Cole."

"Cole. That's precious. Where do you live, Cole?"

"Cherry Creek."

Even Nate knew Cherry Creek was an exclusive Denver neighborhood.

"So, Cole of Cherry Creek, where is Axel Soledad?"

As he asked, Tristan moaned at the mention of the name. It was a warning to Cole not to talk. Nate shifted his weight so he could swing his revolver and smash Tristan in the helmet. Tristan went quiet.

"Where is he?" Nate asked again, putting more pressure on Cole's ear. "I've twisted off a ton of these. I wear them as a necklace. Do you want me to add yours?"

"He's gone," Cole spat out. "Axel left tonight."

"To where?"

Cole told him.

"Prove to me that you saw him," Nate said. "What was he driving?"

"This big truck," Cole said, his words rushing out. "It was like a, you know, delivery truck. Or repair truck. Shit, I don't know. But it was big."

"What was inside of it?"

"Cages. A whole bunch of cages."

"What was in the cages, Cole?"

"I don't know."

"Cole . . ." He gave the ear a quarter twist.

"Birds! Eagles or something like that."

Nate looked up at Geronimo. "Do you believe him?"

"I think I do."

Nate turned back. He released Cole's ear and dug a wallet out of the man's tactical pants. There was a Colorado driver's license in a sleeve and Nate removed it and held it up to Geronimo.

"Take a photo," Nate said. Geronimo did.

Nate tossed both the wallet and the ID aside and leaned down and said, "Cole of Cherry Creek, I know where you live. I've got your parents' address. If you're lying to me, I'll come back for you. I'll find you and tear you apart piece by piece until you're begging me to end it all. Got that?"

"Got it," Cole said. His face was ashen.

Nate stood over the three men. Cole was sobbing. Nate thought about kicking them all before he left, but he had never liked kicking a man when he was down. He didn't mind hurting them in other ways, but kicking was so . . . cheap.

Geronimo stepped into the scrum, but not to kick anyone, either. He bent down over Tristan and hauled him up to his feet by the collar.

"We're taking this one with us," he said.

"Why?"

"I got questions I need answered," Geronimo said.

Tristan protested, "Don't you dare put your hands on me."

Geronimo slapped the side of his helmet so hard it sounded like a gunshot. Tristan wobbled, but he didn't collapse. When Tristan raised his hands to plead his case, Geronimo raised his triple-barrel shotgun and aimed it with one hand at Tristan's chest.

"You have no right to do this," Tristan said.

Geronimo ignored him. He guided Tristan away from his group and pushed him toward the passage to the alleyway. Nate followed behind them.

———

As THEY RETURNED to the Palomino Lounge the way they'd come, Geronimo said, "Well, that was something. I'd heard about the ear thing before, but I never thought I'd see it with my own eyes."

"Thank you for your help tonight," Nate said. "I do appreciate it."

"So you're going after him?"

"Yes. But what was Soledad up to? Why'd he cache all those weapons? Those assholes we met were all geared up already. Who was the intended recipient?"

"I can't say for sure, but I've got a theory," Geronimo said.

"What is it?"

"We ain't got time for it now, but I think our buddy Soledad is playing on a whole different level. A really dangerous level. Tristan here should help us out with getting an answer."

"Please," Tristan said. "Let me go. You can't just kidnap me."

"Call the cops," Geronimo said.

That shut Tristan up.

Nate asked Geronimo, "Why did you talk to them the way you did?"

"What'chu mean?" Geronimo said, reverting.

"That. Exactly that. Why did you go street on them and not me?"

Geronimo grinned bitterly. "They don't expect anything else. They can't see anything beyond my skin color. If I broke out the

King's English on 'em, it would boggle their tiny little minds. It would be too much for them to grasp in the moment."

"You're an interesting guy, Geronimo Jones."

"Thank you, nature boy. By the way, do you need a place to crash tonight? I can text you directions to my piece of property west of town. That's the direction you're headed, anyway. I might want to show off my birds for you in the morning before you take off. You're the rare man that would appreciate them."

Nate thought about it. The adrenaline from the confrontation was wearing off. He'd been on the road for eleven hours and he was exhausted.

"I'd appreciate that," he said.

"Better than sleeping in the back of your van like a damned hippie," Geronimo said with a chuckle.

GERONIMO JONES FOLLOWED Nate to his van on Corona Street. He produced a roll of duct tape from his parka and used it to bind Tristan's wrists and ankles and did a double wrap around the man's head to keep him from talking. Then he pushed Tristan into the back of Nate's van and closed the door.

"It's about last call inside," he said. "I better go make sure all my chickens get home safely."

Nate nodded.

"Are you going to need some help? Taking down Axel Soledad, I mean? I saw what you could do back there with the junior league, but from what I understand your man is a nasty piece of work."

"I appreciate the offer," Nate said. "But I'm better alone."

Geronimo wasn't done. "I don't want you to take this wrong," he said, "but you're no spring chicken. Soledad is a younger and meaner version of you, I take it. It might be good to have someone watching your back."

Nate didn't respond.

"Sleep on it," Geronimo said. "Decide in the morning after we have a conversation with Tristan."

"Okay," Nate said finally.

"One more thing," Geronimo said. "Don't mess with my lady."

"I won't," Nate said with a grin. "I've got one of my own and she's the best. A little girl, too."

"Think of them when you consider my offer, nature boy."

With that, Geronimo tapped the hood of Nate's van and stepped aside.

Nate watched him amble toward the front door of the Palomino with his phone out. He was tapping on it with his big thumbs.

A second later, the directions to his property appeared on Nate's screen. It would be a forty-minute drive into the mountains with a bound and gagged antifa in the back of his van.

Nate wasn't upset to leave Denver in his rearview mirror.

CHAPTER TEN

Hungarian Hay Hook

OUT ON THE COUNTY ROAD, THE TWO MEN IN THE RENTAL SUV sat parked in shadow beneath overhanging branches of a massive river cottonwood tree. A hundred and fifty yards ahead of them on the road was the small sign indicating the turnoff to the game warden station.

"You're sure this is her address?" László asked.

Viktór showed him the illuminated screen on his phone with the map feature on. "Look," he said in Hungarian.

"This might be good," László said. "I don't see any neighbors around. I don't even see any lights."

"What is our plan?" Victór asked.

"We sit here and wait. We don't know how many people are at the house. If she's alone, we can go there tonight."

Viktór settled back in his seat. "I'm hungry and tired."

"I don't care."

"I want chicken-fried steak. Like last night. I can't stop dreaming about it."

"We can't go back to the same restaurant two nights in a row. We'll get noticed."

Viktór cursed and turned his phone screen down on his thigh so there would be no glow inside the car.

"How do we know how many people are at her house?"

"We go and find out."

THEY'D EATEN THE NIGHT BEFORE at a diner in town called the Burg-O-Pardner. It had been a very long day of transatlantic travel and driving eight hours from Denver International Airport to northern Wyoming. Victór had ordered the chicken-fried steak, which came with mashed potatoes. The entire dish was smothered in white sausage gravy. He had thought he was ordering some kind of chicken like his native chicken paprikash—but he loved it. Viktór loved eating beef, and he loved being in a part of the United States that offered it on every menu he'd seen thus far. These people ate meat three times a day, it seemed. He was astonished. He wondered if that was the reason so many of them were fat.

László had ordered "Rocky Mountain Oysters" thinking it was seafood. He liked it as well, but after he did a Google search on his phone he cried out and pushed the plate away.

Victór had a good laugh about that. They even ate the testicles of cows and called them oysters!

This place they were now, Viktór thought, wasn't anything like New York City or Orlando. It was high in the mountains, and the sky was huge and the air was thin. There were very few people or towns, and they'd noted on the highway that they didn't see many oncoming cars. Pronghorn antelope—Viktór had to google them on his phone—dotted the sagebrush plains like domestic sheep. Snow covered the tops of the mountains in three directions. It was cold, but it was an oddly thin cold because there was little to no humidity in the air. He was constantly thirsty and felt like the moisture in his eyes and mouth was being wicked away.

But at least it had lots of beef.

THE KOVÁCS BROTHERS had purchased their clothing at a Walmart in Casper and then discarded what they'd worn on the airplane. So they would look like Americans. Viktór wore a new ballcap with the logo of the New York Yankees. László wore a Denver Broncos sweatshirt that was too small for him. László liked tight clothing that showed off his thick shoulders and biceps.

After sitting for another ten minutes, László said, "Let's go."

"What are we doing?"

"Reconnaissance."

They got out and shut their car doors softly, then moved to the back of the SUV. László opened it, and when the dome light came on he cursed and crushed it out with the heel of his hand.

They pulled on dark jackets, gloves, and balaclavas. Viktór had been tasked with removing all of the sales labels the night before.

Although they'd heard how unbelievably easy it was to buy guns in America and that all Americans in this part of the country walked around with them as if they were living in a cowboy movie, they'd found out differently.

Despite very professional false IDs—László was "Greg Seitz" from Cleveland and Viktór was "Bob Hardy" from Syracuse— they'd discovered that in order to purchase a gun, they needed to endure an FBI background check that the clerk said might take hours or even days. This was a surprise to them. They found out it was the same at several gun stores they stopped at on the way north through Wyoming.

Although Viktór was willing to wait for the background check to clear, László was not. He declared that he didn't like or trust the FBI and he wanted nothing to do with them. What if their new identities didn't check out? What then? He declared they would forego firearms. There were other ways to complete their assignment. And then they could go home.

So instead of guns, they'd purchased hand tools, knives, zip ties, bear spray, and other items that would do. László favored a Pulaski tool used by firefighters in the Rocky Mountains. On a stiff handle was a vertical steel ax blade on one end and a horizontal adze on the other, and it weighed one and a half kilograms, or three and a half pounds.

Viktór chose a hay hook they'd found in a farm and ranch

store. The tool had a triangle-shaped metal handle. At the end of a sixty-six-centimeter, or twenty-six-inch, steel shaft, it curved into a sharpened point. It was used for moving heavy bales. He liked how it felt in his hand and was impressed by the velocity he could generate when he swung it through the air.

THEY MOVED TREE TO TREE in the forest parallel to the road until László pointed out a square blue glow through the branches. When they got close enough, they realized that the glow came from the window of a home in the woods. László motioned to Viktór to come to him. They both dropped to their haunches behind the thick trunk of a pine tree.

"Stay here while I go take a look," László said.

Viktór watched his brother move toward the structure in a crouch until he was directly below the glowing window. There were no outside lights. Slowly, László rose up and peered inside for at least thirty seconds.

He then moved across the front of the structure until he was next to the metal door. He reached up and grasped the door handle. Nothing happened. Viktór could tell that the door was locked.

Instead of coming directly back, László crab-walked along the length of the home until he vanished around the corner of it.

Finally, what seemed like seven minutes later, László reappeared on the other side of the house and made his way in a crouch back to Viktór.

"She's in there," László whispered. "She had her back to me, but she was there, all right. She's sitting on a couch watching television. I could see the top of her head."

"Is she alone?"

"Except for a cat, she's alone. I looked in every window all the way around. The cat saw me looking in, but it ran away and hid under a bed."

"I'm glad she doesn't have a dog."

Viktór raised up so he could see over László's shoulder. He frowned.

"It's not a very nice place," he said. At home very few people lived in mobile homes. They were used as temporary housing at building sites.

"She's a librarian. They don't make a lot of money, I don't think. I'm pretty sure Americans don't read very much."

"Where's her car?"

"There's a car around the back."

"Is it the same van?"

"I think so. It was dark. But I saw something very interesting inside the house next to her on the couch."

Victór waited.

"That bag she was carrying," László said. "The one with the library writing on it. I saw the bag."

Viktór nodded. Then: "So how do we get it? We can't just knock on the door and ask for it. What if she calls the police?"

László seemed to be thinking. He placed his gloved fist under his chin and stared straight ahead.

"There's a way in," he said.

———

ON HIS BACK in the dirt beneath the trailer with a penlight in his teeth, Viktór used a multi-tool to unscrew each of the Phillips head screws of a two-foot-by-two-foot panel near the back of the trailer. He was surprised how easy they came out. Back at home, they would have been rusted into place. Apparently, the lack of moisture in the air kept metal from deteriorating, he guessed. As he worked, flakes of dirt filtered down into his eyes. He'd pushed the balaclava up onto the crown of his head so he could see better and breathe more freely.

As he'd told Viktór, the hatch was indeed too narrow for László's wide shoulders to fit through. He'd been right about that.

At last, the panel was free. Viktór lowered it down and placed it beside him. But there was a problem: the opening was filled with ancient pink fiberglass insulation. He clawed at it until he could see the underside of a similar square panel above. If it was screwed down from the inside, there would be nothing he could do.

He reached up and put pressure on the square and it shifted. When it did, he could hear the muted sounds of a television blaring in another room. He was grateful that he wasn't coming up right next to her.

Viktór folded the multi-tool and slipped it back into his pocket. Using both hands, he pushed up on the inside hatch until it was free of its frame. He slid it to the right side until it butted up against something solid.

There wasn't yet enough room in the opening for him to climb up. So he worked the hatch across the opening the other way. It slid left until he could see the dark ceiling of the room above him and an unlit light fixture. The room smelled like an old person, he thought. Which was odd, because the librarian looked to be much younger when they'd seen her earlier that day.

He tried not to grunt as he grasped both sides of the frame and lifted himself upward into a sitting position. Only his head was inside the room, and he looked around. He was thankful for the glow of a night-light plugged into an outlet near the floorboards.

It was a bathroom. There were towels on racks and a light pink shower curtain. The reason he hadn't been able to slide the panel to the right was because it was blocked by a toilet.

The door was open into a narrow hallway. The sound of the television came from the end of the house to his left.

Viktór shinnied up through the opening and sat on the edge of it with his legs dangling into the space until he could make sure he wasn't breathing hard from the effort. Then he swung his boots up and used the edge of the sink to pull himself to full height.

He removed the hay hook from where he'd tucked it through his belt and fitted his fingers through the triangle. It felt substantial in his grip. He let it hang down as he bent forward to peer down the hall to where the librarian was watching television. He was careful not to let the hook clank against the doorframe.

He couldn't see much of her except the top of her head over the back of the couch. There was a small table between her and the television with a bottle of clear liquid in it and a small paper cup. And, just as László had described, the bag with the library logo printed on the side of it was right there on the floor next to the couch. The bag bulged with its contents.

The librarian was still. Was she sleeping?

Could he pad down the hallway, grab the bag, and get clear without waking her? He envisioned himself scuttling back down the hallway, dropping through the opening, and rolling across the ground until he could fit himself under the trailer skirt and escape. He also envisioned a scenario where she heard him coming and screamed. Or grabbed a gun to protect herself. Or ran for the phone to call the police.

By far the simplest and easiest thing to do would be to sneak up on her and bury the hay hook into the top of her head, grab the photo album, and walk out the front door.

He wished he could consult with László, who was waiting for him outside.

But Viktór didn't want to hurt her. He'd already had enough of that for the day, or maybe for the rest of his life. She was just a librarian, after all.

Just reach down and take the bag and back away. That was his plan.

He took in a deep long breath and moved out into the hallway. He pulled his balaclava down to obscure his face. The hay hook was still hanging along his thigh, just in case he needed to threaten her.

———

VIKTÓR WAS WITHIN six meters of the library bag when a cat appeared from nowhere and yowled and ran down the length of the hallway from behind him. It shot through his legs and leaped on the top of the couch behind the woman, arching its back and hissing at him.

The librarian was startled and woke up flailing. She said, "Cricket, damn you."

Then she turned and looked over her shoulder and saw his face and screamed.

Viktór had never killed a woman before. Especially an old woman who looked like a bird. Especially the wrong woman.

But when she got to her feet and crossed the room and picked up a cowboy-type rifle from where it had been placed next to the front door, glaring at him with wild eyes as she worked the lever action, he had no choice.

THEY RETURNED TO THE SUV the way they had come, from tree to tree. Viktór swung the bloody hay hook in one hand and the book bag in the other. László carried the .30-30 Winchester rifle and a shotgun they'd found in her closet. So it was true what they said about Americans and their guns after all.

They placed all of the items except the book bag into the back of the SUV and covered the guns with a blanket.

László settled in behind the wheel, breathing hard.

"It wasn't her, you know that, right?" Viktór hissed. "You should have looked closer at her car." He was incensed and horrified at the same time.

"What about *that*?" László said, gesturing toward the bag on Viktór's lap.

Viktór twisted on his penlight, placed it in his mouth, and opened the bag. He pulled out a well-thumbed paperback featuring a long-haired blond man with bulging pectorals on its cover. Than another with a pirate and a buxom younger woman in an embrace.

A sticky note was attached to the novel with a list of all of the titles in the bag, as well as a header that read: *For Lola*.

"Who is Lola?" Viktór asked. "What have we done?"

BEFORE LÁSZLÓ COULD RESPOND, a set of headlights appeared on the road far in front of them. They belonged to a panel van with two figures inside that he couldn't see clearly. The van slowed and turned off the county road onto the road that led to the trailer they'd just been at.

The side of the panel van had a graphic of a falcon on it and lettering that read:

YARAK, INC.
Bird Abatement Specialists
Saddlestring, Wyoming

The lights of the van coursed down the road through the trees until they went well past the trailer. There was another house farther down the road. The real librarian's house.

A moment later, the back window of the SUV lit up with the beams of another vehicle coming from behind them.

László recoiled at the intensity of the headlights reflected directly into his eyes from the rearview mirror.

Green bangles pulsed across his vision when he realized the car that had come up from behind them had now stopped next to them on the road. It was right beside them, idling.

László lowered his window and looked out. It was a dark-colored pickup. The passenger window was down and a yellow Labrador peered at him with an open mouth. He could see very little of the driver beyond the dog except for the brim of a cowboy hat.

"Are you fellows doing okay?" the pickup driver asked, leaning forward so László could see his face. He looked like a pleasant man of medium height and build.

"Fine," László replied.

"Anything I can help you with?"

As his vision cleared, László could see that there was an official-looking emblem on the side of the passenger door. It depicted a pronghorn antelope inside the outline of a badge or shield. And a description.

WYOMING GAME AND FISH DEPARTMENT

"No, no," László said while putting on his best grin and making sure his English was as flat and atonal as he could manage. "We just pulled over to look at the map. If you stay on this road, will you get to Winchester?"

"Nope, you'll need to turn around. If you stay on this road, it'll take you to Saddlestring."

"Oh, we must have gotten lost."

"I'd say that's right."

"Thank you, Officer."

"My pleasure."

The window of the pickup hummed up and the truck continued down the road. Like the van just ahead, it turned into the trees going west toward the river.

László eased the SUV into gear and pulled back on the road.

"What now?" Viktór asked with real bitterness.

"We didn't go far enough down that road," László said. "But now we're sure where she lives."

"You said that before."

László fixed Viktór with a dead-eye glare that was quite effective. Viktór looked away.

"We find a hotel," László said. "There is too much activity at that house tonight."

"I'm hungry," Viktór said.

"From now on, we speak in English," László said while he switched languages again. "We don't want anyone to overhear us."

"I'm hungry, Greg."

"We'll find some food, Bob."

CHAPTER ELEVEN

Sheridan Pickett

OUT OF HABIT, JOE JOTTED DOWN THE COLORADO LICENSE plate number of the Nissan Pathfinder SUV on the side of the road and continued on. There was no reason to call it in. This kind of encounter happened quite often on back roads in the Bighorn Mountains during hunting season, even though he'd seen no telltale indications they were hunting. No camo clothing, no weapons, no items of blaze-orange clothing. There was no probable cause to ask them to show him their hunting licenses or habitat stamps.

Therefore, he dismissed them and made the turn to his home. He passed by Lola Lowry's trailer and noted her interior lights were on. A hundred feet later, he could see the taillights of the Yarak, Inc. van ahead of him. That's when the cow moose suddenly stepped out on the path from the timber and stood there blocking his progress.

The moose was tall and ungainly, with stilt-like legs that brought her eye to eye with him in his headlights. Because of their height, moose were a particular danger to motorists who hit them—their high center of gravity could propel their body over the hood and into the windshield.

Joe slowed but didn't stop, expecting her to move on like she usually did. But this time she held her ground. Daisy jumped up from her slumber on the passenger seat and whined when she saw the creature. It was all show, Joe knew. Daisy would run away in terror if she was released.

"Did you notice that she let Liv drive right by her?" Joe said to Daisy. "This proves once and for all that this particular moose is out to get us."

He eased forward until the grille of his pickup was within two feet of the cow. Only then did she finally shuffle off into the timber.

That's when Bert's dog started barking from its crate in the back of Joe's pickup. Joe had lured it to him with a plate of canned dog food. He'd kept Daisy in the cab while he did it. Bert's dog had been wary but also very hungry. Joe had slid the dog food into the open crate and waited, and finally the animal had leaped into the bed of his pickup and entered the crate. Joe then swung the door closed and latched it while the dog ate.

The last thing they needed was another dog, but he couldn't leave it to starve to death or get eaten by mountain lions.

He named it "Bert's Dog."

———

FOR OVER TWENTY-FIVE YEARS of his life and career, Joe used to return home every night to what he often thought of as "The House of Feelings." That's when his daughters and Marybeth had filled their small home.

He was reminded of those years as he entered the mudroom with Daisy and heard the cacophony of female voices inside. He set down a plastic bag with a twelve-pack of beer and the peppermint schnapps Marybeth had asked him to pick up, and was met by Tube and a huge bull mastiff that was so large Joe was nearly bowled over by it.

After hanging up his jacket and placing his Stetson crown-down on the shelf, he kicked off his boots and stepped into his slippers.

"Greetings, everyone," he said as he padded through the living room and into the now-crowded kitchen.

Liv Romanowski sat at the kitchen table with Sheridan and both smiled at his entrance. Kestrel opened her arms and squealed, as if expecting him to scoop her up in his arms, which he did. He noted a quick look of puzzlement in her eyes as he lifted her and he chalked it up to her momentary confusion. For a split second, he realized, she thought he was her father.

April crossed the room and kissed him on the cheek and gently bear-hugged both Joe and Kestrel.

"You're here early," Joe said.

"Wait'll you see my new truck," she said.

"I think I've already met your new dog," Joe said. "Or was that a heifer?"

"Very funny," April said with a roll of her eyes.

Wine bottles were open on the counter and Marybeth, Liv, and Sheridan had a glass. He loved how good it smelled inside and he guessed Marybeth was baking rolls or pies.

"It's good to see you," Joe said to April. "What's with the pink and purple hair?"

"It's a statement," she said, drinking from a long-necked original Coors straight from the bottle.

"A statement about what?" he asked.

"A statement that I have pink and purple hair, silly."

He lowered Kestrel to the floor and the little girl immediately scooted to the cabinet drawers and started pulling out pots and pans. Without being asked, Marybeth handed her a wooden spoon to beat on them with.

Joe winced. He'd gotten used to the quiet since he and Marybeth had moved in.

Like Liv herself, Kestrel was a natural beauty. Both had smooth and flawless mocha skin, perfect teeth, and full mouths. The only feature Joe could see of Nate in Kestrel were her piercing eyes. They were the eyes of a falcon.

Liv was a fierce and regal woman who came off as preternaturally calm. It was her inner strength, Marybeth had speculated to Joe, that made Nate fall for her in the first place. The cut above her right eyebrow was no longer swollen and the bruises on her jaw and cheek were starting to fade. Joe got angry even thinking that someone could lay hands on her as they had. He didn't blame Nate for going after her attacker.

While Joe filled a tumbler with ice and poured a light Buffalo Trace bourbon and water into it, he overheard April good-naturedly challenging Sheridan to a wrestling match.

"I could always pound you," April said. "Nothing has changed."

"That was the old me," Sheridan responded while she flipped her hair, welcoming the challenge. "Back when I was soft. Now I'm a falconer and I rappel from cliffs and do all kinds of physical labor. It's not like retail. I'm afraid I might hurt you."

She demonstrated her belief by posing like a bodybuilder. It made Joe smile.

"No chance of that ever happening," April said as she cracked open another beer.

"Better take it easy on that," Marybeth cautioned her.

"You brought more beer, right?" April asked Joe.

"Yup."

"It's Thanksgiving, isn't it?" April asked rhetorically. "I'm thankful that Dad brought more beer."

"It'll make it easier to pound on her later," Sheridan said.

Joe took a long pull on his bourbon and water and felt it warm him up inside. When the women in his life were going back and forth, he'd known for years that the best thing to do was to step aside.

"So," April asked with a sly grin, "are you guys rich or what?"

"We don't know," Marybeth answered.

"How can you not know?" April asked.

"It's complicated," Joe added. And it was.

Joe still couldn't quite wrap his head around the financial situation he and Marybeth had found themselves in. After a lifetime of existing from paycheck to paycheck and barely supporting the college education of three daughters at the same time, Joe had been given a very unexpected gift.

After his elk-guiding adventure in the mountains that had gone absolutely pear-shaped, his "client," a tech giant CEO named Steve-2 Price, had repaid him with a handwritten IOU, bequeathing him one hundred thousand shares of first-class stock in ConFab, a subsidiary of Aloft Corporation. Before that, Joe and Marybeth hadn't owned a single individual stock and had squirreled away a laughable amount in mutual funds. Both had depended—until very recently—on his state retirement pension and her county retirement for their old age. Neither amounted to much.

Marybeth had told him long ago that she wasn't counting on an inheritance from her mother, Missy, if she passed away. Marybeth assumed Missy would squander away her fortune to the last penny. Joe simply assumed that Missy was too mean to ever die.

Ever since the IOU had been given to him, Joe had tracked the value of Aloft. It was now selling for $45.86 per share, although it had gone as high as $52 and as low as $39 within the previous year.

Which meant, as of today, they might be worth four and a half million dollars. It was incomprehensible.

Of course, the paperwork to back up the IOU had not come through yet. They didn't have stock certificates or even a formal letter from Price confirming the gift. No one knew about it except Marybeth and therefore the girls as well. Marybeth had confessed to him that she'd started watching the stock market on a daily basis.

Would his client come through? Would he renege on his impulsive promise?

Joe didn't know the answer to those questions. He assumed a stock transaction of that magnitude would take time to implement. The last thing Joe wanted to do was to contact the CEO and ask what was going on. The very idea made him queasy.

Marybeth had also mentioned that stock transactions often have conditions attached. For example, she said, they might be prohibited from selling the stock for a period of time. There were other potential provisions that would complicate things. Just because they appeared wealthy on paper, it might not translate to actual hard money in the bank.

But he was starting to wonder. And if it actually happened, what would it mean? Joe had no idea how to be wealthy. Marybeth had grown up with money, but Joe hadn't. Would he feel any different? Would the world look different?

What would it be like to stroll into the sporting goods store on Main Street and buy anything he wanted, like that twelve-gauge over-under shotgun he'd been looking at for the last six months? And to do it without guilt?

"ROUGH DAY?" Marybeth asked Joe as he scrolled through emails on his phone at the kitchen table. Most of them were junk mail or new notices for all Wyoming state employees about insurance or other things he didn't care about. April and Sheridan had taken Kestrel with them down the hall to let her bounce up and down on one of the guest beds.

He looked up at her. How did she know?

"I can always tell," she said. Then: "Were you out at that murder scene today? I read about that on Facebook. An old guy got burned up?"

"His name was Bert Kizer," Joe said. "He was a fishing guide around here for a long time. He was seventy-three years old."

"That's horrible," Liv said. "Do they know who did it?"

"Not yet," Joe said. "But it was pretty awful. The poor old guy. It looked like he was tortured inside his own house and then set on fire and dumped. I really don't ever want to see a thing like that again."

He told them what he knew thus far. He said he'd been listening to the mutual aid channel the rest of the afternoon and evening while the sheriff's department was running all over the county and it didn't sound like they'd developed any leads.

"Is the sheriff up for this?" Marybeth asked. "He was pretty slow on the draw the last time we had a major crime."

Joe said, "I wonder the same thing myself. I hope he's not in over his head."

"Why do you think it happened?" she asked.

"It's hard to come up with an obvious motive. He was an old guy, like I said. A loner with no family that we're aware of. Very few friends. I knew him a little and he pretty much flew beneath the radar around here. It's hard to believe he was involved in anything that would get him killed."

"Was he into anyone for a lot of money?"

Joe shrugged. "It's possible, I guess. But he lived very simply, by what I could see. The most valuable things he owned were the shack itself and a couple of vintage drift boats. Everything else was old and worn-out. So if he borrowed a bunch of money from someone, it sure wasn't obvious that he spent it on anything I could see."

"Interesting," she said. "Maybe gambling debts?"

"Maybe, but I doubt it. We'll find out soon enough if he was a regular at Fort Washakie."

The Fort Washakie hotel and casino on the Wind River Indian Reservation was the only legal gambling facility within a hundred miles.

"But even if he was into them, they'd call the tribal police or the sheriff on him," Joe said. "They wouldn't send out enforcers."

Marybeth said, "Maybe he was one of those people who lives very simply but hoards cash. Guides get big cash tips, right? Maybe he didn't trust banks and he mentioned his stash to one of his clients or a fellow guide?"

Joe stared at Marybeth, then looked to Liv. He said, "She's always a few steps ahead of me. I hadn't even thought about that, and I don't think the sheriff has, either."

Liv smiled her agreement with Joe that Marybeth was the smart one in the family. That kind of annoyed him, but he knew it was true.

"Do you know other facts about Kizer?" Marybeth asked. "Like where he hung out and who his friends might be?"

"Not really," Joe said. "I think he was a regular out at the Wet Fly Bar. I met a couple of his clients once, who said they met him there in order to set up a fishing trip. Maybe the sheriff will follow up there."

Marybeth reacted to that with a look of disbelief.

He said, "At least Tibbs called DCI and asked for help. But he made it very clear he doesn't want me involved."

"Then stay out of it, for once," Marybeth said. "Just let them do their jobs. We need you home for Thanksgiving."

He nodded. But he couldn't quit thinking about Marybeth's theory. Fishing guides received minimal fees from outfitters, but they usually made $80 to $120 per trip in tips. That could add up over thirty or forty years if the guide in question was as frugal as Bert Kizer appeared to be.

"Oh," Joe said. "I forgot to tell you. I brought home Bert's dog. I couldn't leave the guy out there in the woods. He's in a crate out in the garage."

"Another dog?" Marybeth said, raising her eyebrows.

"Sorry," he said.

"Don't apologize. I'd only be angry if you left it out there to fend for itself."

"It's goofy-looking," Joe said. "I named it 'Bert's Dog.'"

"What's another dog?" she said with a rueful smile.

"ANY WORD FROM NATE?" Joe asked Liv after Marybeth refilled their wineglasses.

"He tries to call every night," she said. "I kind of insist on it."

Joe understood.

"He's in Denver right now," she said. "He thinks he's close to finding Axel Soledad."

Denver had been much in the news of late, as rioters had resumed nightly marches and set fire to a few downtown businesses.

"How close?" Joe asked.

"Close. Falconers are a strange breed, as you know," she said. "They don't get along together in person, but in a weird way they stick together. None of them want a guy like Axel Soledad around. So they pass along tips and sightings to Nate."

"Close" meant Axel Soledad was very likely to be maimed or killed at any time, Joe thought. Either that, or they could lose Nate himself. That prospect horrified him.

"I still think Nate should get the federal authorities involved," Joe said. "Transporting stolen wildlife across state lines is a federal crime."

"He'll never do that. He thinks he needs to take care of this himself."

Joe nodded. He knew Nate and Nate's particular code of justice better than anyone. He also knew that Nate's past experiences with the feds had been primarily negative. Several FBI agents still had it in for him.

"Still . . . I wish he'd consider it."

Liv responded with a Mona Lisa smile that conveyed to Joe he was wasting his time.

"Please tell him I'll be there if he needs help," Joe said.

"He knows that."

"Well, just tell him again, please. I suppose this means he won't be here for Thanksgiving."

"I doubt it. You're stuck with Kestrel and me."

"We're happy to be stuck with Kestrel and you," Joe said. Marybeth toasted that sentiment by clinking her wineglass against Liv's.

ALL THREE ADULTS turned their heads when there was a crash from inside the guest room, followed by peals of laughter from Kestrel.

"What's going on back there?" Marybeth called out.

"Sheridan knocked the lamp over," April responded with glee. "She's a clumsy oaf."

"I am not," Sheridan shouted.

"If you two are going to wrestle, you need to take it outside," Marybeth said. Kestrel was obviously enjoying the tussle going on because she couldn't stop squealing and clapping.

Marybeth shook her head, but Joe could tell that she was delighted her daughters were getting along in a familiar way.

He leaned back in the chair and rubbed his eyes. It had been a tough day and the bourbon was working on him. He slid his elbow back along the tabletop until it struck something solid on the edge of the surface.

Joe peeled the spare apron back and revealed the Nazi photo album.

Liv recoiled when she saw it as if she'd been stung. "Are those swastikas?" she asked.

"Yes," Marybeth answered.

Joe could see the symbols stamped or carved into the silver bands that crossed the red leather cover.

"So this is what the fuss was about this morning, huh?" he said to Marybeth.

"Let's let it go for now," Marybeth said as she covered the album again and scooped it up. "Let's save it for later. It's not something you want to look at tonight. This thing can put a spell on you. Trust me when I say it'll spoil the mood."

Joe found it an odd statement, but he trusted her judgment.

"That bad, huh?" he said.

"Let's just say it's as disturbing as it is mysterious," Marybeth said as she found a place for the album in her pantry and closed the door. "I should have put it in here to get it out of the way to begin with."

Joe and Liv exchanged puzzled looks.

Marybeth stopped in her tracks and smacked her forehead with the heel of her hand.

"What?" Joe asked.

"I got so wrapped up in that stupid photo album that I forgot about making dinner for tonight. I was going to make a pan of lasagna."

"Don't worry, we'll manage," Liv said.

"No, you won't. Joe, if I called into town would you please go pick up a couple of pizzas?"

"Sure," he said, trying not to convey his disappointment.

He'd hoped he'd be in for the night. He was thankful he'd only had one light drink. It was unfortunate, he thought, that they lived too far out of Saddlestring to order a delivery.

April appeared in the hallway as if summoned, her hair disheveled from wrestling.

"Get more beer while you're at it."

As she spoke, Sheridan rushed her from behind and threw an arm around her neck and pulled her back. April said, "Ack," but then broke out in laughter. Kestrel followed the two of them back down the hall, clapping her hands for more combat like a little Roman emperor.

Joe climbed back into his boots and clamped his hat on his head and left the House of Feelings with a sigh.

Then he thought of something.

It was only a ten-minute detour to Bert Kizer's place on the mission to pick up pizza and more beer. The home had been taped off with plastic yellow tape and a sheriff's department vehicle was parked in front, idling little puffs of exhaust from its tailpipe.

Joe pulled in behind the GMC Acadia and killed his headlights. Before they went off, he saw the deputy inside the SUV sit up and rub his eyes.

Steck had been sleeping in his car. Joe didn't blame him.

The driver's-side window slid down. "Hey, Joe, you caught me."

"Hey, Ryan. Do you mind if I pop inside for a quick look around?"

Steck arched his eyebrows and thought it over. "Well, I could call the sheriff and wake him up and ask, I suppose."

"Or you could sit tight in your warm car and I'll drop off a pizza to you on my way back home."

"That's a much better idea."

"I'll just be a minute," Joe said. "Did Gary finish all the forensics?"

"He said he's nearly done and that he'll be back tomorrow morning to wrap up."

"Did he find anything that points to the killers?"

"Not that I heard. He's gathering evidence at this point, and I don't think he's started analyzing it yet. What are you looking for, anyway?"

Joe said, "Marybeth had a theory that maybe Bert kept a stash of cash in his house that someone was after. It's not a crazy idea, if you think about it. Why else would someone do that to him?"

"So what do you expect to find?"

Joe said, "Maybe an empty safe. Maybe nothing. Who knows?"

Steck rubbed his chin while he thought it over. Then he said, "Thin crust, pepperoni, onions, mushrooms, and sausage. Oh—and don't touch or move anything inside."

Joe patted the hood of Steck's GMC to acknowledge the order as he walked toward the house. He pulled on a pair of plastic gloves and ducked under the crime scene tape.

———

AFTER TURNING ON all the lights inside the house so he could see better and so Steck could keep an eye on him, Joe did a cursory search of the cabinets, the drawers, the closets, the refrigerator, and the freezer. He noted that black latent fingerprint powder had been left on most of the smooth surfaces and that numbered evidence ID tents were placed across the floor and on the countertops. He observed where swabs had been taken from the dried blood on the floor, walls, and ceiling. The tools had been bagged and removed from the kitchen and although the chair the victim had been bound to was still in the middle of the floor, the duct tape from its limbs had been removed.

From what he could see, Norwood had done a very thorough job. But the forensics tech had been documenting the crime scene. He hadn't been looking for hidden cash.

Again, Joe looked over the framed photos on the wall. Most were much too small to hide a safe. Nevertheless, he tipped each one up and shined his flashlight behind it for a hole in the Sheetrock that he didn't find.

He also glanced behind the framed large print of Charles M. Russell's *The Camp Cook's Troubles* for a safe that wasn't there.

Joe peeled back rugs in the dining area and Bert's bedroom for openings to crawl spaces, but found none.

In his experience over the years, he'd learned that people liked to keep their hidden valuables close to them. That meant in between mattresses or under their beds. Men who wanted to hide things from their wives favored toolboxes and garages as hiding places, but Bert lived alone.

He dropped to his hands and knees and shined his flashlight under the double bed. Beside dust motes the size of tennis balls, there was a green metal footlocker near the head of the bed. When he saw it, Joe felt his heart rate speed up. In the layer of dust on the hardwood were tracks. It was obvious that the locker had been pulled out and replaced very recently.

He reached in and grasped the footlocker by a metal handle and gently slid it out. He noted that it stayed within the tracks in the dust that had already been made.

Joe sat back on his haunches and took a photo of the footlocker on his phone. There was stenciled white lettering on the top and side that read:

R. W. KIZER

U.S. ARMY

He undid six metal side clips that held the lid on tight. A musty odor wafted up from its contents.

On top was a neatly folded green wool army shirt with stiff lapels. He lifted it out and placed it on top of the bed. Underneath the shirt were the uniform trousers and a tightly coiled belt. He removed those as well and put them beside the shirt. Next was a beret emblazoned with a patch of a parachute.

Joe hadn't served in the military, but he knew he was looking at a dress uniform. On the bottom of the locker were a pair of highly polished combat boots and a set of dog tags. R. W. Kizer once had A-positive blood.

There was no cash to be found. But there was enough spare room in the locker, Joe thought, that there could have been several thick stacks of bills.

Joe guessed that the uniform had belonged to Bert Kizer's father. It matched the one in the black-and-white photo in the front room.

He carefully replaced all of the items in the box. Before he did, though, he unfurled the shirt on the top of the bed. D. KIZER was embroidered over the breast pocket. On the right arm sleeve above the single private stripe was a unit insignia of some kind.

It was in the shape of a shield with a ribbon below it. The shield was severed diagonally by a white lightning bolt. On the top left of the bolt were six white parachutes on a field of blue. On the bottom right of the bolt was solid green with the word *Currahee* in formal script on the ribbon.

It meant nothing to Joe, but he took a photo of it.

He carefully refolded the shirt top and placed it exactly as he'd found it, then sealed up the locker and slid it back under the bed.

STECK'S WINDOW SLID DOWN as Joe approached the SUV. "Did you find what you were looking for?"

"Not really, but it wouldn't be a bad idea to ask Norwood to analyze a footlocker under Bert Kizer's bed. There might be some stray prints on it."

"Gotcha."

"See you in a minute with that pizza," Joe said.

As he opened the door to his pickup, Joe's phone chimed with a text message. Marybeth.

We're starving. Are you on your way?

He replied:

Yup. Got sidetracked.

THURSDAY, NOVEMBER 24

The best lack all conviction,
    while the worst
Are full of passionate
    intensity.

Surely some revelation is at
    hand;
Surely the Second Coming
    is
    at hand.

—William
Butler
Yeats,
"The
Second
Coming"

CHAPTER TWELVE

Gargoyle

MARYBETH SNAPPED OPEN ONE EYE IN THE DARK, REACHED for her phone on the bed stand, and looked at the screen. It was four thirty-three. She was on her side in bed with her back to Joe. As usual, they were spooning. His left leg was on top of her left thigh and his arm was thrown over her shoulder. He was deeply asleep, which she chalked up to his full and exhausting day, as well as the two bourbons he'd had when he got back with the pizza.

As gently as she could, she disentangled herself and slipped out from beneath the covers. He moaned and asked her what was up.

"Nothing," she said. "I'm going to put the turkey in the oven. Go back to sleep."

"Mmmmmmm."

It didn't take much convincing. Joe could sleep anywhere, anytime.

She pulled on her robe and slippers and quietly shut the bedroom door behind her.

Marybeth liked how her house felt to her as she padded down the hallway. She loved it that all three of her daughters would be back together in less than six hours. It would be loud, it would be raucous, and she knew she'd love every minute of it.

She was wide-awake and happy.

AFTER RUBBING BUTTER on the cold skin of the big turkey, she slid it into the oven and covered it with a sheet of aluminum foil. Then she heated a mug of water in the microwave for a cup of tea that, she hoped, might induce her to want to go back to sleep for a couple of hours. She doubted it would work because she was jazzed by the impending arrival of her family and friends. Tube heard her stirring and waddled into the kitchen and collapsed in a heap at Marybeth's feet.

Joe had told her about finding the footlocker under Bert Kizer's bed and she was curious about it. As she steeped the tea bag in the hot water, she found his phone and powered it on. She knew Joe wouldn't mind if she looked at the photos he'd taken at the crime scene. After all, her past research in the library and on law enforcement databases had assisted him on investigations time and time again. He encouraged her to get involved in whatever he was working on.

She scrolled in reverse order through the shots of the army

uniform and the insignias and back through his photo stream until she found the unopened locker. That's where she stopped. Marybeth hoped that he hadn't taken any shots of the burned victim earlier in the day and she had no desire at all to find out.

The cover of the old footlocker read:

R. W. KIZER
U.S. ARMY

She shook her head. She'd never met nor heard of R. W. Kizer. It was odd that in a single day she was confronted with two military relics from the bygone past, one German and one American.

Was R. W. Kizer Bert's father? Joe seemed to think so.

She retrieved the album and her laptop from the pantry.

Marybeth booted up her device and googled the name. There were "Kizer Frames" for roller skates and a paper written by an R. W. Kizer on something called Nitrogen Narcosis for the 29th Undersea and Hyperbaric Medical Society Workshop in 1985. She doubted that was Bert's dad.

There was a "Ray W. Kizer" on Ancestry.com and she clicked on it. She'd found something, she thought. Ray Kizer was listed as military and his name was taken from an archive called *U.S. Navy Cruise Books, 1918–2009*. Her excitement dissipated when it was revealed that he was a Lieutenant Junior Grade C in the navy. The photo on Joe's phone was clearly an army uniform.

She could smell the aroma of the turkey heating up and it was enticing. So was the dizzying feeling she got when she was on the hunt.

Marybeth changed the search criteria. As far as she knew, Bert had lived in the area his whole life, which meant his dad might have been local as well. She keyed in "Kizer," "Saddlestring," and "Wyoming."

She got a hit. It was a link to a short obituary from the Saddlestring *Roundup* dated February 5, 2001.

It was titled "Richard 'Dick' Kizer."

Longtime Twelve Sleep County resident Richard "Dick" Kizer passed away at the Bighorn Mountain Senior Center on February 2, 2000. He was 79.

Dick Kizer was born September 3, 1923, in Medicine Bow, Wyoming, to a pioneering ranch family. The Kizer family moved to Casper in 1930 and later to their sheep ranch east of Saddlestring in 1938. Kizer graduated from Saddlestring High School in 1940.

In 1941, 20-year-old Kizer joined the U.S. Army and was assigned to Easy Company of the 2nd Battalion, the 506th Parachute Infantry Regiment, under Major Dick Winters. As one of the "Band of Brothers," Kizer landed in Europe during the invasion of Normandy and remained with the unit all the way through the Battle of the Bulge and beyond. Easy Company was the first American contingent to reach "The Eagle's Nest"—Hitler's Alpine retreat of Berchtesgaden. He was one of two Wyoming soldiers to stay with Easy Company throughout the war.

After World War II, Kizer returned to the valley and married Lorena "Dottie" Neil. He worked as a ranch foreman, a roofing contractor, a school janitor, and a fishing guide. Dick enjoyed hunting, fishing, camping, and attending rodeos.

Dick Kizer was preceded in death by Dottie. They had one son, Wilbur "Bert" Kizer, also of Saddle-string.

Bingo.

Marybeth sat back in her chair, her head spinning.

She leaned over her keyboard and keyed "Easy Company" and "WWII" into the search engine and was suddenly awash with items pertaining to the "Band of Brothers," "Major Dick Winters," "Stephen Ambrose," and scores of other hits. What interested her most was the shoulder insignia of Easy Company.

It was the same patch Joe had photographed on the army uniform.

She sipped her tea and tried to imagine what it must have been like for a local ranch boy who had probably never traveled out of state in his young life, much less internationally, to be sent to Europe to storm the beaches of Normandy and then push through France, Holland, Belgium, and into the heart of Nazi Germany. The things he must have seen and experienced!

And then to return home after the war to be a . . . school janitor.

It boggled her mind. But his service and exploits must have impressed his son, she thought. Bert kept his father's military uniform and souvenirs close to him. Although Marybeth knew nothing about Dick Kizer, she imagined him to be similar to older men she'd met who survived World War II, Korea, and Vietnam. They kept to themselves, spoke very little about their experiences during the war, and went on with life.

She contrasted that to the self-aggrandizing photo album of Julius Streicher and thought, *Thank God the good guys won.*

THE REFERENCE IN THE OBITUARY to another Wyoming resident in Easy Company intrigued her. Always the least-populated state in the nation, Wyoming had only 250,000 residents in 1940. That two of them were in one of the most storied units of World War II was a remarkable coincidence.

After checking the internal temperature of the turkey, she returned to her laptop and did a new search using the words "Band of Brothers," "Wyoming soldier," and "Major Dick Winters."

No mentions of Dick Kizer came up, but there were plenty of quotes from Major Winters and many more items about the *Band of Brothers* television miniseries and the book by historian Stephen Ambrose.

A photo of Major Winters showed him to be a strikingly handsome and masculine man. After the original *Band of Brothers* book and series came out, he'd apparently written a book of his own titled *Beyond Band of Brothers: The War Memoirs of Major Dick Winters.*

She did a new search, this time using the words "Band of

Brothers," "WWII," "Easy Company," "Dick Kizer," and "Wyoming."

Again, nothing with Kizer's name appeared, but another highlighted name came up several times. The name was Alton More.

She continued down this rabbit hole until she found several quotes from both Ambrose's book and Winters's memoir. They were in regard to the fact that Alton More was one of the very first soldiers to enter Hitler's Alpine Eagle's Nest at Berchtesgaden in 1944.

According to Ambrose, American soldiers looted the Nazi sanctuary room by room, scooping up everything they could find. Alton More located two of Adolf Hitler's personal photo albums and pilfered them. The albums were reportedly filled with original photos of the famous politicians of Europe who had been guests of the Führer. When a superior officer learned of the find, he ordered More to hand over the albums, and later a high-ranking French officer demanded the same thing. Winters, who had commanded More across all of Europe, blocked the orders. He told More he could keep what he'd found.

According to Winters in his memoir, he protected More and his loot from being confiscated by French, Russian, and British high command. Since More was his personal driver, the two of them concocted a scheme in which More could keep the albums hidden out of sight in a secret compartment in Winters's Jeep until he could smuggle them back to the States.

Winters himself was proud of what he'd liberated, and wrote, "We walked into the main dining room where we encountered one very brave waiter . . . Today we are still using the silverware from the Berchtesgaden Hof in our homes."

Marybeth dug deeper.

Alton More, like Dick Kizer, returned to Wyoming immediately after the war. More went back to his hometown of Casper, where he married and went to work as a traveling salesman for Folger's Coffee. As word got out that he had in his possession two of Hitler's photo albums, he was approached by both private collectors and the German government to sell them. Before he could decide what to do with the albums, More was killed in 1958 when his car hit a horse seventeen miles outside of Casper. He was thirty-eight years old.

What happened to the albums?

There the internet trail went cold. There was speculation that More's widow sold them to a private party, and additional speculation that she'd been swindled and the con artists had vanished into the ether. There were additional photo albums owned by Hitler and their sale by international auction houses, but nothing on the specific albums More had brought home.

Top Nazis were apparently very big on photo albums of themselves.

"So," Marybeth asked herself out loud, "if Alton More came back with two of Hitler's personal photo albums, maybe fellow Easy Company soldier Dick Kizer returned to Saddlestring with Julius Streicher's?"

It was *not* the craziest coincidence she could come up with.

She felt Tube suddenly scramble to his feet and growl.

That's when Marybeth sensed a foreign presence and looked

up to see a man's face staring at her through the window over the kitchen sink. She gasped and felt her throat constrict. When their eyes met, the man turned away quickly and vanished.

She screamed and swept her arm, accidentally knocking her tea off the table with a crash.

JOE THUNDERED DOWN the stairs and rushed to her.

"What happened?"

"There was a man outside looking in at me," she said. "He looked like a damned *gargoyle*. It scared me to death."

"Are you sure?"

"Why would I tell you otherwise?"

"Sorry." Joe approached the window and looked out. "He's gone. Do you know who it was?"

"I don't," she said. "He was . . . not a good-looking man. Probably late thirties, early forties. He was bald and had very scary eyes."

"A hunter, maybe?" Joe asked.

"It's possible. But why didn't he call or knock on the door?"

"Good question. Hold tight."

HER HEART WAS still beating fast when Joe reappeared, this time with his gun belt fastened around his bathrobe and slippers on his feet. He'd also clamped on his hat. She'd seen this getup before and he still looked ridiculous. But she appreciated his concern.

The door banged after him as he went outside.

She stood and moved to the window. Joe was walking briskly across the frozen lawn toward the trees in the direction of the road. His right hand was on the grip of his Glock semiautomatic. Puffs of condensation floated back over the shoulder of his robe.

He went into the trees and she couldn't see him anymore. She didn't want him to go that far out of her sight.

Marybeth held her breath, hoping she wouldn't hear cries or gunshots.

But there was silence.

SHE WAS STANDING on the front porch hugging herself against the cold when Joe walked back out of the timber.

When he got close, he said, "Yup, someone was here. I followed his tracks in the frost all the way from the window toward the county road. Then I heard a vehicle start up and speed away."

"Did you see him at all?"

"Nope. He was gone when I got to the road."

"Should we call the sheriff?"

Joe gave her a look. "And tell him what? Besides, he has enough on his plate right now."

"I'm sorry I screamed."

"Don't be."

They went inside and Joe unbuckled his belt and placed it in a coil on top of the refrigerator. He rubbed his hands together quickly for warmth.

"The turkey smells great," he said.

"Happy Thanksgiving, my hero," she replied with a smile that was only a little bit forced.

"You say he looked like a gargoyle?" Joe asked.

"A *big* gargoyle. He had big ears and a shaved head and kind of grotesque features. I've never seen him around here before, and believe me—I'd remember that face."

Joe narrowed his eyes. "I might have seen the guy you describe last night out on the county road. He was with another guy in a Nissan Pathfinder with Colorado plates. He claimed he was lost and trying to figure out how to get to Winchester."

"It could have been him," she said. "Why would he come back?"

"I don't know. But he's gone now."

She shivered involuntarily, recalling his face at the window.

"I took down his license plate," Joe said. "I've got it out in my truck. Let me go call it in."

"Do that," she said. Then she nodded toward her laptop on the table. "I'll wait until you come back in to show you what I've learned."

CHAPTER THIRTEEN

The Razor City

Viktór was pacing the floor and kneading his fingers together behind his back in the shabby little motel room an hour and a half away from Saddlestring in Gillette, when he heard the crunch of gravel outside the curtained window. A car had arrived outside. He picked up the rifle from the table and held it to the side as he parted the curtains to see László park the Nissan just in front of the door.

It was a strange little motel, very American and car-centric. It was built in a squared-off horseshoe design with outfacing doors and no interior hallway. The lobby, which also served as a residence for the owner/operator, was at the end of one of the wings closest to the street. Although there had been ten or more vehicles at the motel when they arrived, only two remained. All of the vehicles in the lot the night before had been dirty utility pickup trucks from energy companies. This town called Gillette was obviously a workingman's town. He'd seen a sign welcoming visitors to "The Razor City," but he didn't understand the significance of that. This place they were staying at was a workingman's motel. László had paid cash for the room.

There was a small television bolted to the wall and the cups in the bathroom were made of thin plastic. Even the art on the walls—faded prints of cowboys and geysers spouting in Yellowstone Park—were screwed to the paneling so they couldn't be easily removed.

Viktór heard his brother swipe a keycard in the outside lock. A rush of cold air came into the room with him, along with grit blowing in from the dirt parking lot.

László entered holding up a bulging white paper bag as if offering a gift. He had to use the weight of his big butt to close the door against the wind.

"Where have you been?" Viktór asked angrily in Hungarian. "I woke up and you were gone. And you took the car so I couldn't go anywhere."

"Have you looked outside?" László said with a sheepish grin. "There's no place to go. This town is completely closed. Hardly anything is open today."

"Then where did you go?"

"English," László said. "Remember that we must speak in English in case someone overhears us."

Viktór snorted and crossed his arms across his chest. He glared at his brother.

"The only place open was a McDonald's," László said as he

handed the bag to Viktór. "I got you two McMuffins and two hash browns. Those are fried potato wedges."

"I know what they are," Viktór said. He angrily opened the bag and grabbed a breakfast sandwich. It *did* smell good. He ate half of it wolfishly before he narrowed his eyes and inspected what the sandwich consisted of. It was an English muffin with an oval of processed egg and a thin slice of ham.

"No beef?" Viktór moaned. He was still upset that they had arrived so late the night before that the diner with chicken-fried steak in Gillette he had located on his phone had been closed.

"They don't put beef on those things."

"Why not?"

"It wasn't an option."

VIKTÓR SAT AT the wobbly little table in the room and ate sullenly. He liked the hash brown wedges, but he didn't want to give László the satisfaction of knowing it.

László sat on the side of the bed with his big hands hanging down between his thighs watching Viktór eat. He'd mentioned that he'd eaten in the car on the way to the motel.

As far as Viktór was concerned, things were going from bad to worse since they'd arrived in Wyoming. First, the old man in the woods played stubborn and wouldn't help them, even when László threatened him. That led to his brother going medieval on the man with such ferocity that Viktór was helpless to stop it. Only when it was too late into the process did the old man admit what he'd done with the item they were seeking. Viktór couldn't help but think it all could have been accomplished without the horror that had occurred.

But then there was the old lady who, rather than cower or scream before Viktór like an old lady should, went straight for her rifle. He hadn't expected that reaction and he'd had no choice but to defend himself. Her last seconds on earth, when she was on the floor looking up at him with hate in her eyes and the point of the hay hook embedded in her head, would stay with him for the rest of his life. That image had burned into his mind and he'd awakened several times during the night with it in front of him. He could see her now.

And for what? A bag of romance novels.

Then he'd finally, finally drifted back to sleep, only to wake up and find that his brother had left him in a motel room in a town he didn't know. László had taken the shotgun and their rental car and he hadn't even left a spare keycard.

The breakfast sandwiches László had brought him had done little to make up for what he'd been put through.

László had insisted that they not stay the night anywhere around Saddlestring or Twelve Sleep County where they could be seen, so they'd driven over an hour to the east on Interstate 90. Similar to the trip north, there were very few cars on the road except tankers and big trucks. As they drove, the landscape changed completely. Gone were the mountains and trees. The land flattened and the only lights were from oil rigs in the distance. László took the first exit into a town called Gillette. From what Viktór could tell, it was an energy town where everyone drove pickup trucks.

But the only place he'd been thus far was in a beat-up room in a place called the Tumble-On-Inn.

László said, "Today is an American holiday. I didn't know anything about it until I saw signs on buildings that said 'Closed for Thanksgiving.' I was going to buy ammunition for the guns, but every store is closed."

"We need ammunition," Viktór said. The only cartridges he had for the rifle were the five .30-30 rounds that had come with it, and they looked old. László needed twelve-gauge shotgun shells.

"Where did you go for hours?" Viktór asked.

"I couldn't sleep, either. You kept thrashing around and yelling. So I got up and drove back and found the librarian's house. We didn't go far enough down that road last night."

László left it there, but it was obvious to Viktór that his brother had more to say.

"Did you get the album?"

László shook his head. "I didn't have the opportunity. There were too many cars there, too many people, and too many dogs. I don't know how many, but I couldn't chance it. I looked inside her house through the window."

Viktór paused, mid-bite. "Did she see you?"

László looked down at the top of his boots. "She might have for only one second."

"Mi a fasz bajod van?" Viktór hissed in Hungarian.

"English."

"What the fuck is wrong with you?"

"I wanted to make sure we knew where the librarian lived. I didn't want to make another mistake."

Viktór saw the sense in that. "So when do we go back and get it?"

"Not today," László said. "There will be too many people there."

"How do you know that?"

"When I looked in the house, I could see a big dining room table that was set with a lot of place settings. I think they're going to have a big feast with a lot of guests. I suppose that's what Thanksgiving is all about."

"Why didn't we know this?"

László shrugged.

"We have to stay here? In this shithole?"

"We have to lie low. It's best that we don't get noticed," László said. "I thought about that guy in the pickup who saw us on the road last night, so I stopped at a rest stop on the way back here and took a set of license plates off of a car and put them on ours. We're not from Colorado anymore. Now we're from the state of Illinois."

"What did you do with the Colorado plates?" Viktór asked.

"I threw them in a trash can."

"So we go get the album tomorrow?"

"I think so."

"What if the guests stay there?"

"Then we wait. But I don't think they'll stay. Americans don't ever stay very long in one place," László said.

"So you think you know Americans now?"

"Yes. They're always moving. Walking fast, talking loud,

waving their arms around. They don't like to sit still ever. They're all like that. I don't understand why they're all so fat, the way they move around."

To make extra money when he was in college on the wrestling team, László had worked as a waiter and bartender on a small luxury cruise ship in Budapest where the majority of the guests were from the U.S.

"I think those were different people," Viktór said. "They were rich Americans. Not like here."

"All Americans are rich."

"How can you say that? The old man wasn't rich. The old lady wasn't rich. People who stay at a shithole like this aren't rich."

László didn't respond, but his cheeks flushed red. Viktór knew that as an early warning signal. László had a volcanic temper, especially when he thought he was being mocked. Or when someone wouldn't do what he demanded. *Ask the old man about that*, Viktór thought.

"These Americans are different, I think," Viktór said. He kept the challenge out of his voice so as not to further provoke his brother. "We've been led to believe that Americans are soft, stupid, rich, and weak. But there is something different with these people here. They're stubborn and mean and it means nothing to them to grab a rifle and aim it at my face. We can't think that they'll give us what we want."

Viktór paused, then said, "Even a librarian."

"Even a librarian," he echoed.

———

AN HOUR LATER, they were both laid out on twin beds beside each other, watching the television. They hadn't slept together in the same room since they were boys.

American football was on. Viktór understood that one of the teams was the Detroit Lions. The Dallas Cowboys would play later in the day.

"This is a stupid game," Viktór said. "I don't understand it. There's a lot of standing around having meetings. Then they try to kill each other. What's the point of it?"

László tried to explain the rules. "If you get the ball across the goal you get more points. One team tries to get it across the goal and the other team tries to stop it. It's kind of like rugby."

"It's not like rugby at all."

There was a knock on the door and the brothers looked at each other. They'd not heard a car approach outside.

The door opened inward as far as the safety chain would let it. "Housekeeping," a man said.

"We don't require a service," László responded.

A young man with thick glasses and a wispy beard peered in through the crack of the door at the two of them on the beds.

"Are you sure?" the man asked.

"We are sure," László said firmly. With a side-eye, Viktór could see his brother reach beneath the bed for something. Probably the Pulaski tool.

"Not even towels?" the man asked.

"We're okay, I said," László replied. "Close the door. You're letting the cold in." He was getting angry.

"Who's winning?" the housekeeper asked.

"Not the Lions," Viktór said.

"I'm not surprised. I can't remember the last time they won. I'm from Michigan."

Viktór didn't know what that meant. He looked to László, who was lifting the ax from the floor to lay it across his thighs. Viktór signaled to his brother with his eyes to calm down.

"It's none of my business," the housekeeper said, "but they're serving free Thanksgiving meals at the community center if you guys are interested. Turkey and all the trimmings."

"We're okay," Viktór said. "Please close the door."

He could feel László tense up next to him, ready to leap to his feet and swing the ax through the gap in the door.

"Well, suit yourself," the housekeeper said. He sounded disappointed. But the door eased closed and Viktór let out a deep sigh of relief.

Then the door opened again.

"Happy Thanksgiving," the housekeeper called out. Then he quickly pulled the door closed.

His shadow passed across the curtains of the outside window and Viktór could hear the squeaking of laundry cart wheels on the cement sidewalk. A few seconds later, he heard "Housekeeping" called out in front of the room next to theirs.

"These people," Viktór said. "They're a pain in my ass."

CHAPTER FOURTEEN

Northwest of Boise

NATE ROMANOWSKI AND GERONIMO JONES WERE OVER HALF-way on the nineteen-hour, thirteen-hundred-mile drive from Denver to Seattle. Nate was at the wheel of the van. The landscape was rolling grassland and wide-open vistas and there was no longer much snow in the mountains. The sagebrush was gone. They'd outrun it.

As they traveled, Nate got used to the van rattling with empty cages on rough blacktop. It was a sound that he hoped would go away once the crates were filled with his recaptured Air Force. The rattling would be replaced by the shrieks of falcons and the heavy odor of hawk shit. He welcomed it.

They'd soon leave Idaho and enter the state of Oregon. Eastern Oregon, like eastern Washington, struck Nate as more Rocky Mountain West than Pacific Northwest. Dry, flat, and lonesome. The change in terrain and atmosphere was subtle and it came slowly over hundreds of miles traveled. He'd noted it before. Beef cattle still grazed in the fields and the small rural towns they passed through were ranch-oriented. Farming towns and green fields would soon replace them in a kind of change-over that came with the subtle drop of altitude and the heavier air. Once they left the Yakama Indian Reservation and crossed over the Cascades in Washington State, it would all be different: wet, green, and more than a little insane.

As he drove, Nate eyed every car they passed on I-84 for a glimpse of Axel Soledad's vehicle. They'd learned from Tristan that Soledad had swapped out the Chevy Suburban he'd used in Wyoming for a black Mercedes-Benz Sprinter transport cargo van. Presumably, it was loaded with Nate's falcons and one, maybe two, associates of Soledad's. If Tristan's information was correct, Soledad was bound for Seattle with a stop along the way in Baker City, Oregon.

Tristan had let the Baker City reference slip when he talked to them and it determined the route Soledad would take. Interstate 25 north to Fort Collins, US 287 to Laramie, I-80 West to Salt Lake City, I-84 to Ellensburg, Washington, then I-90 West to Seattle. The fastest possible route, less the stop.

Nate and Geronimo planned to stop in Baker City as well, if they didn't overtake Soledad's vehicle en route.

TRISTAN, LAST NAME RICHARDSON, had spent the previous night bound and gagged in a heated outbuilding on Geronimo's land in the mountains west of Denver. Nate had been given a well-appointed guest bedroom on the second floor in the Joneses' spectacular log home. He'd gone to sleep overlooking a stunning view of the twinkling city lights far below them.

From that distance, downtown looked quiet and peaceful. The fireworks had apparently stopped.

Jacinda Jones, Geronimo's attractive wife, had made scrambled eggs and bacon for breakfast. She was obviously six to seven months pregnant with their first child. It was clear to Nate that she was peeved at Geronimo, likely because he'd told her what they were about to do. She kept her distance during breakfast to maintain civility, but she couldn't help but ask Nate about his "circumstances."

Men always asked what he did for a living. Women always asked about his family.

He showed her photos of Liv and Kestrel on his phone and her eyebrows arched.

"I didn't know there were any Black people in Wyoming," she said.

TRISTAN HAD BEEN SEATED on the floor in the corner of the utility shed when Nate and Geronimo took him a plate of breakfast. Geronimo had cut the tape from Tristan's wrists and removed the tape from his mouth so he could eat. He refused and said he wasn't hungry.

Relieved of his black bloc clothing and heavy boots, Tristan looked even less impressive than Nate had imagined. He was pale, sallow, with a sunken chest and acne scars on his neck and jaw. His eyes darted toward them like a cautious ferret and he kneaded his fingers together to hide the fact that his hands were shaking.

Turned out, Tristan Richardson had grown up wealthy in the Highlands Ranch suburb of Denver. His father was an insurance company executive and his mother was a buyer for an outdoor sports clothing chain. He'd graduated from the University of Colorado in Boulder and . . . he lived at home.

Tristan hated his parents. He hated the government. He hated all politicians, whether local, state, or federal. They were all corrupt fascists, and their party didn't matter. He hated the police. He hated capitalism most of all, and he was determined to "fight the fascists who benefitted from it at the expense of the downtrodden, the oppressed, and those without a voice or rights."

He said he was "anti-fascist," just like the Allied troops that invaded Hitler's Europe on D-Day.

While he went on, Geronimo scrolled through Tristan's iPhone 12 Pro. He'd gotten Tristan's password earlier by pointing the triple-barrel shotgun at his knees.

Tristan seemed befuddled by the fact that Geronimo was distracted and wasn't more sympathetic to his views.

Nate didn't care about any of that.

"How do you know Axel Soledad?" he asked Tristan.

Tristan said his associates referred to the man by his first name primarily. Axel.

Axel was kind of a patron saint of antifa cells across the country, Tristan said. Axel had set up legal defense funds with sympathetic attorneys in most of the major western cities to bail out those that got arrested, and he funded the defense for antifa who actually appeared in court. Axel was influential with many local district attorneys and he encouraged them to release people who'd been arrested without charging them.

Axel had become more important in the past few years, Tristan said. He'd become more active. He was like a ghost who knew where to show up and when at just the right time to provide weapons, food, tents, clothing, and spiritual backup. He was unbelievably well-connected.

Even though no one was certain where he lived, Axel knew where to be. Whenever there was serious street action, Axel was there. Portland, Seattle, Denver, Minneapolis, Los Angeles, San Francisco, New York, Kenosha, Omaha, Louisville, Washington, D.C. His support kept the movement simmering at all times.

He was a *legend*.

Geronimo was more focused on the nuts and bolts of what had happened the night before.

"Who knew about the cache of weapons he dropped off?"

"Everybody. The geocache site went out over social media," Tristan said.

"When you say everybody, do you just mean antifa assholes like you?"

"No—everybody."

"They use Signal, Telegram, and Gab and other software to communicate," Geronimo explained to Nate. "Encrypted shit no one can trace. Everybody knows where the weapons are located except for the cops."

Tristan nodded his head in agreement.

Geronimo said to Tristan, "Looking through your contacts here, I can't find his name."

"He's not listed by his name," Tristan said, blushing with apparent embarrassment.

"What's he listed under?"

"Shaman."

Nate rolled his eyes while Geronimo located the contact details.

"Found him," he said. "Does he know you well enough that if we sent him a text, he'd respond?"

"Probably not," Tristan said. "Plus, he doesn't communicate by text because someone might intercept it."

"Sticks to threads on encrypted sites, then?"

"Yes."

Gernonimo suddenly looked up. "Who selects the items in the weapons caches he leaves?" he asked.

"Axel, I guess," Tristan said. "It's not like we place an order or anything."

Nate was confused by the question.

"I'm keeping your phone," Geronimo declared.

Tristan's reaction was visceral. He thrashed and tried to kick out of his bindings. "No—*you can't take it*. You have no right to take my phone," he shouted.

"You don't have any rights on my property," Geronimo said. He patted his shotgun and arched his eyebrows when he said it.

"Please, don't do that," Tristan begged. There were tears in his eyes.

"Why is he going to Seattle?" Nate asked.

Tristan said, "There's a lot going on up there, man. A lot

brewing right now. We've got the fascist Nazis on the run up there. It's the place to be." Then: "Can you give me back my phone?"

THEY'D LEFT TRISTAN RICHARDSON on the side of US 287 near Tie Siding, Wyoming. There wasn't a single building in sight and the only man-made objects were electrical transmission lines in the distance and wind turbines in various stages of construction. The wind howled and rocked the van.

Nate watched Tristan fade to a tiny black dot in his rearview mirror.

He said to Geronimo, "I'm kind of surprised how few antifas there were in Denver. I thought there was more."

"Not really," Geronimo said. "People out there think there are thousands of them in every city. But from what I can tell, there's just a loud few. Like I said, they could be rounded up in one night, but it doesn't happen."

"You have a really nice house and I like your falcon setup."

Geronimo had two impressive mottled white gyrfalcons in perfect physical condition. Gyrfalcons were the largest of all North American raptors.

"You mean, how can a Black brother my age afford such a nice spread?"

"No, because you make a living offering protection to Denver bars. And don't use that race crap on me. It won't fly."

Geronimo chuckled. He winked. "Yeah, okay, nature boy." Then: "Jacinda's from Chicago. Her mom invented Afro Chic. Ever heard of it?"

Nate recalled the name from tubes of hair-care goo that had annoyed him in his bathroom at home. "I have."

"She sold it to Procter and Gamble a few years back and she gave all her kids a nice trust fund," Geronimo said. "I hit the jackpot marrying her."

"I know the feeling," Nate said. "And now you're expecting your first child."

"Uh-huh. I'm still trying to wrap my mind around *that* development."

"Boy or girl?"

"We don't want to know, but I'd guess that Jacinda will give in at some point and we'll find out."

"I've got a little girl," Nate said. "Kestrel."

Geronimo grinned at that. "Smallest falcon in the species. I like that. Does she boss you around?"

"She's got me wrapped around her finger," Nate said. "She's another reason why I have to find Soledad and take him down. He frightened her and she hid from him. I don't know what would have happened if he'd found her. I can't even think about it."

"So what about you?" Geronimo asked. "Tell me about your business now that you've supposedly gone straight."

Nate did. He said the bird abatement business was growing every year and that Yarak, Inc. was getting calls from as far away as Southern California and Michigan to get rid of problem birds infesting farms, zoos, wineries, and large-scale industrial facilities. Liv ran the day-to-day operations of the business and Nate oversaw the deployment of falcons. They'd recently hired Sheridan Pickett as an apprentice falconer.

Geronimo asked, "Is it true that when you put a peregrine in the sky, all the shitbirds like starlings see it and run for the hills?"

"It's true," Nate said. "All they have to do is see the silhouette of the falcon in the sky. It's imprinted into their DNA that if they don't leave the area immediately, they'll die a horrible death. Which they will. So that alone usually does the trick."

"Amazing, man. It sounds like a good gig."

"It is," Nate said. "Which is why we need to find Soledad fast and recover my Air Force. He stole five peregrines, two red-tailed hawks, three prairie falcons, a Harris hawk, and a gyrfalcon. Twelve out of fifteen birds. He killed three and left them."

Geronimo whistled and called up Tristan's calculator app on his phone. He punched in a series of numbers and mumbled while he did it.

"Peregrines are worth fifty K on the black market . . . redtails go for twenty-five K each, prairies and the Harris hawk go for the same, and an Arab sheikh will pay up to forty-five for a gyr like mine . . . that's fucking four hundred and forty-five thousand dollars!"

"Yes."

"Jesus. I'm in the wrong business," he wailed.

"It's not just that, as you know," Nate said. "It's the capturing of fledglings in the nest and years of flying them to the lure. Building up fourteen birds to a state of perfect *yarak*—well, it would take years to do it again. This guy stole our company and our livelihood. I can't let him get away with it."

Geronimo agreed.

"Tell me something," Nate said. "You've got that patch on

your coat and you seem to know a lot about antifa. How in-volved are you?"

Geronimo hesitated while he formed his answer. "Don't get me wrong," he said, "I'm totally down with the movement. BLM—not antifa. Don't get confused. BLM and antifa are in two different lanes and those lanes don't merge, even though some ignorant folks think they do. Anyway, like I said, I've been pulled over for Driving While Black too many times. I get it and it pisses me off and I want to see progress made. But I'm not a follower. I'm a free man with a will of my own. I don't go for the shit some of the BLM honchos go on about. But something bad is happening."

"You asked Tristan about the choice of weapons that were put in the cache we found. What was that about?"

"Ah, you picked up on that."

Nate nodded.

"That's not the first street cache I ever found," Geronimo said. "But this one was a little different."

"Meaning what?"

"Well, it had the usual stuff: bats, rods, bricks, rocks, fire-works. That's pretty standard."

"Interesting," Nate said. "Go on."

"What this cache *didn't* have were plastic shields for protec-tion. There are usually shields there like the cops use. And in this case there were those *axes*. I've never seen axes before.

"Another thing," Geronimo said. "That cache was untouched before we found it, even though there was street action going on downtown. Don't you find that kind of odd?"

"What does it mean?" Nate asked. "You still haven't told me why you're helping me shut down Axel Soledad."

"I'll tell you when I'm ready," Geronimo said. "I need more proof than I've got. I don't want you to think I'm one of those conspiracy nuts."

Geronimo leaned back in his seat with Tristan's phone perched between his thighs. He tapped it and said, "There's a lot of information we can use from this. It's like our own little captured Enigma machine. We can follow message threads and weigh in as Tristan Richardson if we want to. We can really screw with those people when they're planning street action or coordinating their movements."

SIX HUNDRED AND eighty-five miles later, north of Boise, Nate asked Geronimo, "Did 'Baker City' ring any bells for you?"

"No. Never heard of it."

"Have you ever heard of an outfit called Wingville Enterprises?"

"No, man."

"Have you ever heard of Ken Smisek or Bob Prentice?" Nate asked.

Geronimo shook his mass of dreads. Meaning no.

"They're more my age," Nate said. "Falconers gone bad, like Soledad."

"What about them?"

"They live near Baker City."

CHAPTER FIFTEEN

Wingville

Baker City, Oregon, was a town of fewer than ten thousand people in the high desert between the Wallowa Mountains to the east and the Elkhorn Mountains to the west. Nate found it charming. The downtown was historic and well-preserved, with ambitious early nineteenth-century stone buildings. The structures had obviously been put up by residents who at one time had believed the place would boom into a major city. There were so many of those once-ambitious towns in the west, he thought. Showpiece architecture that shouted optimism for something that would never come. It was kind of depressing.

It was also largely closed due to the Thanksgiving holiday. Driving through the deserted downtown reminded Nate of the bad old days of the pandemic.

Ken Smisek and Bob Prentice lived eight miles outside of

Baker City on US 30 near an unincorporated town called Wingville that was more of a location on a map. All that remained of the settlement was a historical sign and the Wingville Cemetery.

Smisek and Prentice had obviously taken the name of the location for their business. Wingville, Nate thought, was a clever name for a falconry brokerage business.

Smisek and Prentice were former bounty hunters and falconers who were partners in business as well as in life. They had a side business trafficking small arms as well. They'd been in operation for over twenty years. Nate knew about Wingville from back when he was in special operations and his mission was to facilitate the purchase of rare North American falcons for rich tycoons and members of royal families in the Middle East. The purpose of the mission had been to infiltrate the elite caste of men who not only employed official falconers but also financed terrorists, including Osama bin Laden. Mark V had paid Wingville to locate peregrine falcons and gyrfalcons to provide to the targets. The prices per bird were equivalent to what they were today, and money was no object.

In many Arab countries, the art of falconry was considered regal and of exceptionally high status. Billionaires employed official falconers, and they spent hundreds of thousands of dollars to equip their charges with top-quality raptors and temperature-controlled mews. There were even custom-designed four-wheel-drive vehicles to transport falcons and falconers across the roadless desert. Relatives of the royal families sometimes flew private 757s to desert encampments to hunt and fly their birds.

Bin Laden had been located in one such encampment, but the potential collateral damage of taking him out had been considered too risky at the time. That fact would forever haunt Nate, and it had turned him against his own commander.

As new laws were enacted domestically and across the world to prohibit the sale of wild falcon species, Smisek and Prentice hadn't closed shop. Instead, they'd gone underground.

Like Axel Soledad, the owners of Wingville breached the falconers' code in addition to breaking international wildlife trafficking laws. Prentice and Smisek bought and sold birds that had obviously been poached or stolen, and they placed birds with unscrupulous falconers in other countries. Their clientele was still largely in the Middle East, where falconry remained revered and spiritualized, but they also served customers in Scotland, Wales, Australia, and New Zealand.

After briefing Geronimo on Wingville's background, Nate said, "It only makes sense that Soledad would come see the Wingville boys on his way to Seattle. My hope is that he sold them my birds and we can liberate them before they get sold again."

"So your birds might be here?" Geronimo asked incredulously.

"That's what I hope."

"If we get them back, will you still want to find Soledad?"

"Yes. But it might be delayed a while."

It was obvious to Nate that it wasn't the answer Geronimo wanted to hear.

"I'm giving up Thanksgiving dinner and football at home," Geronimo said.

"Me too."

"Our ladies aren't very happy with us as it is. I'd hate to think this adventure is a waste of time."

Nate said, "If I get my birds back, it's half-successful."

"I want full-successful."

"We'll see."

THE ROAD DETERIORATED as they drove north from Baker City, and Nate had to slow down. He used the mapping feature of his phone to get to the physical location of Wingville, although he wasn't sure how much longer he'd have a strong cell signal.

He nearly missed the turnoff to "Wingville Ranch" because the sign for the place had fallen off its mount and was now propped up against the pole. He slowed even more as he turned onto a rough two-track dirt road.

"These guys are in the middle of nowhere," Geronimo said.

"I think they like it that way," Nate said.

The terrain was treeless and high. The road took them over an undulating series of soft benches. At the crest of each hillock, Nate searched for the ranch headquarters itself. He wanted to surprise Smisek and Prentice with his arrival. He didn't want to tip them off that he was coming.

As he topped another grassy hill, he saw a collection of buildings far below in the bottom of a swale. Nate hit the brakes and backed up until he could no longer see the compound—and where someone down there couldn't see him.

"Hold tight," he said to Geronimo.

He got out of the van and walked up the road with a spotting scope mounted on a short tripod. There was a set of recent tire tracks in the dust of the road. Someone had been just ahead of him.

Nate crept to the summit and kept low. He didn't want to skylight himself and be seen. He set up the scope and leaned into the eyepiece.

The ranch headquarters was entirely in the open. It reminded him of his own compound in Wyoming. There was no way someone could drive to the buildings below without being seen and tracked from a great distance. Nate assumed Smisek and Prentice had picked the location for exactly that reason, as had Nate. It was mimicking the defense mechanism of a pronghorn antelope: stand boldly in the open so as to see potential predators long before they could get there.

The compound was a collection of outbuildings surrounding a Victorian two-story brick ranch house in the middle. He could see the snout of a Jeep poking out from one of the outbuildings, and the back of a pickup was next to it. Someone was home, but there was no Mercedes transport visible.

There were several satellite dishes on the roof of the ranch house that he guessed were for internet access. The brokerage of falcons was now largely done on the web, and even in such a remote location it enabled them to communicate with potential buyers anywhere in the world.

A small, shallow creek serpentined through the swale floor

and through the corrals next to the house. The creek was choked with brush on both banks, which were relatively high, and he could see only a few openings with water.

Nate nodded to himself and went back to the van to lay out his plan to Geronimo.

FORTY-FIVE MINUTES LATER, Nate gently splashed down the middle of the ankle-high creek and pushed through brush that seemed determined to choke out the sun. Geronimo followed and cursed under his breath at the hazards. The temperature was in the low sixties and there was a slight breeze from the north. It was much warmer than it had been in Wyoming or Colorado.

They'd hiked down the side of the hill far upstream from the compound. He'd chosen to approach on foot via the creek bed because it was the only route available that couldn't be watched easily by someone in the house.

"I'll need new boots after this," Geronimo said.

THE CREEK WIDENED as they approached the headquarters, and the brush became more sparse. Nate couldn't get any lower to stay out of sight. He turned to Geronimo and gestured toward the side of an old barn fifty yards away.

"You ready?" he asked.

Geronimo indicated he was.

Nate broke into a run with Geronimo just a few feet behind

him. They dashed to the barn in the open, hoping no one would glance through a ranch house window and see them. The barn would hide them from the house if they made it.

They made it.

Nate stood with his back to the barn wood and Geronimo joined him. Geronimo reached into his coat and drew his shotgun out and held it down the length of his thigh.

"I think we're good," he said.

Nate waited until his breath returned to normal after the sprint, then sidled down the wall toward a four-pane window. He dropped below it and then slowly raised up to see inside.

He motioned to Geronimo to come over.

The interior of the barn was dark except for natural light that came from the windows and a discolored fiberglass covering on the roof that served as a skylight. On the floor of the barn were long rows of wooden crosses pounded into the dirt. Thin leather straps hung from the Ts of the crosses and the ground was spattered with splashes of white.

In the background were lights on stands and plywood panels painted primary colors.

Nate whispered, "This is where they keep the birds they're going to sell. Jesses are hanging from those crosses to keep the birds in place. You can see that they photograph them against different backgrounds and they post the shots to their site on the dark web."

"I see that," Geronimo said. "But where are your birds?"

"I hope there's another mews in one of the other buildings."

"Or they aren't here at all," Geronimo said. Nate noted the

slight elation in his voice. He obviously didn't want to be done with their mission.

THEY LOOKED IN THE WINDOWS of two other outbuildings. One was a smaller mews, but the crosses were just as empty. The other building was filled with typical ranch junk: broken-down pickups, a tractor with three flat tires, an old trailer wagon that had probably come with the place.

Nate was frustrated and angry. He said, "I think it's time to pay a call on Smisek and Prentice."

"Will they be armed?"

"What do you think?" Nate said. "They're outlaws running two illegal operations: falcon smuggling and gunrunning. They're hated by legit falconers and targeted by federal wildlife agents. They're probably paranoid as hell."

Geronimo checked the loads in his shotgun, even though he'd already done that before they'd left Nate's van.

"Lead the way," he said to Nate.

NATE APPROACHED THE BACK DOOR of the ranch house slightly from the side, moving from Russian olive bush to Russian olive bush. He kept his eyes open for movement from behind the windows and storm door and he swept his vision across the back of the house for trip wires or motion sensors. He didn't see any.

He made his way across a flagstone patio toward the back concrete porch stairs. Geronimo stayed with him.

They pressed themselves against the brick wall on the back of the house and listened. There was a slight murmuring sound inside. Nate guessed it was from a television or radio.

He reached up and grasped the storm door handle. It wasn't locked. He eased the door open and stepped between it and the back door. Geronimo held the storm door open so it wouldn't slam shut on them.

Nate held his weapon next to his temple as he peered through the door's window into the kitchen. He could see two plates on the table as well as silverware. A pot of something was on the stove and a red light glowed on the control panel.

"They're home," Nate mouthed to Geronimo.

Geronimo mimicked knocking on the door and raised his eyebrows in a question.

Nate shook his head.

The wooden door was unlocked as well. Nate turned the knob, pushed the door inward, went in, and moved to the side in a shooter's stance. Geronimo navigated the storm door and let it ease shut behind him, then moved into the kitchen to Nate's right.

He could smell roasting turkey from the oven and it made him salivate. Prentice and Smisek were cooking their Thanksgiving meal.

A radio on the kitchen counter next to the stove was playing classical music at low volume. Nate could sense no movement from any of the rooms in the house. He checked out the pots on the stove. One was filled with mashed potatoes and the other green beans. Gravy in a saucepan had been simmering on the burner for a while. It wasn't yet fully congealed, but it appeared to be the thickness of wet plaster. He turned the burners off but kept the radio on so as not to alert anyone inside of their entry.

He lowered his revolver and pressed it against his thigh. An opening in the kitchen revealed a hallway leading to a sun-filled great room at the front of the house. Nate moved slowly and deliberately down the hall, ready to sprawl out or dart into a side room if necessary. Even as he did so, he noticed the framed photos on the walls of Smisek and Prentice. There were shots of them with falconers in the Middle East desert, sipping drinks on the beach of what looked like Mexico, skiing together, and embracing at what looked like a drunken wedding reception.

Nate smelled it before he saw it—the comingling of roasting turkey, gunpowder, and blood in the air.

He entered the great room following his raised weapon. It settled first on Ken Smisek, who was sprawled out in a lounge chair with his arms out and his head flung back. There was a dark-tinged hole beneath his chin and the top of his head was missing. Blood spatter and bone fragments covered the wall and ceiling. A heavy Ruger Redhawk .357 Magnum revolver lay on the floor under his open hand in a pool of blood.

Bob Prentice lay on his back on the floor in the middle of the room. He'd been shot twice in the chest, and the carpet below him had been dyed red by blood from the exit wounds in his back. His face was frozen into a grimace.

"Oh, man . . ." Geronimo said, sniffing. "This just happened. Murder-suicide?"

Nate nodded. "Or meant to look like it."

Then he gestured to Geronimo that they should split up and clear all the rooms in the house to make sure no one was hiding out.

"Don't touch anything," Nate whispered.

There was no one in any of the rooms of the house, including the basement and attic. Nate was struck by how clean and orderly it was. Prentice and Smisek were meticulous housekeepers.

When they were alive.

Nate pushed open the door to a spare bedroom that also served as a home office. It had been ransacked. An extra-large gun safe dominated one wall. The door to the safe gaped open and it was empty inside.

WHEN THE TWO OF THEM returned to the great room, they holstered their weapons. Nate kneeled down over Prentice's body and pressed his fingertips to the man's neck. He was surprised to feel a very slight and wavery pulse.

"He's alive," Nate said. Then to Prentice, "Bob? Can you hear me?"

Prentice was long and thin with wavy ginger hair and a tattoo of a falcon on his neck. He was extremely pale from lack of blood.

He opened his eyes and they settled on Nate's face above him.

"What happened here, Bob?" Nate asked.

Prentice worked his mouth, but no sounds came out. The bright red blood on his mouth looked like lipstick.

"Remember me, Bob?" Nate asked.

Prentice tried again to speak. He croaked, "*Nate Romanowski.*"

"That's right. What happened here, Bob? Did Ken and you get into a fight?"

Prentice closed his eyes and shook his head in slow motion. His lips moved again, but all he could do was wheeze.

"Bob, was it Axel Soledad?" Nate asked. "Did he stage this? Did he clean you out of guns?"

Prentice's eyes widened. "*Axel,*" he whispered.

"Man, we gotta do something," Geronimo said. "The guy in the chair is long gone. But maybe we can call someone. Or take him into Baker City . . ."

Nate looked up at Geronimo and shook his head. Prentice had nearly bled out. It was a miracle that he'd even made it this long.

And as if on cue, Prentice shuddered and emitted his last communication: a death rattle. His head flopped over to the side.

Nate reached down and closed his eyes.

"Why did he do this?" Geronimo asked. "Why would he murder the guys he needs to sell his birds?"

"Maybe they wouldn't pay him what he wanted," Nate said. "But I think he decided to eliminate the middlemen. There's no commission to pay this way."

Geronimo whistled. "So what do you think happened here? He shot the guy on the floor and then forced the other one to shoot himself?"

Nate got to his feet. "My guess is the other way around. Axel shoved that revolver under Ken's chin and pulled the trigger, then turned and shot Bob. He positioned the Ruger to make it look like a lover's quarrel that went bad."

"Jesus."

Nate nodded. He said, "Soledad had a partner in Wyoming for a while. Another antifa. When the partner got injured and was of no good to him, Soledad broke his neck and left him in an old ranch house. And now this. That's the kind of psycho we're after."

"He needs to be put down," Geronimo said.

Nate agreed and looked around the house. He said, "Make sure to wipe down anything you touched. Let's back out of here. We can make an anonymous 911 call to the Baker City cops once we're clear. I hate to just leave these two bodies here for who knows how long before someone finds them."

"How far is he ahead of us, do you reckon?" Geronimo asked.

"The blood's congealed, but it isn't dry," Nate said. "Just like the gravy. I'd say couple of hours at most."

"We're closing in on him," Geronimo said. "He's not going to know what hit him."

CHAPTER SIXTEEN

The Shaman

"Hit me again," Axel Soledad said to Randy Daniels.

"Doesn't it hurt?"

"Yeah, it hurts. But it gets the GSR off me."

Gunshot residue. Randy knew that much.

He raised the wand inside the car wash and squeezed the trigger. Hot water and steam shot out of the nozzle in a V with enough force to make the wand kick like a gun. He pointed it at Soledad's naked flesh and swept it across his body. Soledad stood with his legs spread and his arms held out away from his body. The hot spray turned his skin red with force and heat. It didn't seem to bother him.

They had stopped at a manual car wash on the outskirts of Pendleton, Oregon. The car wash was coin-operated, so it was one of the few businesses open on Thanksgiving Day.

It wouldn't be that far before they crossed over into Washington State. They'd washed down not only the exterior of the Mercedes transport, but now Axel as well.

Soledad had stripped to his boxer briefs and had crumpled his clothing and stuffed it into a dumpster on the side of the facility. He now stood inside the bay in a pose that looked like Jesus on the cross. He'd asked Randy to do the honors. Which Randy did.

Randy had never seen Axel Soledad out of his tactical gear or black bloc before. Axel was wiry and fit and very white. There were angry-looking scars on his back and across his shoulders, as if he'd once been whipped.

"That's good," Soledad said after Randy had circled him once again with the high-pressure wand. "Now clean yourself up. You stink of blood."

WHILE RANDY DID HIS BEST to clean himself with the wand—unlike Soledad, he avoided the center mass of the hot water and used the periphery of the cone instead—Soledad dressed in a set of clean clothes in the corner of the bay.

Randy was a pale twenty-six-year-old ginger with a concave chest and a smattering of freckles across his nose and cheeks. Unlike Soledad, Randy didn't have human blood or gunshot residue to wash away. But he did have bloodstains on his cargo pants, his shirtsleeves, and beneath his fingernails. It had been his job over the length of the trip to get out on the highway and gather roadkill in various stages of decomposition and bring the carcasses back to the transport to show to Soledad for inspection. If the roadkill was fresh and not putrid, Soledad gave a thumbs-up.

Randy used a cutting board on the center floor of the vehicle to dismember the rabbit, or fox, or coyote, or hapless domestic dog, and feed the pieces to the hawks in their cages.

It was disgusting. The transport was disgusting. It smelled of dead animals and live falcons that squirted pungent white shit all over the floor. Feathers floated in the air. And it seemed like every time Randy relaxed and started to take a nap, one of the birds would let out a screech that made his anus pucker up and his toes curl. None of it seemed to affect Soledad, who drove in silence.

Randy hated the birds. He hated their smug bearing and their black, beady devil eyes. If they could free themselves from their cages, they would swarm him and slash him to ribbons with their talons and beaks.

Although he'd asked in Denver if he could accompany the Shaman on his journey to the northwest and he'd been pleased and honored that Soledad had picked him (it was probably his lean and hungry look as well as his long rap sheet, Randy surmised), he now regretted making the ask. Randy didn't really know Soledad well except by reputation. Randy had hoped to be inspired, for his commitment to the cause to be not only renewed but amplified by learning all he could from Soledad. But although an undeniable charisma surrounded Soledad like a kind of aura, he'd revealed nothing about himself or his intentions.

What Randy did know about the Shaman was that he was a

true believer. Everybody said that. Soledad showed up when he was needed and provided backup, weapons, logistics, and assistance. Then he vanished like a cipher. And he never got arrested.

Soledad had promised Randy ten thousand dollars once their mission was complete. That seemed like a lot of cash at the time, especially since Randy had recently been let go from his internship at a graphic design firm. The boss hated him. That was why they'd fired him, he was sure.

All Randy knew was that Soledad was delivering a whole bunch of wild raptors from somewhere to buyers somewhere else. And that the proceeds from the transaction would be used to help the cause. It didn't take him long to figure out the two of them were bound for Seattle, and then probably somewhere else. Soledad had insisted that he disable the GPS app on his phone and that he was to stay off of it as much as possible.

"Don't tell anyone where you are," he'd said as they left Denver. "*Anyone.*"

And Randy hadn't, even though he knew by now his parents would be worried about him. He had an appointment with his therapist that day and his mom usually drove him.

BECAUSE HE HADN'T had the opportunity to pack a change of clothes and wasn't perpetually on the road like the Shaman, Randy had to dress in the wet clothes he'd hosed down on the floor of the bay. He did his best to wring them out, but they were still damp. Pulling them back on made him shiver.

Meanwhile, Soledad looked like a million dollars, Randy thought. Crisp white shirt, clean black jeans, sports jacket, and running shoes to replace the combat boots he'd worn up until now. He looked like a corporate lobbyist.

"Maybe we could stop somewhere so I could get a change of clothes?" Randy asked.

"Maybe," Soledad said vaguely. He was distracted by something on his phone.

"I'd guess they have a Walmart or Target here in Pendleton. One of them should be open today."

Randy knew nothing about Pendleton, except he thought it might be a rodeo town. It certainly looked like it from the billboards he'd seen on the way there. Something about blankets and a Roundup.

Randy had asked Soledad about what had happened in that brick ranch house. Soledad had told him to stay in the transport and feed the rest of the birds while he went inside. Even through the cacophony of screeching falcons at mealtime, Randy had thought he heard three distinct shots.

Five minutes later, Soledad had returned. His demeanor was just as cool as when he went in. The only difference in appearance were the tiny flecks of blood on the back of his right hand and a spot of it on his right cheek.

"Follow me," Axel had said. "I need some help."

It took four trips to completely empty the upstairs gun safe of weapons and ammunition. Shotguns, rifles, pistols, wicked-looking submachine guns were all among the cache. Randy didn't know guns. He was surprised how heavy they were.

The weapons had filled three large duffel bags in the back of the van.

Randy wasn't sure he wanted to know what had happened. They'd entered the house through a side door and he couldn't see the front room. And Soledad offered absolutely no clue other than to say that "a problem had been solved."

"WELL, WELL, WELL," Soledad said as he looked at his phone. His face was animated.

"What?"

"Look at this," Soledad said. He held the phone to him, but didn't let go of it. Randy leaned in to make out what it was.

He saw a blurry photo of a white van taken from the side. There were words painted on the exterior of the vehicle that he couldn't make out.

Soledad swiped the screen and there was the van again, this time pointed in the opposite direction.

"I don't get it," Randy said. "What am I supposed to be seeing?"

"Do you remember when I stopped on the way out of the Wingville ranch?"

Randy did. Soledad had halted half a mile from the compound. After rummaging around through a gear bag in the back of the transport, he'd gone outside and shut the door, then come back five minutes later without an explanation.

"I hid a trail cam in the brush," Soledad said. "That way, I'd know who went in and out after we left. The trail cam sends shots to my phone as long as the batteries hold out."

Randy nodded for him to go on.

"This van showed up an hour after we left. Drove down the road one way, then back out. Can you see what's written on the side of it?"

Randy reached out to steady Soledad's hand. He peered at the screen and pinched it out with his fingertips to zoom the shot.

"Yarnick?" he asked.

"Yarak, Inc.," Soledad corrected. Then: "Bird abatement specialists from Saddlestring, Wyoming."

Randy was befuddled. Soledad laughed, but not at Randy. He was laughing at the photo of the van.

"Nate Romanowski is after us," he said.

"Who?"

Soledad chinned toward the transport. Meaning the birds inside. "He wants what we have."

"Who is he?"

"You've never heard of him," Soledad said. "You're not a falconer. He's old-school, from another era. He was considered to be a big man back then: deadly, full of mystery and crackpot ethics. But he left the life to become a pussy capitalist. His time has passed."

"Why is he following us?" Randy asked.

Soledad didn't answer. He had already spoken longer than at any time Randy had been with him. Soledad, if anything else, kept his own counsel. His description of Nate Romanowski, even. It seemed like it was something Soledad was saying to himself, not to Randy.

Then Soledad checked the clock on his phone and said, "Time to go."

"Where?"

Soledad didn't answer.

THEY TOOK THE US 30 exit off I-84 and drove through central Pendleton until it became Southeast Court Avenue. They passed a Walmart Supercenter and Randy pointed out that it was open, but Soledad kept driving. They merged onto Westgate and crossed the Umatilla River, and Soledad slowed down and drove into the parking lot of the Eastern Oregon Correctional Institution.

The facility was sprawling and multistoried, constructed of blond bricks and topped by a red-slate roof. Randy thought it looked more like a college campus than a medium-security prison.

"What are we doing here?" he asked Soledad.

"Picking up a buddy," Soledad said. "You'll need to move into the back."

"What, and sit on the floor? With the hawk shit?"

Soledad shrugged. Then he gestured toward the large building in the center of the complex that appeared to be the headquarters. "There he is."

Randy squinted toward where Soledad was pointing.

Four men emerged from the side door of the building. Three were obviously correctional officers. They were dressed in dark blue and wore EOCI ballcaps.

The fourth was a small man in ill-fitting civilian clothes. A baggy short-sleeved shirt over a dark long-sleeved Henley. Only when the man stopped at the gate and turned his back to the COs to have his handcuffs removed did Randy realize it wasn't long underwear but full-sleeve tattoos.

"Well, get in the back," Soledad said to Randy with impatience.

"Who is this guy?"

"Let me give you a tip," Soledad said. "Don't challenge him."

SOLEDAD AND THE RELEASED INMATE fist-bumped in the front seat as they left the parking lot. The new man turned and glared at Randy hunkered down behind him. His gaze was not kind.

The inmate had dark hollow eyes, sharp cheekbones, and an overlarge mouth barely covering a mouthful of sharp yellow teeth. He looked feral, Randy thought. Not a man to be messed with.

"How do you two know each other?" Randy asked.

"The Blade and I were baptized in blood together," Soledad said.

"What does that mean?"

The Blade turned in his seat and his gaze froze Randy to the floor of the van.

"It means shut the fuck up."

Randy did.

The Blade grinned crookedly at Soledad.

"Happy Thanksgiving, I guess," he said.

WHAT RANDY DIDN'T KNOW and would never know, Soledad thought, was about that baptism in blood. Soledad and the Blade were bonded together in a way that a civilian trust-fund boy like Randy would never comprehend.

It had happened halfway around the world in Myanmar, formerly Burma, in 2012. That's where they'd lost not only their comrades but also their faith in the U.S. government. And they'd pledged to each other that if they ever got back to the States alive, they'd burn it down.

Their team of eight Mark V special operators had scrambled out of a black helicopter just inside the border of Rakhine, the westernmost state in the country. Their mission had been to accompany an ethnic Rohingya warlord from his village and get the man safely to Thailand. From there, other operatives would whisk him away to Australia.

Myanmar government forces wanted to stop the passage of the warlord and either murder him or put him into a concentration camp. It was part of their campaign to annihilate and ethnically cleanse the entire Rohingya population. With the warlord out of the picture, the resistance would weaken even more.

Although the geopolitical reasons for the mission were never explained to the operators—they never were—Mark V did what it always did. It carried out orders.

Mark V existed off the books and their existence was denied to anyone, including Congress. The word within Mark V was that their presence was not even briefed to certain U.S. presidents.

Every Mark V operator had to not only pledge lifelong secrecy about what they'd done around the world on behalf of the Pentagon, they'd all signed powerful nondisclosure agreements, which, if broken, would result in immediate secret imprisonment or worse.

Axel Soledad commanded the squad of Peregrines. They moved through the jungle like predators, living off the land and maintaining radio silence. Like every mission Soledad had been on, they'd been ordered not to radio for assistance or pickup until the mission was accomplished.

They'd located the warlord in his village, but the man had been stubborn and frightened and didn't trust them. He'd delayed his departure while government forces moved into the province in a pincer movement. Within two days, the eight Mark V warriors had been ambushed by government forces that had surrounded the warlord's village.

Wave after wave of them came for three straight days and nights. The warlord tried to surrender, but he was cut down the minute he showed himself. But the onslaught continued.

Most of the enemies they killed were child soldiers who had been conscripted into the Burmese army for forty dollars and a bag of rice. Soledad and his men killed hundreds of twelve-, thirteen-, and fourteen-year-old boys.

At the time, Soledad's younger brother, Trey, had been the same age as the Burmese boys he slaughtered. It was awful. Their superiors loaded up the children with drugs that included cocaine and a mixture of sugarcane syrup and gunpowder that turned them into savages. Combine that with the bloodlust frenzy only teenage boys were capable of, and it was horrific.

The child soldiers were undisciplined and poorly trained, but there were too many of them. Five Peregrines were mortally injured in the fighting. Soledad then pulled the plug on the mission and called for the three remaining men—Corporal Butler, Sergeant Spivak (the man known as the Blade), and himself—to evacuate the village and be airlifted to safety.

There was no response.

One of the primary and central tenets of special operations was to leave no man behind. Special operators risked their lives countless times recovering wounded soldiers and those who'd given the last full measure. The tenet was sacrosanct.

"Leave no man behind" might have been valid back when old guys like Nate Romanowski served in the unit, Soledad thought. Lots of noble lies might have existed then.

Among the more experienced special operators, it was sometimes discussed how quickly the U.S. government walked away from allies and agreements with foreign fighters. There was a long list of "friends" that had been forgotten and left for dead by the stroke of a pen or a few words in a presidential speech. But special ops was different. Or so they thought.

They'd been betrayed and abandoned for reasons Soledad later learned were treacherous, petty, and inexcusable. It all had to do with internal politics within the executive branch in Washington. In a speech, the octogenarian president had misread his teleprompter, somehow mangling the U.S. policy of support for the Rohingya into support for the Myanmar government. Rather than admit the president's error, his aides had reversed the official policy instead. Since Mark V didn't officially exist, the result had stranded them without support or even acknowledgment.

Soledad, the Blade, and Butler had fled to the west toward the Bay of Bengal through some of the most inhospitable jungle terrain in the world. They'd eaten monkeys and snakes, and Corporal Butler had been struck in the neck by a king cobra that killed him within hours.

Unaware of the abrupt change in policy, Soledad and the Blade had made it to the coast, stolen a fishing boat, and navigated south for days until they'd finally beached the boat and plunged on foot into Thailand. Both were wounded, sick, and exhausted. Their calls and texts to Mark V HQ in Colorado Springs were unanswered.

Soledad had discovered that his passwords no longer worked to access Mark V data or communications, and his encrypted satellite phone had been remotely disabled.

They'd been disappeared.

They later learned that their families had been notified that they'd died bravely in action on a covert mission that couldn't be disclosed. Pensions paid for their deaths had been more than magnanimous.

While recovering anonymously in a Thai hotel room, Soledad and the Blade had discussed what to do next. They could blow the lid on the operation and the high-level policy change, expose the existence of Mark V, bring legal action against commanders who didn't exist on any official payroll, and violate their NDAs.

Or they could quietly come home and turn on their masters. They chose the latter.

And now that the Blade had served his time for assaulting a federal agent in Portland two summers before, they could resume their legacy together.

AFTER A HALF HOUR of silence in the transport, after Soledad had once again gotten on I-84, the Blade said to him, "Seattle, right?"

"Yes. We're going to get in and get out."

The Blade nodded that he understood. Randy didn't.

"Guess who is after us?" Soledad asked.

"Who, besides everybody?"

"Nate Romanowski. He wants the birds."

The Blade whistled. "Nate Romanowski? *That* Nate Romanowski?"

"The same. But he's *not* the same. Instead of fighting back after he left the unit, he went off the grid and now he's pretending he's legitimate."

"I don't get that," the Blade said. "If anybody should be on our side, it's him."

"He doesn't have any fight left in him," Soledad said. "He's washed-up."

"Damn," the Blade said. "I used to look up to the guy. The stories I heard about him . . . he was *badass*."

"He's old and soft now. He's married and has a kid."

"Are we gonna get rid of these birds in Seattle?" he asked.

"Not yet."

The Blade chuckled at that. He and Soledad seemed to share a private joke.

"Then what are we going to do in Seattle?" Randy asked finally.

"We're going to light the fuse," Soledad said.

CHAPTER SEVENTEEN

Lola Lowry

Joe loosened his belt and settled into his lounge chair in front of the television in the living room. He was happy, sleepy, and a little bit drunk. The Dallas Cowboys game was a few minutes away and he hoped it would be dull and boring so he could squeeze in a nap.

For the first time since he and Marybeth had moved in, the house felt *full*. The aromas from the feast still lingered and he couldn't think of anything that smelled better.

The Thanksgiving meal had been wonderful, although rounds of dessert were still to come. The women of all ages in the dining room were howling with laughter and they'd scarcely noticed that he'd slipped away. The shady exit from the dinner table was a move he'd worked on for years and, by all accounts, nearly perfected.

Daisy had found him, of course, and she was collapsed on

the side of the chair. April's big dog, LeDoux, seemed to worship Daisy, and soon there were two dogs on the carpet. Tube had come out of the dining room long enough to assess where Joe was, but he'd turned and gone back because, although he was only half Corgi, his outlook toward humans was all Corgi. Tube instinctively knew that the people in the house had gathered primarily to appreciate and admire *him*. He'd gone back into the kitchen so as not to deprive them any longer.

Lucy had arrived with her friend, Fong Chan, an hour before they ate. Fong was petite and polite and she spoke perfect English. She told everyone during dinner that she had been texting her parents in Hong Kong about the trip with Lucy and the Thanksgiving dinner and that they were happy she'd met a friend. She read out a text from her parents thanking Lucy and everyone in the family for the special occasion.

She mentioned that her parents were considering a move from Hong Kong because of the Communist oppression there. They favored California, but Fong said she'd now convinced them to take a look at the Mountain West because she'd found people to be especially welcoming.

Lucy was courteous and attentive to her friend—she was always the perfect host—but she'd slip out of character to parry a jibe from one of her older sisters or slip in a good-natured insult when they were talking. As always, Lucy read the room better than anyone in the family other than Marybeth, and she knew just what to say at the perfect time to either delight her parents or enrage her sisters. It was good to have her home.

Kestrel was too busy to eat. Instead, she cruised from diner to diner to get bits of food, which everyone gave her. Liv said she didn't like the idea of her baby girl imitating a dog, but even she fed the toddler a piece of turkey with gravy.

Sheridan reveled in playing the big sister, the one with the actual job who lived in the real world. She chided April about being "practically unemployed" and Lucy for being cocooned at college. Her comments, made good-naturedly, were greeted with rolled eyes from both of her sisters.

April switched from beer before the meal to wine after, and she got louder with each glass. She was already challenging Sheridan to another wrestling match at some point. Fong was alarmed, until Lucy assured her there would be no real violence.

Liv had brought a pot of cornbread and oyster stuffing that she said she'd learned to make from her grandmother back in Louisiana. Joe loved it and had eaten way too much of it. When he burped in his chair, he could taste oysters.

From where he sat, he could see out through the living room window to the front lawn and the woods beyond. He glanced over from time to time to make sure the gargoyle-looking man Marybeth had encountered that morning wasn't coming back. The day was cool and still, marked by errant swirls of wind that picked up fallen leaves and danced them around in pirouettes, then dropped them again. There were still a couple of late elk-hunting areas open in the mountains, but the season was winding down. He didn't feel guilty taking the day off and not patrolling. Even the few elk hunters remaining usually made their way into town for a Thanksgiving meal at a restaurant or church.

He periodically checked his phone for text messages from Sheriff Tibbs or Gary Norwood in regard to their day-old murder investigation. Both of them were apparently taking the day off as well. Either that or they had nothing new to report.

The plate number he'd written down from the car on the road the night before proved to be a dead end. It was a rental belonging to Budget Rent A Car. It had been rented by someone called Bob Hardy from Syracuse, New York. A New York DMV quick records check had come up empty.

HIS EYELIDS WERE DROOPING when he noticed Liv hurrying out of the dining room with her phone pressed to her ear. As she walked by, she mouthed, "Nate" to Joe.

"I'd like to talk to him when you're through," Joe said, instantly awake.

Ten minutes later, Liv came back from where she'd spoken to Nate in the mudroom. Her eyes were moist, but Joe could tell she wasn't upset, just emotional.

She handed Joe her phone.

"Hey there," Joe said. "Happy Thanksgiving. You missed a heck of a meal."

"So I heard," Nate said. He sounded distant and subdued, as if he didn't want to raise his voice. "I'd hoped I'd be back by today, but it didn't work out."

"Liv said you're getting close."

Joe knew not to mention specific names or quiz Nate on strategy or his location on the cell call. There was no way to know who might be listening in. Nate was certainly on the radar of the feds and Joe was a known associate.

"I am. It could be any time now."

"Does he know you're on to him?"

"Probably."

"Will that screw things up?" Joe asked.

"It might, but I don't have a choice but to move on him fast and hard. I *can't* let him get away."

"Is there anything I can do?"

Nate paused, which surprised Joe. Then: "No. It's important that you're there keeping an eye on Liv and Kestrel."

Meaning, Joe knew, *If I lose him somehow, he might double back and come after my family again.*

"Are you doing all right?" Joe asked.

"Mentally or physically?"

"Either one."

"I've done hours of windshield time and I've taken a few hits," Nate said.

Joe wanted more details but knew not to ask for them. "Are you completely on your own?"

"Not completely. I've got a few friends. One in particular."

"Do you trust him?"

"I do."

"When can we expect to see you?"

"Soon, I hope." There was another pause, as if Nate was contemplating saying, *Or never.*

"You can always come back," Joe said. "You don't have to finish this."

"Wrong. I *have* to finish this."

Nate said it in such a definitive way that Joe knew it was pointless to try to talk him out of it.

"Well, we miss you," Joe said. "Kestrel is a firecracker, just like her mom."

Liv reacted to that with a grin.

"I miss her," Nate said. "Being away from her and Liv is harder than I imagined. Now I know what you've been dealing with all of these years."

"But it's not so bad, is it?" Joe asked, smiling. "It's certainly better than sitting naked in a tree watching the river flow by." Which was one of Nate's pastimes when he was single and off the grid. That, and submerging himself in the reeds near the bank of the river with a breathing tube to "experience what a fish feels like."

Nate didn't respond. Joe imagined his friend covering the mike on his phone and talking to someone.

"I've got to go," Nate said in a whisper.

"I understand," Joe said, although he understood nothing. "Be safe."

"You've been a good friend," Nate said as he terminated the call.

Joe felt the hairs on his neck prick up.

"What?" Liv asked Joe as he handed the phone back to her.

"He said I was a good friend," Joe said.

"You are."

"I just wish he hadn't said it in that way. Did he tell you where he was?"

"Not specifically," Liv said. "Somewhere in Washington State. He was 'in the heart of the beast.' Which I took to mean Seattle."

Joe nodded. He said, "If it were anyone else, I'd be really worried."

"You're telling me," Liv said. "I've had a knot in my stomach for days. Today was the first time I feel like I've cut loose for at least a few hours."

"Go back and have some more wine. It's okay."

"I hope so," she said.

He hoped so, too.

IT WAS THE SECOND QUARTER and Dallas was down by nine and Joe was awakened by Marybeth shaking his shoulder.

"I'm worried about Lola," she said.

Joe sat up and rubbed his eyes. "I forgot about her," he said.

"I thought she'd come by for dessert at least. I've been waiting for her to call for a ride before I slice the pies."

"Did you call her?"

"Twice. She doesn't have a cell and her phone just rings and rings. She doesn't have it set up for messages."

"I hope she didn't fall down and break her hip or something," Joe said. "Maybe she had a little too much peppermint schnapps."

Marybeth said, "I suppose she could have driven into town for a holiday meal at the senior center. But to ease my mind, I think you should go check on her."

Joe glanced at the game. Dallas was now down by sixteen. But he really didn't care.

He sat up. "Okay."

"Thank you, Joe."

WITH DAISY ON HIS HEELS, Joe walked to his pickup and out through the front gate. The day had warmed into the fifties and the clouds had parted over the Bighorns. It was a remarkably temperate Thanksgiving Day.

Sunlight streamed through cloud holes to bathe sections of the timber in bronze light. A golden eagle hovered in place over the tops of the trees to the north, looking for mice in the undergrowth.

He opened the passenger door and Daisy bounded in. It was less than a five-minute drive from Joe's house to Lola's trailer. For once, the cow moose wasn't there to block his progress. He'd fooled her, he thought, by mixing up his routine. She was prepared to interfere with him at dawn and after dusk as he came home, but she wasn't ready to lumber out on the road when he was driving from his house in the midafternoon.

He became concerned when he saw that Lola's older-model white SUV was parked behind her trailer. She hadn't driven into town. The porch light was on over the metal front door as well, which was unusual. Lola was a stickler for not "wasting electricity."

Joe left Daisy in the cab. He didn't want his dog barking at Lola's cat.

He rapped hard on her front door. "Lola? It's Joe. Are you in there?"

There was a faint muffled sound from inside. The audio was from her television.

He knocked again. "Lola?"

There was no response. He tried the door handle. Locked.

Since there wasn't a window or peephole in the trailer door, Joe moved to the right side of her wooden porch and leaned over the railing so he could see inside her front room from a window that he knew looked in on her living room. Her blinds were open.

He could see images flickering across the screen of her television. The back of her couch was to him, but he couldn't see her head above the top of it. Her cat was curled up on the armrest of a recliner and it eyed him coldly.

"Lola?" he said while rapping on the glass.

Nothing.

Then, almost out of his angle of vision to his left, he saw her shoes. They were heavy orthopedic shoes and her feet were in them. Lola was on her back on the floor and her legs were splayed out on the linoleum. Joe couldn't see Lola's upper torso from where he was on the porch.

Her legs weren't moving.

As quickly as he could, Joe jogged back to his truck and dug out a heavy crowbar from the gear box in the bed and returned to the front door. He jammed the blade of the tool in between the door and doorframe above the locked handle and wrenched it hard. The lock broke with a *clunk* and the door swung inward about a foot until it stopped. He pushed on it and it gave a little, but he could tell by the feel of it that the door was blocked by Lola herself. If he forced it open, he'd slide her across the floor. If she was already injured, he didn't want to compound it by shoving her around.

Joe tossed the crowbar off the porch and wedged his head through the opening.

She was on her back and the bottom of the door was touching the top of her head. Her face, which was directly below him, was pale and waxy and her hands were balled up into tiny fists. Her eyes were closed and there was what appeared to be a neat round bullet hole in the middle of her forehead. Her glasses were askew on her face. He couldn't see any blood on the floor.

Joe dropped to his haunches on the porch and withdrew his head from the opening. He reached in and around the door and pressed his fingertips to the skin on her neck below her jawline. She was cool and stiff to the touch. There was no pulse.

"*Oh no . . .*" he moaned aloud.

Another body of an elderly local. Another crime scene.

He stood up and fished his cell phone out of his breast pocket and speed-dialed Sheriff Tibbs directly.

"Joe?" Tibbs said. "We're right in the middle of Thanksgiving dinner."

"I know and I'm sorry."

"I really don't have any updates from the Kizer case."

"That's not why I'm calling, Sheriff. There's been another murder. This time it's our neighbor, Lola Lowry. I just found her body in her trailer and it looks like she was shot in the head last night or really early this morning."

"Oh no."

"That's what I said."

"On *Thanksgiving*?"

"Unfortunately. She was supposed to come to our house today. When she didn't, Marybeth asked me to check on her. That's how I found her."

Tibbs was quiet. Joe could hear the tinkling of utensils in the background as well as the play-by-play call of the Dallas game.

"Text me the address," Tibbs said wearily. "I'll call Steck, Bass, and Norwood so I can ruin their holiday as well."

"Sorry again," Joe said.

"Can't you just stay home and mind your own business?" Tibbs asked with sudden heat. "Every time you go out, you create another goddamn headache for me and my department."

Joe punched off without responding.

Then he called Marybeth with the bad news and ruined *her* holiday.

CHAPTER EIGHTEEN

Northern Lights

SEVERAL HOURS LATER, JOE SAT OUTSIDE HIS HOME AT DUSK IN a rocking chair with a blanket on his lap and his twelve-gauge Remington Wingmaster shotgun across his thighs. Daisy was at his feet. He smoked a cigar and sipped on a tumbler of bourbon and water and watched errant strobes of red and blue lights flash across the tops of the trees in the direction of Lola Lowry's trailer as sheriff's department vehicles came and went.

The news about Lola had cast a definite pall on the festivities inside, although no one had yet left. He'd described what he found at the scene to hushed silence. His daughters, Liv, and Marybeth speculated on what had happened and what was going on around them. Two murders in two days in Twelve Sleep County was a remarkable and unwelcome development. Fong Chan quietly followed the discussion with wide eyes, suggesting that she couldn't quite believe what a barbaric environment her sweet friend Lucy had come from.

Even though there were law enforcement vehicles on the access road, Joe kept a close eye on the wall of trees to the east in the direction of the county road. If the gargoyle that Marybeth saw that morning came creeping back, he was ready for him.

Joe had informed Sheriff Tibbs when he met him at the crime scene about the gargoyle, as well as the two men parked on the side of the county road he'd encountered the night before. He'd described the men—what he could see of them—and said the driver had heavy features that could be described as "gargoyle-like." And he'd given a description of the SUV with Colorado plates.

Tibbs had taken down the information in a notebook, but in a dismissive and cursory fashion, Joe thought. As if Joe's tip was just another item designed to complicate matters.

All Joe knew about the cause of death was Gary Norwood's initial proclamation that it "wasn't a gunshot wound." The hole in her forehead had been caused by a sharp weapon yet to be determined.

That poor old lady, Joe thought. She was now the primary focus of a literal locked-room mystery scenario. Who could have killed her and how had the bad guy gotten into her trailer? And what was the motivation?

"ARE YOU GOING TO SIT out here all night?" Sheridan asked in the dark. She slid a lawn chair over next to Joe and sat down.

"Probably for a while," he said. "I hope I can head off any more surprises before they happen."

"I didn't know you smoked cigars."

"This one was a gift. I checked on a bunch of hunters at an elk camp last week and one of them gave me a cigar. I kind of like it. He was probably guilty of something."

"Mom told us about that Bert Kizer guy," she said. "Do you think Lola's murder is connected with him?"

"That's what I'm trying to puzzle out. I don't know if they even knew each other or why someone would go after them. Maybe they knew each other from the senior center? There are a lot of questions about what's happened in the last two days and I don't have any answers. Problem is, I don't think the sheriff has any, either."

"He isn't really on the top of his game, is he?" Sheridan asked. She'd had experiences with the sheriff when Joe was lost in the mountains.

"He might surprise us," Joe said.

"Doubtful." Sheridan was a harsh judge of character, Joe thought. Like her mother.

"Are you going to investigate it yourself?" she asked.

"You know how that works. The sheriff has to invite me in. He hasn't done that."

"When has that ever stopped you before?"

Joe grinned. Good point.

"If you do decide to get involved, I hope you'll let me know," she said. "With Nate gone, I could be your partner."

Joe was touched. He reached out and grasped her hand.

"You need to stay close to Liv and Kestrel and keep an eye on them," he said. "That was the deal with Nate, wasn't it?"

"Yes, even though Liv is tough and fully capable of handling herself."

"But not Kestrel."

Sheridan's silence was an indication that she had to agree with her father.

"Not that I wouldn't appreciate your company," Joe said. "We'd make a pretty good team, I think."

"I think so, too," she said. "I learned a lot of things when I used to go on ride-alongs with you back in the day."

Joe's phone burred and he checked the screen. Deputy Bass.

Bass told Joe he was making the rounds at all of the lodging facilities in Saddlestring, looking for the SUV with Colorado plates that Joe had seen the night before. He hadn't found a vehicle matching the description yet, but he'd put the word out county-wide and said he'd keep looking. If the vehicle couldn't be found, he said, he'd do the same at the three motels and two bed-and-breakfast outfits in Winchester.

Joe thanked him for the update and punched off.

As IT GOT darker outside and more still, Joe could hear the volume increase inside his house. His daughters had broken out board games and opened more bottles of wine, and there were whoops and shouts. He continued to watch the tree line and catch occasional flashes of wigwag lights from the crime scene.

Marybeth came outside and stopped abruptly as she looked around.

"Look at that," she said, pointing over the roofline of the house. Joe turned in his chair to follow her gesture.

Blue and pink northern lights shimmered and pulsated across the big sky. This was a rare occurrence in Wyoming, but not unprecedented.

"It's beautiful," she said. "The sky is on fire."

"From both directions," Joe said. "Wigwags to the east and northern lights at the same time. It's like living on the Vegas Strip."

She sat in the chair Sheridan had left.

"They're having so much fun in there I don't want to break it up," she said.

"Why break things up at all?"

"Do you think it's safe for everyone to stay here tonight?" she asked. "That intruder spooked me. There was a *reason* he came to our house. I just don't know what it was."

"I'm ready for him next time," Joe said, patting the receiver of his shotgun.

"I think I'd rather have everyone here under our roof than scattered in the wind where we can't keep an eye on them," she said.

"I agree."

"I've got a question for you," she said. "When you were in Lola's trailer, did you see the tote bag full of books I brought her from the library? I left it on the floor on the side of her couch."

Joe looked over, not understanding.

"It had our logo on the outside. It's like the ones I always bring home."

He shook his head. "I don't remember seeing it."

"Do you think you could go back there and look? I see that they're still investigating Lola's place."

Instead, Joe called Gary Norwood's cell phone. Norwood sounded weary and out of sorts.

"Gary, are you still at the scene?"

"I am, but I'm about to put a lid on it for the night. I'll be back tomorrow. Joe, I left a half-eaten turkey leg on my plate for this."

"I'm sorry."

"I know. It isn't your fault—but try telling Tibbs that."

"Did you determine what killed her?" Joe asked.

"Not definitively, but, like I said, it wasn't a gunshot wound. I'd describe the injury as almost like a very large ice pick. It must have been sharpened and delivered with a lot of force because it really penetrated her skull. My guess is she died instantly, which is probably the only good thing about this situation."

"Does the sheriff have any leads?" Joe asked.

"Other than your mystery SUV, I don't think so," Norwood said. "Whoever did it got in through the *floor*. And he either wore gloves or cleaned up—just like the scene at Kizer's. Like Bert's place, there's no sign of forced entry. I haven't found anything of note yet, and as far as I know there aren't any suspects."

Joe noticed that Marybeth had leaned closer to him so she could overhear Norwood.

"I've got a quick question for you and then I'll let you go," Joe said. "Do you see a Twelve Sleep County Library tote bag anywhere inside the trailer? Filled with . . ."

"Romance novels," Marybeth whispered.

". . . Romance novels," Joe said.

"Just a sec," Norwood said. Joe could hear him place his phone down on a hard surface. He came back a minute later.

"Nope. No bag full of books. Why?"

"Marybeth was wondering about it. She dropped the bag off for Lola yesterday."

"Well, it isn't here now."

"Thank you, Gary. Now go eat that turkey leg. And Happy Thanksgiving."

"You too, Joe. And my best to your family."

Joe disconnected the call and lowered the phone to his lap.

"You heard," he said.

"It's interesting. That means either she got rid of the books—which doesn't sound like Lola—or somebody took them."

"Who would take romance novels?" Joe asked. "Who would even want them?"

"That isn't necessary," Marybeth admonished him. Like a true librarian.

"Sorry."

The missing book bag obviously took her aback. She paused, deep in thought. While her mind worked, her eyes sparkled. Joe loved to watch her puzzle things out in real time. He found it wildly attractive. And he knew better than to interrupt her.

"Give me your phone," she said.

He handed it over. She called up the photo app and scrolled through the Kizer crime scene in reverse chronological order. She grimaced in anticipation when she viewed the shots of the interior, not knowing when images of the burned body would begin. He intended to warn her when she got close.

But she didn't get that far.

"Here," she said, jabbing at the screen with the tip of her fingernail with a *click*. "Do you see this long-billed cap on his table? And the jacket hung over the back of the kitchen chair?"

She turned the phone to Joe and he looked at it. It had appeared to him at the time that the items were haphazardly placed there, as if Bert had entered his home and tossed his cap on the table and draped his coat over the chair.

"Okay," Joe said, raising his eyebrows. "That's a long-billed fishing cap with black under the brim. The black helps with the sun's reflection off the water. Some guides really like 'em."

"This indicates to me that he'd come home before the bad guys arrived. He took off his coat and hat and then he answered a knock at the door. He probably wasn't expecting company, is my guess."

Joe nodded. "That's what Norwood thought, too. There was half-eaten bacon and eggs on the counter," he said. "Maybe Bert thought it was a prospective client coming to see him."

"Maybe. Now this coat. Was it a fishing jacket?"

"It said 'Simms' on the sleeve," Joe said. "So, yes, it was a fishing jacket. That doesn't seem odd for a fishing guide."

She looked up. "The man I saw yesterday morning in the

alcove of the library was wearing a cap like this and a jacket like this. Do you think it's possible it was Bert Kizer?"

"I don't know."

"Do you have a recent photo of him? I know the one in your phone isn't probably something I could use to identify him."

"True," Joe said. "And please don't try."

"Here," she said, handing him back his phone. Marybeth dashed inside the house and returned with her laptop. The glow from the screen illuminated her face as she quickly logged on and tapped out passwords on a series of screens.

Joe recognized the layout of the Wyoming Department of Transportation website. He often accessed the site to identify hunters by matching their driver's license information with their hunting licenses. He'd caught a few out-of-state hunters pretending to be residents that way. The violators had been motivated to commit fraud because nonresident licenses cost much more.

"How do you have access to that?" he asked her.

"Don't ask."

A few more taps and she found what she was looking for: Bert Kizer's motor vehicle license photo. She studied it.

"I think it was him," she said. "The man who left the photo album at the library was Bert Kizer. I'm ninety percent sure of it. And I think the album belonged to his dad, who'd been in the Band of Brothers during World War Two. He probably kept it in that footlocker you found under his bed."

"How did you get all of that from my phone?" Joe asked, perplexed.

"All I got from your phone was the name on the footlocker," she said. "I researched the rest online this morning while everybody was asleep and the gargoyle showed up. Anyway, I looked up R. W. 'Dick' Kizer and found his obituary. It said Bert was his son and that Dick was in the Band of Brothers."

"You're *kidding*," Joe said.

"I'm not. Dick Kizer was one of two Wyoming soldiers in that unit. He landed at Normandy and stayed with the regiment all the way across Europe. They were the first Americans to enter Hitler's Eagle's Nest, where one of them—a guy from Casper, believe it or not—stole two of Hitler's personal photo albums and brought them back."

Joe was stunned by the implication. "So did Dick Kizer take the album that was dropped off at your library?"

"I don't know for certain, of course, but it's possible. He was there in Berchtesgaden."

Joe felt a chill that had nothing to do with the cold evening. There had been enough spare room in the locker for the album to have been there. He thought of how pressed the uniform had been, as if something heavy and flat had weighted it down for years before it had been removed.

He asked, "Why would Bert decide yesterday, after all these years, to donate that album to your library if that's what happened?"

"I don't know," Marybeth said. "But maybe he did it because he thought someone was going to come and take it from him. Maybe he did it just a couple of hours before the bad guy showed up at his house and tortured him until he told him where it was?"

"Stay with me on this," Marybeth said, racing ahead. "Let's say that Bert somehow found out that somebody was coming for his father's photo album. How he learned that, I have no idea. But his reaction to the possibility was to get the album out of his house and leave it somewhere secure where no one would make a big deal of it. Believe it or not, that's one reason people trust our library. They trust us to be discreet.

"So Bert does this early yesterday morning. He thinks he's found a safe place for it. Maybe his intention was to come back later and retrieve it. Or maybe he hoped we'd send it on to some national archive so no one could get to it. I don't know his thinking."

"I'm following you," Joe said, urging her on.

She said, "Bert goes home after dropping off the album to find a guy—or maybe a couple of guys—waiting for him. I'm going to say it was at least two men because I don't think one guy could do to Bert Kizer what was done to him, do you?"

"No."

She said, "They strong-arm him and demand the album. For whatever reason, he won't tell them anything at first. But when he won't hand it over, they get nasty with him. Why it means so much to them, we don't know. And we don't know how they knew he even had it. It obviously means enough to them that they torture him for it. At some point he breaks and tells them what he did with it. But they can't just let him go. He's seen their faces. Maybe they even told him why they want it. So they take him out back and set him on fire and dispose of the body. Then," she said, leaning in close to Joe, "they drive to my library. By this time, they know we have it."

"Go on."

"So what are they going to do?" she asked. "Are they going to storm a public library and start asking about a package that was left on the doorstep? Would they call that kind of attention to themselves in a public place knowing what they just did to a poor old man? No, I think they did surveillance. They were watching for me the entire time."

Joe felt another chill. "They saw you take it out of the building in a Twelve Sleep County Library tote bag. Then they followed you at least to our access road."

"That's what I'm thinking," she said. "But they're not from here. They knew what road I took, but they didn't know there was another house at the end of it. Maybe they looked into Lola's trailer and saw the tote bag and thought it belonged to *me*."

"Oh no," Joe said. "They killed Lola for a bunch of romance novels instead of a Nazi photo album."

"And if they're desperate and violent enough to kill two old people because of it, I doubt they'll just go home," she declared. "They realized they'd made a mistake—that they'd gone to the wrong house. So at least one of them came back this morning to scout things out. That was the gargoyle."

"Whew," Joe said. "I've got to really think this over. This is a lot to digest."

"There could be holes in it," she said. "But how many times have I been wrong about things like this?"

He couldn't think of any. There had to be at least one time, he thought. But no instance came to mind.

"It's the only explanation," she said. "The only thing that connects Bert Kizer and Lola Lowry is that photo album. The photo album that's in our house right now just a few feet from all of our girls, plus Liv and Kestrel."

Joe nodded and began to raise his phone to make a call. He was buzzing inside.

"Don't call the sheriff just yet," Marybeth said. "He's completely overwhelmed. Let's think about all of this and try to come up with something that makes more sense. I doubt the bad guys would come for it tonight with all the activity in our house and all of those cops working just up the road."

He lowered his phone. That made sense.

"Let's sleep on it," she said. "Maybe we'll wake up tomorrow with another scenario that works."

"Like I'll be able to sleep," Joe said.

"Me either."

If Marybeth's speculation was correct, he thought, the gargoyle and his toadie could have come to their house the night before when everyone was sleeping. Instead, they'd gone to Lola's trailer. It had been a close call.

Marybeth was thinking along the same lines. "If I hadn't dropped those books off to Lola, she might still be alive."

"Don't say that. If you hadn't, *you* might have been targeted."

They looked into each other's eyes, each running would-have, could-have instances through their heads. There was no reason to say them out loud. They'd been together so many years it was no longer necessary.

Finally, Marybeth said, "What is it about that album that would motivate someone to kill for it?"

Joe shrugged.

Marybeth stood up and hugged herself against the cold. "I think I'll go back inside and pour myself a big glass of wine."

"Good idea. I'll be right behind you. But I'm going to walk our tree line first just to make myself feel like we're safe tonight."

"Take Daisy."

"Of course."

She turned to him with a sad smile. "Is this the worst Thanksgiving we've ever had?"

"Yup."

FLASHLIGHT IN HAND and Daisy snuffling the grass, Joe walked the tree line at the edge of the property. He saw nothing of note except the cow moose lurking in the dark timber. Her eyes glowed back like two orange sparks in the beam.

Daisy stopped abruptly at a game trail that wound out of the trees from the woods. She braced her legs stiffly and her tail shot back and forth like a metronome. It was the stance she took when she narrowed in on a game bird hidden in the brush.

The gargoyle had left his scent, Joe thought. He'd used the

game trail to walk through the forest from the county road to their house that morning.

Joe swept the trees with light, but no one was there. Then he called Deputy Tom Bass. Since Bass was the rookie in the department, Joe asked, "Are you on duty tonight?"

"Unfortunately, yes."

"Doing time at the newest crime scene?"

"Affirmative," Bass said. Bass was new enough, Joe thought, that he still spoke in radio jargon rather than simply saying yes.

"Could I ask you a favor?" Joe said. "Could you swing by my house a few times tonight and let me know if you see anything suspicious? Like a guy on foot in the trees?"

Bass hesitated. Then: "Sure, I could do that."

"Keep an eye on the county road for parked SUVs as well."

"What's going on?"

"It's just a precaution. You might have heard that my wife saw someone on our place this morning. We don't want him to come back."

Joe didn't want to explain yet the possible connections between the gargoyle and what happened to Lola, and certainly not to Bert Kizer or a wild theory involving a Nazi photo album.

"Will do," Bass said. "Over."

"Over," Joe said.

Then he checked his wristwatch. It wasn't yet nine.

CHAPTER NINETEEN

The Wet Fly

THE WET FLY BAR WAS LOCATED AT THE SOUTHERN EDGE OF Saddlestring. It had been open less than a year and a half, but the owners appeared to have discovered a niche that kept it going: steady but not flashy, unpretentious, always open. It was the kind of place with three or four older-model pickups parked out front from when it opened at ten in the morning to when it closed at two a.m. It seemed to have a steady clientele, but it was rarely packed. The Wet Fly catered to shift workers as well as locals who simply wanted to drink at any time of the day.

Plus, Joe had heard, they let regular customers keep tabs. That was helpful to those who had seasonal employment. They could charge their light beers and drafts during lean times and pay them off during flush months. It was perfect for on-again, off-again fishing guides like Bert Kizer.

The Wet Fly was also the kind of establishment that would

be open on Thanksgiving night when most people were at home with their families and friends and the small downtown was closed up tight. The bar attracted loners and outliers and people with no place else to go.

Joe TURNED IN to the unpaved parking lot from the highway and parked in front of a hitching post. Neon Coors signs glowed from the windows and onto the hood of his pickup. As usual, there were three other cars out front.

It was a long, low-slung building with a metal roof and faded siding. The front door was metal and painted yellow.

Marybeth hadn't been crazy about the idea of him running into town at night and leaving all of them, but she relented when Deputy Bass began a circuit between Lola's trailer and the river house. Additionally, she was as curious as Joe was to find out if he could learn more. He'd promised to get back as soon as he could.

He swung out of the cab and his boot heels thumped on the frozen ground. He'd deliberately not changed into his uniform shirt and he wore his holiday Cinch shirt untucked to help conceal the Glock clipped to his belt. His old down vest was stained with leather treatment from when he'd wiped down his saddles and tack the month before. He didn't want to look official.

The first thing that struck him when he entered the saloon was the pall of cigarette smoke that hung in the air. He sometimes forgot people still smoked, and he recalled that the Wet Fly was officially located in the county and not the town and that smoking wasn't prohibited. He liked it. It made it seem like a real bar, even though he knew his clothes would stink of tobacco smoke later.

The interior was dark, but not gloomy, with most of the light provided by lamps above the backbar and a bright light that hung from the ceiling over the unique L-shaped pool table in the side room. Both pool players looked up and squinted at him as he entered. It was obvious from the way they leaned against the table for stability that they'd been at it for hours. Empty beer bottles littered the side tables.

"Looking for a challenge?" one of them asked him.

"Not on that," Joe said with a smile. He'd heard that previous owners of the bar had found the L-shaped table somewhere in New Orleans and had driven it back. He'd never seen another one like it and he had no wish to try to play on it.

"Suit yourself, game warden," the man said.

Joe hadn't fooled anyone, including himself. Everyone in the valley knew who he was, whether he was in uniform or not. The game warden's whereabouts was always a hot topic in a hunting and fishing community.

There were three people seated on stools at the bar with their backs to him. An older man with a billy-goat beard and a crumpled slouch hat nursed a draft beer at the far left end, and a portly middle-aged couple sat side by side at the center of the bar, looking up at the late football game on a television set mounted to the wall. Pittsburgh versus Baltimore. It was nearly over.

Joe chose a stool between the billy-goat man and the couple.

The bartender was a woman he recognized, even though he couldn't recall her name. He'd given her a warning citation the previous summer for fishing without a license and being inebriated at the same time out at Saddlestring Reservoir. Her real violation in his mind was that she'd been fishing with a can of worms—but he hadn't told her that.

At the time, she'd been in a white tank top, jeans so short that the pockets stuck out from the hem, and flip-flops. Behind the bar, she was still sleeveless, but dressed in tight Realtree elk-hunting camo tactical pants and top. She had dyed orange-red hair, full-sleeve tattoos, and green eyes nearly blacked out by a raccoon-like application of eyeliner. She greeted him by flinging a cardboard beer coaster toward him on the bar from a column of them on the backbar. It landed directly in front of him and stopped. It was a good trick.

"I'll have a Coors, please."

"Sixteen or twenty ounces?"

"Sixteen."

"I bought a fishing license, if you want to see it."

"That's okay. I'm not working right now."

She fetched the beer and placed it on the coaster. "On the house," she said. Then: "Happy Thanksgiving."

"Same to you."

"Just tap your glass if you want another one."

He nodded. She gave him a long, suspicious glance—*What is he doing here?*—then walked around the bar to gather empties from the pool players.

———

JOE SIPPED HIS BEER and took the place in. Although he'd spent many hours over the years in the Stockman's Bar downtown, he'd not been in the Wet Fly. He hoped it wasn't because he was snobby about it, but he knew part of that was true.

The decorations, as such, were a pastiche of items left over from previous occupants. Golden Thai lions perched from shelving on the side wall, a reminder of when a local Vietnam vet and his Thai bride had tried to make a go of the place as a restaurant before it became an ill-fated barbecue joint. There was the ax-throwing chute on the other side of the pool table, where it appeared that the last contestants had buried their blade in a thick cross section of wood and simply walked away. Dusty trout mounts were festooned everywhere, as were ancient display cases of salmon flies under glass.

The ceiling was littered with dollar bills that had been signed by customers and stuck up there with tacks. And there was that L-shaped pool table.

Joe had learned over the years that often the best way to get information during an investigation was to ask absolutely nothing. Instead, he waited until the subjects came to him. There was something about people feeling the need to fill a vacuum. It was the same impulse he'd seen borne out time and time again when he knocked on the door of a suspect and said, "So, I guess you know why I'm here."

Obviously, Joe was in the Wet Fly on Thanksgiving night for

a reason. He knew it, the bartender knew it, and the customers knew it. So it was only a matter of time before someone broke down and attempted to find out.

Joe didn't put his money on the billy-goat man at the end of the bar. The man was still.

He was on his second beer and the Steelers were driving to seal the win when the woman slid off of her stool next to her partner and sidled over. She was unsteady on her feet, and when she mounted the stool next to Joe, it was not a graceful move.

"I haven't seen you in here before," she said.

He kept his face pleasant and blank. Joe noted that her partner was watching and listening to their exchange closely, while trying not to appear that he was.

She had pale gray eyes and a pug nose and a puffy face. Her hips were wide and they fit over the barstool like a hand gripping a tennis ball. Her husband had a thick head of wavy ginger hair and the darkened nose and mottled cheeks of a serious drinker. He wore a half-smile and appeared to be alert and not unintelligent.

"Can I buy you and your friend a beer?" Joe asked.

"He's my husband," she said. "I'm his long-suffering wife." She laughed a hoarse laugh.

"I'm Joe," he said.

"I know who you are. Your wife is the librarian, right?"

"Correct."

"I'm Connie and that's my husband, John. Sheftic. Connie and John Sheftic."

"Nice to meet you both," he said. He raised his glass to John, and John nodded back a greeting.

"Connie, Joe, and John," John said with a chuckle. "Jeepers. I hope we can keep it straight."

"Do you have a bet on the game?" she asked Joe, probing.

"No."

"We're Steeler fans," she said. "We used to live in Mount Lebanon. That's a suburb of Pittsburgh. Steeler Nation is in our blood."

To demonstrate it, she reached over the bar for a used bar rag and waved it over her head. "Pretend this is a Terrible Towel," she said.

Joe ducked so the rag wouldn't hit the top of his hat. She waved it with such force that she nearly lost her balance and toppled over. Joe quickly reached out and steadied her by grasping her arm and helping her regain her balance on the stool.

"Connie . . ." John cautioned. Then to Joe: "Sorry about that. She gets overexcited when the Steelers are on." He pronounced it *Still-ers.*

"Gotcha."

"Thanks for the beer. Happy Thanksgiving."

"Same to you."

John studied Joe for what seemed like an extended amount of time. Then he gathered up his glass of beer and moved down the bar to sit next to his wife.

"Tell me," John said, "weren't you the guy who discovered Bert Kizer's body yesterday?"

"I was."

"Was it as bad as I've heard?" John asked. "He was tortured with hand tools and burned up?"

Joe hesitated. "I'm afraid so."

"What kind of low-rent bastards would do such a thing?" John asked. Connie made a sour face and Joe realized she was about to cry. Tears formed in the corners of her closed eyes.

"I don't know," Joe said. "It was pretty bad. Did you know him?"

It was the money question.

John indicated that he did. His eyes were moist as well. "Salt of the earth, that was Bert. Just a good, solid guy. Give you the shirt off his back. We was friends with him, but we couldn't afford to book him for a trip. He took us out a couple of times, though. We brought the beer and he rowed. I must have lost twenty flies in the bushes, but he kept giving more from his tackle box. Tied them himself. That's the kind of guy he was."

Connie raised her hands and covered her face. Behind her fingers, she squeaked and wept. Joe reached out and touched her shoulder and said he was sorry for what had happened to her friend.

"He never did nothing to deserve what happened to him," she said through sobs. "When you walked through that door tonight all alone, for a second I thought it was Bert. He always came alone."

Joe didn't respond for a moment.

"It's not like it looks," Connie said, suddenly defensive. "We don't spend every Thanksgiving at the bar. We're not here twenty-four/seven. But we like to sit here and unwind and watch the Steelers. I just didn't feel like cooking for myself today, so . . . we ate down at the Catholic church. Then we came for a beer and ended up staying the whole damned night.

"I'm a *good* cook," she said emphatically.

Joe looked at John. Behind her, John shook his head, indicating she wasn't.

"How well did you know Bert Kizer?" Joe asked. "Did you know him pretty well?"

Connie swiveled on her stool to John and they both arched their eyebrows in unison, as if agreeing among themselves that it was okay to talk.

John said, "I guess we knew him as well as anyone. He kept to himself, but you tend to have all kinds of conversations when you're sitting side by side with a guy drinking beer for hours. Some of them you even remember later." He laughed. "We solved a lot of the world's problems, Bert and me. Too bad no one listens to us."

"To me, Bert wasn't a big talker," Connie said. "I think he was divorced and he might even have had a kid somewhere, but he never talked about them. But ask him a question about fishing or hunting . . . *Christ*. He'd go on and on."

"What about that guy at the end of the bar?" Joe asked sotto voce. He glanced at the billy-goat man surreptitiously over his shoulder. The man was either listening intensely or lost in his own thoughts. "Did Bert talk to that guy?"

Both Connie and John shook their heads emphatically, as if to say, "No one talks to *him*."

"Okay," Joe said, nodding. "What I'm trying to figure out is who could have done this to him and why. Did he ever talk about having enemies?"

Connie and John looked at each other again. John said, "Not really. He was pretty pissed at a couple of out-of-state clients who stiffed him last summer, but I never got the impression they were enemies of any kind. He didn't like politicians and he wasn't shy about insulting them, but I can't think of anyone else who might not have liked him. At least enough to do this."

"What kind of situation was he in financially?" Joe asked. "Any idea?"

"Bert couldn't rub two nickels together the whole time I knew him," John said, shaking his head.

"Not that he wasn't generous when he was flush," Connie interceded. "When he got a big cash tip, he was in here buying for the rest of the night until it was gone."

"So it's likely he wasn't saving any of it?" Joe said. "That was some speculation I heard: that maybe he was hoarding cash and somebody wanted it. Or that they *thought* he was hoarding cash."

John shook his head again. "Anybody who knew Bert or saw his place would know he was dead broke. Money just burned a hole in his pocket."

Joe sipped the rest of the beer and tapped his glass for another. He indicated to the bartender to serve another round to the Sheftics as well. They gladly accepted.

"Since you two seem to have known him about as well as anyone, did the sheriff talk to you about Bert?" Joe asked.

They said no. He wasn't surprised.

Joe said, "If he did, is there anything you would tell him about Bert? For example, did he indicate to you that he was expecting company?"

"No, nothing," John said. "Believe me, we'd try to help out. Whoever did this to Bert needs to go down. Connie and I have been talking about it all day. For the life of us, we can't figure out why anybody would want to hurt him. We wish we could help."

Joe believed them.

"I think it was strangers," Connie said. "Itinerants. I think it was random."

Joe looked at her.

She said, "Since the pandemic, there have been a lot of strange homeless people out there." She indicated "out there" with a wave of her hand in the general direction of the mountains. "People left cities and now they're just drifting around. We seen 'em in campgrounds last summer and they're still out there. I think some homeless people found Bert's place and hurt him for no good reason."

"It's a theory," Joe said to be conciliatory.

"Connie has lots of theories," John said with an eye roll.

The billy-goat man at the end of the bar suddenly cleared his throat with a wet, hacking sound that made Connie and Joe cringe.

"Tell him about the treasure," the man croaked. He'd obviously been eavesdropping the entire conversation.

"The treasure?" Joe repeated.

Connie and John again exchanged glances.

Connie said, "That's what Bert called it, anyway. He told us about it once when he was really, really hammered. Bert said he had a treasure that belonged to his old man and he was trying to figure out how much it was worth."

Joe tried to keep his face still. But inside, he felt a mild electric jolt.

"Did he say what the treasure was?"

John opened his mouth to answer, but Connie cut him off. "He found out John here used to be a gold coin and collectibles dealer back in Pennsylvania. That got Bert really excited that night and he asked John if there was a market in World War Two memorabilia. He said his dad brought home some stuff from the war."

"Like what?" Joe asked.

John waved his thick hand in the air dismissively. "Most people think that crap is worth a lot. You know, medals, helmets, that kind of crap. But that stuff is a dime a dozen. Our boys brought back mountains of it and it isn't exactly rare at all. I showed Bert where a German steel helmet was for sale on the internet for two hundred bucks, is all. Medals and that kind of memorabilia goes for even less. Hell, you might make more melting that stuff down than trying to sell it as is."

Joe let him go on.

John said, "What I told him didn't even faze Bert. He said what he had was special and worth a ton of money. He was convinced of it. He said he'd prove it to me. I told him there were swap meets and conventions where all that stuff gets exchanged, and that it was all low-rent even all these years later.

People who collect Nazi memorabilia are a strange bunch, I'd say.

"So the next time we were in here drinking a lot, he pulls out a sheet of paper," John said. "He'd been carrying it around with him for a while. I think he printed it off the internet. It was a news article saying that Hitler's phone had sold at auction for a quarter-million dollars or something like that. I looked at the picture and said, 'Bert, it has his *name* on it. Otherwise, it's just an old phone.' It was the *name* that was valuable, not the phone. I thought that would put Bert off, but it got him even more excited. He said that his 'treasure' had a name on it like that, but he wouldn't tell me what it was."

Joe knew what it was.

"Bert might have tried to contact some of those World War Two memorabilia places," Connie said. "I think I heard him talk about it once. Like he was shopping this treasure around, maybe. But I never heard that it came to anything."

"He sure never got rich," John said. "He's been adding to his tab the whole month."

"Interesting," Joe said, thinking about the implications of what he'd just heard. If Bert Kizer was contacting collectors, collectors might start reaching out to potential customers. And if the right customers had wanted the album desperately, perhaps they'd bypassed the dealer and come straight to the source.

He couldn't wait to tell Marybeth.

"I thank you for your time," Joe said to Connie and John. "But I better get going home."

"Thank you for the beers," Connie said. She reached out and

caressed his shoulder. "Don't be a stranger around here. I heard you were some kind of by-the-book Goody Two-Shoes, but you're all right."

"*Connie . . .*" John said, embarrassed.

"Thank you, I think," Joe said. "Maybe I do need to get out more often."

He handed them one of his cards. "If you think of anything else, please give me a call. My cell phone number is written on the back. I'll pass any information you give me along to the sheriff for his investigation."

"I don't think that sheriff could find his ass with both hands," John said.

Joe didn't comment.

As he passed by the billy-goat man, Joe patted him on the shoulder. "Thanks."

The man swiveled on his stool and leaned into Joe. He said, "If this is about that Nazi photo album Dick Kizer brought back, I seen it."

"*What?*"

"I seen it."

Joe froze. The man spoke in a low tone so that the Sheftics couldn't overhear. As Joe leaned in, the stench of alcohol and fetid breath was almost overwhelming.

"I ain't talking in here where certain people can hear me. Go outside and I'll follow you."

Joe agreed and went out the door. He lingered on the wooden sidewalk porch and leaned a hip into the hitching post rail. It was cold and he crossed his arms for warmth.

A moment later, the billy-goat man came out. He didn't wear a coat and he swayed from side to side as he spoke.

"I knew Vern Dunnegan, too," the man said. He was referring to the game warden who had preceded Joe in the district years before. "Vern used to look at things a different way than you. He was a good guy. You ran him off."

"Actually, I didn't," Joe said. "He resigned on his own. But what is it you wanted to tell me? Who are you?"

"Quinton Thirster. I've been around here a long time."

Joe had heard of him. He'd been a notorious deer and elk poacher who had spent time in prison. Thirster was infamous in the valley for cutting a Jeep in half with a chainsaw after a divorce settlement with his ex-wife.

"Dick invited me out there once and we ate scrambled eggs and calves' brains on Nazi plates," Thirster said. He wriggled his fingers around in the air as if tracing an oval.

"Little swastikas all around the rim of the plate. It was crazier than hell."

"You're not kidding, are you?" Joe said.

"I even looked through the album," Thirster said. "I don't remember much about it, except there was some photos of old Hitler himself. I can't remember the name of the guy who owned it. Some Nazi big shot."

"Julius Streicher?" Joe asked.

The man nodded. "Might have been it. Like I say, I can't remember for sure. It was fifty years ago. Dick and me got into an argument over a cow and we never spoke again. Bert wouldn't talk to me, either. But I saw what I saw."

Joe thanked the man and gave him a card.

Thirster turned and pointed at the red metal door. He said, "Those two, they're not all innocent. They wanted to take advantage of Bert. I could see it. When Bert told them about his treasure, suddenly John was his best friend on earth. Once a dealer, always a dealer, is what I say. I wouldn't be surprised if it was them who called the collectors. Those two might have blabbed what Bert had and caused this whole thing to happen. No, they ain't all innocent and good, if you ask me."

He said it in a conspiratorial way, as if unspooling a great revelation. The man reached out and grasped Joe's arm.

"Things aren't always what they seem," he said, his eyes sparkling. "Just like those Nazis. Just like Hitler. They weren't all bad, you know."

"Gotta go," Joe said, jerking his arm loose.

CHAPTER TWENTY

Voilà!

Two hours before, when he returned from the Wet Fly Bar, Joe found Marybeth awake and seated at the kitchen table with the photo album open in front of her. He wasn't surprised to see her still up. It was nearly midnight.

"The girls went to bed, but I can hear them talking," she said. "The four of them are sleeping together in the first bedroom. I gave Liv and Kestrel the spare room for the night. I wanted to keep everyone here in one place. Liv agreed with that when I told her what was going on."

"What are you up to?" he asked.

She gestured to the album. "I'm trying to figure out what it is in this book that these people want. Or why they want it. I can't believe it's the album itself. It can't be that valuable except maybe to historians of the war. There *has* to be something specific in these photos—or somebody—the bad guys don't want anyone to know about. Something personal."

Joe sat next to her and told her what he'd learned over the past two hours. He ended it with "So you were right. The album belonged to Bert Kizer. Somehow, he found out people were coming here for it and he ditched it at your library."

"But why, we'll maybe never know," Marybeth said. "I just can't help but wonder what it is in this album that would make somebody do what they did. Do you think it's a couple of crazy Nazi war memorabilia collectors?"

Joe shook his head. "Not according to the Sheftics. They say there's a real market for this kind of stuff, but that it's limited. I have to say I believe them. I just can't see how it would be worth killing over."

He told her about the swastika plates that Thirster claimed he had used at the Kizer residence.

Marybeth took it all in.

She said, "This is pure speculation, but I want to try to tie together what we know so far."

"Go."

"Bert's father, Dick Kizer, along with Alton More from Casper, were two of the first American GIs to enter Hitler's Eagle's Nest. Along with the rest of the Band of Brothers, they looted the place and brought back what they could get away with. Alton More hit the motherlode: Hitler's personal photo albums. Dick got honorable mention with this Julius Streicher album, but it was still something he was very proud of. And he brought it back. Maybe some Nazi dishware as well."

"That he must have gotten rid of at some point," Joe said. "I would have seen it at Bert's place. Or Norwood would have said something when he searched it."

She said, "Bert worshipped his father, or at least he had a lot of respect for his service, so he kept Dick's wartime souvenirs in that footlocker under his bed for decades. He could have donated all that to the local museum or to an archive, but he kept it all close."

Joe nodded for her to continue. Thus far, it all fit.

"For whatever reason, Bert decides after all this time that he wants to find out what the album itself might be worth to someone. Maybe he was on hard times or he just realized he was getting older and he wanted to see if he could get a reward for it. I don't blame him. Or it could be that Bert wanted to find out the value of the album so he could borrow against it."

Joe liked that. He said, "Maybe Bert wanted to use the loan to buy a new drift boat. The one at his house looked pretty beaten up."

"Maybe," she said before plunging on. "Bert knows next to nothing how to go about either trying to sell it or find out its value. Who would? But then he meets John and Connie Sheftic, who have a background in collectibles. The Sheftics, unlike Bert, know what channels to use and who out there might be interested in the album—and what they might pay for it. Maybe the Sheftics post to World War Two sites, or military forums. Or creepy neo-Nazi sites. Who knows?"

Joe said, "They didn't get into the details at the bar, but they did something like that."

Marybeth said, "Artifacts like this album are worth whatever someone is willing to pay for them, I do know that from the library world. That's how rare books get exchanged. So by the Sheftics getting the word out on this thing, it was kind of gambling. They had no idea what they were getting into, and neither did Bert for that matter."

Joe said, "I need to ask them more questions, like did anyone express interest? Did anyone out there offer a price? I should have asked."

"Don't beat yourself up," Marybeth said. "We can fill that in later. But for the sake of my theory, let's say that the existence of the album reaches the right—or wrong—people. They contact the Sheftics or more likely Bert himself. After all, I was able to connect Bert's dad to the album using public information from the internet about the Band of Brothers. Anyone in the world could do the same thing. My guess is that they contacted Bert directly and bypassed the Sheftics."

"That sounds right," Joe said.

"For whatever reason, Bert got cold feet after being contacted by the potential buyers. Maybe they didn't offer enough, or Bert didn't trust them. He would have felt a lot of pressure if the reason he went public in the first place was to ascertain the value of the album, not to sell it outright. So he didn't go through with the transaction."

"But they still wanted it," Joe said.

"They did. Maybe they were *very* aggressive. And Bert got the feeling that they'd come and get it no matter what. After all, they knew his name and address. So to get it off his plate he drops it off at the library and makes it my problem."

Joe winced at the implications of that.

"Why he didn't just sell it to them or even give it to them to spare his life, we'll never know," she said. "Maybe in the end he thought it would dishonor his father's memory. That kind of fits."

"It does," Joe agreed.

She closed the circle. "They want this album so badly that they murdered poor Lola for it. That will always hang over my head. But now," she said, patting the red leather cover of the album, "they know we have it. The gargoyle saw me with it this morning."

Joe said, "What we know is that they'll do just about anything to get it."

"Correct."

"I think it's time to bring the sheriff in," he said. "This will make his head explode."

"I wish Nate was here right now," Marybeth said. His wife would always prefer to have Nate around than any kind of law enforcement personnel. Joe couldn't disagree.

"So it's up to us," he said.

"I'll make coffee."

"WE HAVE TO lure them in and trap them," Marybeth said as she returned to the table with two mugs. "They're in the area. We know that. If we want to get them we've got to set them up."

Joe looked at her a long time. "How?"

"Think about it," she said, again tapping the album. "This is kind of a sensational story. Imagine the hook: 'Nazi Photo Album Appears at Small Wyoming Library.' The background of Julius Streicher is as salacious as it can get and right now *Der Stürmer* is kind of a thing again with the extremists in our own country. Plus you've got the Band of Brothers angle. Thanksgiving is always a slow news weekend. If we spun it right, the story could go viral in a hurry."

"How could we do that?" he asked.

She said, "We announce a press conference tomorrow at the library to reveal the contents of the photo album to the world."

"Who will show up?" Joe asked, puzzled. Saddlestring was a long way from major media centers.

"Everyone, if we do it online," Marybeth said. "We have all the technology we need at the library from the pandemic."

"How do we get the word out?"

"I'm doing it now. And when the girls wake up, we're going to enlist them to do something they won't believe. We'll ask them to bring their phones down to the table. We can have them take photos of the album and some of the photos inside. Between the four of them, they're connected to every social network out there. Especially Lucy. Fong can post it on Asian networks, I'd guess. This story, if we package it right, could go around the world in no time."

Joe took a deep breath. He knew she was on to something.

"And we've got a secret weapon," Marybeth said. "Your new best pal: Steve-2 Price. I bet if you asked him he could make it trend on ConFab and get it out to millions of his followers. One way or another, our bad guys will hear about it and be forced to act. That's when we nail them."

Price's contact information was in Joe's phone. He just hadn't used it.

"*Then* I'll call the sheriff," Joe said.

"That sounds like a plan," she said, grinning. Then: "Joe, why are you looking at me like that?"

He reached out and grasped her hand, then stood up to lead her to their bedroom.

"*Now?*" she asked. "With all of our girls in the house?"

But she squeezed back and followed.

"I'll try not to shout," he said.

CHAPTER TWENTY-ONE

The Brothers

László and Viktór exchanged looks inside the motel room when they heard a car pull up directly outside their door. Headlights bathed the outside of the window blinds and leaked through. When they heard a car door slam shut, Viktór launched himself off his bed and approached the window in stocking feet. Behind him, László grabbed the shotgun and checked the loads.

The football game was long over and local news flickered on the television screen in the dark room. A pizza box on the table yawned open, revealing two remaining slices. Empty beer cans from a twelve-pack of Miller Lite stood like chess pieces on the chest of drawers against the wall.

There was a half-inch opening on the right side of the closed blind and Viktór pressed his eye to it. When he saw who was out there, he moaned softly.

"Who is it? Is it that housekeeping guy again?" László whispered.

"No. It's a cop. He's walking around our car."

"*Szar!*" "Shit" in Hungarian.

Viktór moved slightly to the side so he could keep his eye on the patrolman. The man wore a bulky open jacket over a brown uniform shirt and khaki trousers with a dark stripe down the legs. He had a flat-brimmed dark hat with a silver star-shaped badge on it.

The cop circled their rental Nissan, holding a long black flashlight to see inside.

Once again, Viktór regretted that they had picked this motel. The rooms had only one door and that was to the parking lot. There was no inside door to a hallway. If they needed to escape, they would have to run past the cop outside.

"What's he doing?" László asked.

"Looking inside our car. Did you leave anything incriminating on the seat?"

"No."

"Now he's looking our way."

"Is he on his radio?"

"Not that I can see."

"I'm glad I changed the plates on it."

Viktór let out a breath of relief. He'd forgotten László had done that. So what did the cop want? It was rude that he hadn't turned off his headlights.

"I'm going to find out," Viktór said.

"Maybe that's not a good idea," László said, standing so close to him with the shotgun that Viktór could feel his brother's body heat.

"It's a normal reaction, I think. It's more suspicious to not open the door when he's right outside."

László grunted an agreement. Then: "Don't invite him in."

"Of course not."

"Speak English."

"Of course," Viktór said defensively.

"I'll be ready," László said.

"We don't kill cops."

"Then don't invite him inside. And remember the cover story."

Viktór nodded and shot the bolt back on the lock. He cracked the door about a foot and looked out. He shaded his eyes against the headlights with his outstretched hand and tried to appear like he'd just awoken.

"What's going on, Officer?" he asked. "Those lights . . ."

"Oh, sorry," the cop said. "Just a second."

The cop reached into his vehicle through the open driver's-side window and the lights doused, leaving two pulsating orbs in Viktór's eyes.

"Sorry about that," the cop said. "I didn't mean to wake you up."

"Is there something wrong?"

The cop hesitated. As the orbs dissipated, Viktór could see him better from the ambient lighting from under the eave of the motel. The cop was young and fresh-faced with blue eyes and a wash of acne along his jawline. Despite the dark uniform and semiautomatic weapon on his belt, he looked like a teenager.

"Deputy Tucker Schuster, Campbell County Sheriff's Department."

"Bob Hardy. That's my car."

"Nice to meet you, Mr. Hardy," the cop said. "Where are you from?"

"Syracuse," Viktór said. He was glad he remembered the city.

"New York?"

"Yes."

"With Illinois plates?"

Viktór felt his chest tighten. Why couldn't László have stolen New York plates?

Next to him, he heard his brother whisper to him.

"It's a rental," Viktór repeated. Then: "Is there some reason why you're looking it over and waking me up?"

"Sorry to disturb you. I really am. We got a call from the next county to look out for a green Nissan Pathfinder in the area. When I saw this one, I pulled in here to check it out. But we're looking for a car with Colorado plates. In the light from the motel, I thought the plates were green like Colorado, but I see now this one is kind of a shade of blue. And it's the wrong state, so I apologize again for disturbing you on a holiday."

"It's okay," Viktór said. "Good night, Officer."

Then Deputy Schuster did something Viktór didn't anticipate. Instead of climbing back into his cruiser, he stepped from the dirt parking lot onto the sidewalk of the motel directly in front of the open door. "What brings you all the way out here to Gillette, Wyoming, Mr. Hardy?"

"I'm looking for property out west," Viktór said. "You've

heard what it's like back there. No jobs, no future. I need to get away. I like wide-open spaces."

Deputy Schuster said, "You know, I understand. I watch the news. People on top of each other, lots of crime. I can't say that sounds like much fun."

"It isn't. Now, if you don't mind . . ."

"I've never been east of Nebraska myself," Schuster said. "I've never felt the need. Can I offer you a piece of advice?"

Viktór didn't want to close the door in the man's face, but the back-and-forth was taking a direction he didn't like. And the cop took another step closer until he was standing in the threshold of the door. If Viktór closed the door, he would literally hit the man. It could be construed as an assault.

In his peripheral vision, Viktór saw László raise the shotgun on the other side of the open door. There was an inch and a half of cheap compound board between the double-barreled muzzle of the weapon and the ear of the deputy.

"What's your advice?" Viktór asked, not really wanting to hear any.

"Gillette is a real nice town, don't get me wrong," Schuster said. "I grew up here so I know. It's got the nicest people in the world. Real friendly folks. But it's an energy town. Coal, and coal's dying. There are probably other towns in Wyoming you'd like better to settle down in. Have you been to Sheridan?"

"No," Viktór said morosely.

"Buffalo? Cody?"

"No, no."

"I wouldn't recommend Jackson Hole unless you can afford

it. Judging by your choice of accommodations, I'd say that's a long shot."

"Okay."

"You might want to try those places out, is what I'm saying."

Viktór felt his face flush with anger. He was grateful the cop wasn't shining the flashlight at him to see it. "Thank you, Officer. Now I'm really tired and I want to get an early start tomorrow."

"Is there just one of you in there?" Deputy Schuster said.

Viktór felt his scalp twitch. "Why?"

"Well, this SUV we're looking for had two men in it. So I was just wondering if you were alone."

"I'm here with my brother, Greg," Viktór said. "He's sleeping and I don't want to wake him up."

"Yeah, I can see through the door that you two did a number on a pizza and drank plenty of beer tonight. Kind of a sorry-ass Thanksgiving. Is your brother looking to move out here, too?"

Viktór heard a muffled *snick* from his right as László thumbed the safety of the shotgun off.

"Do you want me to apologize to your brother as well?" Deputy Schuster asked, leaning in to peer over Viktór's shoulder. Viktór was astonished. Was this cop going to force his way in? Or get his head blown off trying?

"Please, I need to go," Viktór said.

The cop grinned and cocked his head. "Your accent—I can't place it. You say you're from New York, but I'm getting like an Eastern European vibe. I had a teacher once from Hungary and he talked kind of like you. Weird, huh?"

Suddenly the door was wrenched open, causing Viktór to backpedal across the room. It was László, and László was enraged.

He grabbed the deputy by his collar and pulled him into the room. The deputy went down hard on the floor and László was on top of him. László clubbed the man's head with the butt of his shotgun, then he plucked the officer's weapon out of its holster and tossed it on the bed. In the same movement, László kicked the door shut. He flipped the deputy over and jammed the muzzle of the shotgun into the flesh beneath his nose.

Viktór was reminded there was nothing like his brother when it came to displays of sudden violence. It was one of the reasons he'd been such a good wrestler. László *liked* hurting people.

"*What is wrong with you?*" László bellowed at the cop.

Deputy Schuster looked up at László. He was terrified. His eyes shifted over to Viktór, as if pleading his case.

Viktór placed his hands on top of his head and paced the room. "What have you done?" he asked out loud. "What have we done?"

"I've got his keys," László said. "I'm going to go move his car."

"*He's a cop*," Viktór said.

"He's a stupid cop."

Viktór couldn't argue with that. He watched as László removed handcuffs from the deputy's belt and had the cop sit up. His brother ratcheted the cuffs tight on the man's wrists behind his back. László also removed a canister of pepper spray and a handheld radio from his belt and tossed them on the bed out of reach.

"Here," László said, handing the shotgun to Viktór. "Hold this on him and don't let him move or talk."

"Where are you going to hide his car so that no one can find it?" Viktór asked.

"There's a ditch behind the motel. I'll get it out of sight for now."

"What are we going to do with him?"

László shrugged. Before he left the room with the keys, he gave Deputy Schuster a hard kick in his ribs. The officer moaned and tipped over to his side, writhing on the floor. Viktór kept the shotgun on him.

"What *is* wrong with you?" Viktór asked.

AFTER DEPUTY SCHUSTER got his breath back, he answered the question. "I was just trying to be friendly."

"Look where it got you," Viktór said.

"Yeah. My mom always tells me I need to work on my inter-personal communication skills."

Viktór had no response to that. The cop's hat had been knocked off his head in the scuffle and it sat upside down next to the foot of the bed. With his hat off, he looked even younger than Viktór had originally thought.

"Is he really your brother?" Schuster asked.

"Yes."

Schuster nodded. Then: "Are you the two we're supposed to be looking for?"

"No." It was an easy lie.

"I'll tell you what," Schuster said. "How about you let me go before your brother gets back? I'll pretend this never happened and you two can go on your way. It's a big deal for a cop to get jumped and have his weapons taken away from him. You'll be in big, big trouble for assaulting a police officer."

Schuster didn't want to add that he was a rookie and he'd never live it down. He needed the job after being laid off at the coal mines the year before.

Viktór didn't encourage him to go on.

"Look," the deputy said, "my shift ends at six. Here's what we can do. I'll get my car back and I'll drive to the department like normal at the end of my shift. I'll pull in to the department, clock out, go home, and no one will be the wiser. But if you detain me here, they'll know something is wrong. They'll come looking for me. And they'll find you."

Viktór didn't know how much of that to believe. He said, "You were giving me advice. Now I want to give you some advice. Stop talking. I can't control László when he gets angry."

"László?" the cop said. "I thought you said his name was Greg."

"Shut up."

Schuster shifted himself on the floor so that his back was against the footboard of the bed. As he did so, he winced. It obviously hurt him to move.

"What are you two wanted for, anyway?" he asked. "What are you running from?"

"You should listen to your mother," Viktór said.

"I'm guessing you're the two they're looking for over in Twelve Sleep County. Am I right? You did something over there and they're after you. I heard some back-and-forth on the radio about the homicide of an old man and the possible homicide of an old woman. Please tell me you weren't involved in that."

"Of course not. Shut up."

"And maybe they got the plate wrong on your car. Or you switched plates?"

"No one is after us," Viktór said. "We're here for a different reason."

Viktór thought: Deputy Schuster was a dead man. Viktór knew it. The cop probably knew it, too. The only question was how and where it would happen.

"So what's the reason?" the cop asked.

Viktór said, "It's a different reason. Now shut up."

As he said it, Viktór heard his brother swipe the keycard in the outside lock.

"What are you two talking about?" he asked suspiciously as he entered the room.

VIKTÓR DIDN'T FILL HIM IN. The cop wisely didn't, either.

László's phone trilled and he drew it out of his coat pocket and looked at the screen. Before punching it up, he said, "It's Hanna."

Their older sister. Viktór felt dread. Hanna scared him even more than László.

In the quiet room, he could hear the high-pitched tone of her shrill, rapid-fire voice without getting all the words. She was obviously very angry about something.

László responded in Hungarian: "Hanna, we've located it, but we don't have it in our possession. We've had some difficulties we didn't expect. No one could have expected them. But we think we'll have it tomorrow and we can come home . . ."

Then László froze at something Hanna told him. His eyes bulged and his face flushed red.

"*What?*" he shouted. "*When? How is that possible?*"

Hanna went on for another minute and then terminated the call. László stood there, locked in place. Something was terribly wrong.

László missed his pocket when he tried to put the phone back. It bounced off the floor near his feet.

He slowly looked up at Viktór and said, "Pack up. We've got to move out of here now."

"Why?"

"I'll explain in the car."

"What do we do with him?" Viktór asked, gesturing to the cop with the muzzle of the shotgun.

Viktór could see László's mind work and he was horrified by what would likely happen next. But László said, "Bring him with us."

Then, in Hungarian so the cop couldn't understand, he said, "I have an idea how we can use him."

"Okay, we use him," Viktór replied. "But we don't kill him. We can't kill a cop. If we do that, everyone will be looking for us. Everyone. We'll never get home."

Viktór could tell that László thought otherwise. But maybe, for once, he was listening.

Deputy Schuster looked back and forth between the two brothers as they spoke. "Where are we going, fellas? Or are you going to let me go?" he asked.

"Shut up," Viktór explained.

CHAPTER TWENTY-TWO

Seattle

EVEN THROUGH A TORRENTIAL DOWNPOUR THAT LASHED THE black walls of trees in waves bordering the highway and sluiced down the borrow ditches with the look and force of miniature whitewater rivers, Nate and Geronimo could see the emerging nighttime glow of Seattle ahead to the west. It was an hour away from midnight.

Nate was still behind the wheel. Geronimo was working through Tristan's phone, finding items that caused him to hum and moan and exclaim, "*Holy shit.*" His face was illuminated by the screen of the phone in the dark.

"What?" Nate asked.

"I'm using Signal with Tristan's log-in," Geronimo said. "Our pal Axel is still ahead of us and he's announced his arrival to the antifa assholes and BLM folks in Seattle."

"How far ahead?"

"His last post was nineteen minutes ago. He's leaving another cache for them and he's posted the coordinates of it. Have you ever heard of the Gum Wall?"

Nate shook his head.

"It's in an alleyway real close to the public market center downtown. Just like Denver—he chose a place to stash weapons within easy reach of where the street action is planned, but out of view of the cops. *If* there are cops, anyway."

"Why wouldn't there be?" Nate asked.

Geronimo shrugged. "Sometimes the mayors of these cities are spooked, so they tell the cops to stand down. Sometimes they send them in only when it's too late. You never know."

"How far away from the Gum Wall are we?"

Geronimo swept away the Signal screen and pulled up the mapping application.

"Twenty-five minutes if we push it," he said.

"He should still be there," Nate said, feeling a surge of anticipation course through his limbs.

Twenty-five minutes.

Although he risked hydroplaning over the standing water on the highway, Nate goosed the accelerator and grasped the wheel tight.

THEY'D DRIVEN FROM Pendleton to Seattle via I-84 to I-82, and they'd soon merge onto I-90 to enter the city from the east. Their only stops had been to buy gasoline, fast food, and a charger so Tristan's phone wouldn't go dead en route.

They'd crossed the Columbia River hours before, and as they neared Seattle, the pine trees got thicker and closed in on them, and the interstate seemed more like a tunnel than a highway. Traffic was sparse that time of night.

The rain was mist at first and it obscured the mountains, but it picked up in volume and intensity as they drove. Nate was astonished by the amount of water falling from the sky and he guessed it was comparable to a summer's worth in Wyoming. The wipers could barely keep up, and the thrumming sound of rainwater produced by the tires on the van created a kind of white noise that forced them to shout inside.

"Who called for the street action tonight?" Nate asked.

"I don't know, but Axel is obviously aware of it."

"What will this rain do to the protest?" Nate asked.

"Who knows?" Geronimo said. "If it was Denver, everyone would stay inside. *I'd* stay inside. But this is Seattle, so maybe they're used to it."

THEY MERGED ONTO I-90 and the traffic increased. Plumes of rainwater shot out from beneath the tires of oncoming cars in the eastbound lane.

Despite the downpour, Nate thought Seattle was stunning and beautiful. The lights looked like diamonds flung across undulating black felt. The glistening city stopped abruptly at the dark bay itself. City lights reflected double and triple from the wet streets in a maelstrom of technicolor electricity. Out in the dark harbor, oceangoing vessels with blinking red lights punctuated the blackness. And the Space Needle knifed its way straight upward into the low-hanging clouds.

"Why do they want to tear down a city like this?" Nate asked.

"This is what they do," Geronimo replied.

"Axel deliberately went to Wingville to gather up a bunch of firearms," Nate said. "Maybe he'll pass them around tonight."

Geronimo whistled at the implications of that. Then he dug his triple-barrel shotgun out from beneath his seat and once again checked the loads. As he filled his parka pockets with stubby twelve-gauge shells from an ammunition box he'd brought along, he said, "Stay on I-5 North up here. It'll take us where we want to go."

NATE NOTED wet highway signs for the Central Business District, First Hill, and Pike Place Market. Geronimo kept him on track: "Take Madison Street/Convention Place," he said. "Merge onto Seventh Ave. Left on Madison Street. Right on Western Ave."

The Central Business District was dark and not well lit. Thus far, there were no people on the streets.

They passed by an abandoned brick building that looked like an old warehouse. All of the windows on the ground floor had been smashed out. Spray-painted graffiti covered the exterior.

Geronimo seemed nervous and kept up a running commentary while pointing out and interpreting crude graphics he saw.

"FTP means 'Fuck the Police,'" he said. "ACAB is 'All Cops Are Bastards.' Did you see those numbers back there, '1312'? That's numeric code for 'ACAB.'"

Scrawled in block letters on the pavement of the street they were on was NO BORDERS, NO WALLS, NO USA AT ALL. Then: WE DON'T WANT BIDEN—WE WANT REVENGE!

"I think I got all that," Nate said before Geronimo felt the need to read it out loud. "Are you ready to get my birds back?"

Geronimo Jones grinned and Nate could see his teeth.

"I'm ready," he said.

CHAPTER TWENTY-THREE

The Gum Wall

TWENTY MINUTES EARLIER, AFTER HALF OF THE LOADED FIRE-arms had been laid in the alleyway and covered by a canvas tarp, Axel said to Randy Daniels, "Go out to the street and take a position where you can get a visual on everything that's going on. Keep me informed of what you see."

Randy nodded and grunted. He was in a foul mood and didn't want to talk.

"Give me your phone," Axel said.

"What?"

Axel held out his open hand.

"How do I call you if I see something?" Randy asked.

Axel gave Randy a handheld radio. Reluctantly, Randy took it and gave Axel his phone.

"Leave it on channel twenty-two and keep the volume low," Axel said. "Don't talk on it unless you have something to say."

"It's raining out there," Randy said.

Axel leaned into Randy so his mouth was inches from his ear. Randy could feel the full force of Axel's menace in a way he hadn't felt before.

Through gritted teeth, Axel said, "Go."

Randy went.

RANDY WAS IN a foul mood because this wasn't what he'd signed up for. He'd accompanied the Shaman to be his colleague, to learn from him. Maybe to bask in the glow of his dark celebrity.

Not to sit on the floor of a van breathing in hawk shit and stray feathers for hundreds of highway miles. Not to do all the physical work of loading heavy firearms into the van and stacking half of them in an alleyway just a few hours later. Not to be wet and freezing most of the day. Not to be talked down to and mocked by Axel and the Blade.

And now he was being sent to stand out on the street in the open during an epic rainstorm the likes of which he'd rarely experienced growing up in Denver.

He could hear Axel and the Blade talking behind him in the alley. No doubt, they were making fun of him again. They stayed back there, Randy guessed, because that's where the cache of guns was located and because it was dry. The alleyway was covered on top back there.

Randy wished he had his phone so he could use the flashlight on it. There was something very weird about the alleyway they were in. The walls seemed to undulate with misshapen, multi-colored globules. Like fungus growing—or acne on bad skin.

It wasn't until he emerged from beneath the covered part of the alley into the open rain near the street that he got it: the brick walls of the passage were covered by hundreds of thousands of wads of used chewing gum. It repulsed him and he made sure he stayed in the middle of the alley away from either side, which were no doubt teeming with bacteria from the mouths of unclean strangers.

Disgusting.

So *that's* why they called it the Gum Wall.

RANDY DISOBEYED AXEL the minute he emerged onto the empty street. Instead of standing there like a dutiful soldier getting soaked to the bone by the rain, he ducked into a dimly lit bodega whose windows and glass door were covered with iron bars. Printed in block letters on a piece of cardboard was:

NO PUBLIC TOILETS. DON'T EVEN ASK!!!!!

He pocketed the handheld and pushed his way inside. An electric buzzer signaled his entrance. It was hot and close inside and the aisles were so narrow he had to turn sidewise to get to the counter.

The cashier was an Asian man whose features were distorted

by the thick plexiglass that separated him from his customers. Business was done through a small open slot cut from the bottom of the barrier.

"What you want?" the man asked. He sounded hostile, Randy thought.

"I was hoping I could buy a raincoat."

"No raincoat! You antifa?"

"I'm just a brother trying to stay dry," Randy said.

"Get out! No raincoat here. Soda, cigarettes, beer."

Randy looked around. The shelves were packed with items on both sides. He smiled when he saw a box of thirty-five-gallon plastic garbage bags.

"I'll take one of these," Randy said. "I don't need the whole box."

"Whole box or nothing."

"That's robbery."

"What? Get out if you don't want to pay."

Randy looked around for an alternative choice but couldn't find one. He cursed and approached the counter.

"Twenty dollars," the cashier said.

"Twenty dollars? For ten garbage bags? That's ridiculous."

"Twenty dollars or get out."

He thought for a second about putting the box under his arm and exiting the store without paying. Better that than agreeing to be robbed by this man.

"Twenty dollars or put it back," the man said. "Then get out, *antifa*."

Randy tried to stare down the clerk, but he couldn't see his eyes well enough through the thick plastic. What he *could* see was that the little man seemed very agitated.

He considered his options. If he left the plastic bags, he'd be forced to stand in the street and get soaked. If he walked out with them, the store owner might either pull a gun and shoot him in the back or call the police. If the Asian store owner called the cops, he'd be easy to find since he'd be standing at the mouth of the alley a block away.

Or he could pay the ransom.

Randy slid a twenty through the slot and exclaimed loudly that it was *fucking highway robbery.*

Before he pushed open the door, Randy paused and looked over his shoulder at the man. He was still there, wavering behind the uneven plastic like an apparition.

"You'll get yours, you fucking . . . *capitalist.*"

He whispered the last word. He hoped the owner heard it and it stung.

"Get out and don't come back. Store for neighborhood, not you."

As Randy stood on the street punching a head hole and armholes through the plastic garbage bag before pulling it on, he looked back at the bodega and thought, *Yours will be the first place we burn down, old man.*

STILL STEAMING FROM the encounter at the bodega, Randy returned to his position as sentinel and realized right away he'd missed nothing on the street. Hard rain came down in sheets and angry black water shot down the gutters into storm drains.

There were no protesters out, nor cops. The only vehicles he saw were delivery vans sluicing through the running water.

Across the street was a small urban park. There were benches and some kind of sculpture and several small dome tents lit from the inside. Probably homeless, he thought. Aside from the tents, there were no live human beings milling around there. Wasn't this the square designated as the staging area for the street action?

Had Axel got the date or time wrong? Or the location? That didn't seem like Axel.

Randy drew out the radio and keyed it near his mouth.

"There's nothing going on out here," he said. Then: "Over."

"Stay in position," Axel responded.

Randy sighed and rolled his eyes. Rainwater pattered incessantly on his makeshift plastic raincoat.

AFTER TEN MORE MINUTES of nothing to report, Randy wiped his wet face clean with the cuff of his shirt and retreated back down Gum Wall alley. He wanted to get under the overhang and out of the rain. What could it hurt? He could still see most of the street.

The pounding of the rain hushed when he reentered the covered alley. He kept to the shadowed side of the right wall so that if Axel looked in his direction, he wouldn't see his outline from the streetlights on the square. Randy didn't want to invite Axel's wrath.

The mouth of the alley provided an odd kind of acoustic

anomaly. Even though Randy couldn't see Axel and the Blade deep in the shadows near the cache, he could hear them very clearly.

Axel was holding court. And it sounded to Randy like Axel was talking about antifa.

"They really don't have any realistic goals," Axel said. "It's all bullshit from trust-fund militants with daddy issues. They say they want to abolish the police. They say they want no government and no capitalism and they want to return the country to indigenous tribes. But they all have the newest iPhone. It's all just fucking insane."

The Blade laughed. He said, "But, man, they *love you*."

"Yeah, they do. That's how smart they are."

Randy felt a chill run through him. He felt as if someone had punched him in the chest.

Axel said, "Remember those child soldiers in Myanmar? How fucking incompetent and fucked up they were? Well, compared to the antifa guys I've met, those boys were highly trained warriors.

"There really aren't that many of them altogether," Axel continued. "It's a media myth. There are maybe just a couple hundred in the whole country at most. Most of them are concentrated in Portland. The reason people think antifa is a big deal is because they keep recirculating. They get arrested but not prosecuted, and they're back on the street in hours. It's a shell game.

"And they're only good for one thing," Axel said. "They'll help us destabilize the status quo, even though they don't know it. Them and the hard-core BLM guys. They're a means to an end, as far as I'm concerned. Both groups are easy to manipulate if you press the right buttons. With BLM, of course, you need cops to confront them and injure or kill one on video. With antifa, you just turn them loose and don't arrest them or prosecute them for anything. It emboldens them if they don't get any pushback."

"You've been thinking about this for a while," the Blade said.

"Yeah. We can't go at the leaders in D.C. directly for what they did to us. It's impractical and they're all hiding behind walls and fences. But we can light the cities on fire and expose them as weak and spineless. The media will be on our side. They always are."

"So how's this gonna work?" the Blade asked.

"We need to be in the right situation," Axel said. "We need to be in the middle of a full-fledged riot. Fog-of-war conditions. That's what all of this has been leading up to. We need a situation with absolute chaos. Cops fighting antifa or BLM. Or antifa just burning everything down."

"Then what?"

"Then we light the fuse," Axel said. "That's why I'm dressed like this."

"Like a golf pro or some such?" the Blade said, chuckling.

"Yeah. I need to look like a local white businessman who maybe found himself in the wrong place at the wrong time. Naturally, I'll choose to be on the side of the cops in their riot gear. I'll keep my head down until the time is right. Then I'll pull this," he said.

Randy imagined Axel showing the Blade one of the guns they'd stolen earlier in the day. He imagined it to be one of the .40 Glock pistols Axel had claimed "were the weapon of choice" for law enforcement personnel across the country.

"You'll be positioned in a window or on a roof with your sniper rifle," Axel said to the Blade. "I'll pop a couple antifa or BLM guys from within the crowd of cops. I'll take down as many as I can without exposing myself. It'll all get caught by people on the side with their phones and on police body cams. No one will know who did the shooting, but they'll know it came from the cops."

"Meanwhile," the Blade said, "I'll target a couple of cops in the cross fire."

"*Exactly*," Axel said. "The scene then will go absolutely ballistic with dead bodies on both sides. Someone will remember our Signal post of where to find the weapons cache. It doesn't matter to me whether it's antifa or BLM. I just want them finding those guns and going back out on the street to hunt cops. A few citizens will get taken out in collateral damage, but that's to be expected.

"It won't stop here," Axel said, his voice rising. "Not if there are actual bodies in the streets. Especially if there are bodies in the streets and actual video showing it started from within the line of cops. Maybe someday they'll work it out and realize it wasn't a cop that fired first. *Maybe*. But in the meanwhile the riots will spread from city to city like it's done before. We'll burn this motherfucking country to the ground, just like we swore we'd do when they left us over there to die."

The Blade whooped. "You think big."

"What's the point of thinking small?"

Randy closed his eyes. He'd never felt so betrayed. He slumped against the wall and didn't even care if his plastic bag wrap stuck to the wads of chewing gum.

Just then, his radio crackled.

"Anything going on?" Axel asked. His voice had returned to normal. It was the passive tone of a sociopath, Randy thought.

Randy had trouble speaking. Finally, he keyed the mike and said, "Nothing."

"Shit. Shit-shit-*shit*. Keep me informed." Axel keyed off.

Randy let the handheld drop to the pavement. He wasn't sure he had the strength to stand back up and walk away. Then he heard Axel curse again from the shadows.

"What is *wrong* with them?" Axel shouted to the Blade. "What kind of pussies are we dealing with? A little *rain* keeps them away? *Rain?* Imagine if they had to hike a hundred miles through enemy territory in a rain forest like we did? See what I mean about them?"

Randy waved his hand as if dismissing Axel for good. He'd had it. He wasn't even going back for his phone. Instead, he'd find a pay phone somewhere and call his parents and beg them to buy him a plane ticket back to Denver. They'd object at first, but then he knew they'd cave. They always did.

That's when a cop suddenly appeared on the other side of the street. One cop, on foot. Eyeing him. Randy turned his head away and picked up his pace. But instead of the cop giving chase, he turned toward the alley where Axel and the Blade were located.

Randy had no way to warn them, since he'd ditched the radio. And he had no good reason to do it anyway, since Axel had revealed his true colors.

AXEL LIFTED HIS RADIO to contact Randy again when he heard a grunt from behind him and scuffling shoes on the alley pavement. The Blade heard it, too. Someone was approaching them from the gloom, from deep within Gum Wall alley.

Axel clipped the handheld to his belt and drew a flashlight from his blazer pocket and turned it on. He choked down the beam and shined it behind them.

Two disheveled men were shuffling toward him and both stopped and held up grimy bare hands against the bright light. They were homeless men, obviously, and Axel caught a glimpse of several makeshift tents farther down the alley.

The vagrants were Black men, both in their fifties or sixties. They wore several layers of clothes, which made them appear bigger than they actually were. One had an impressive snow-white beard and the other was so dark-skinned Axel could barely make out his facial features.

The bearded man growled, "This is our alley, motherfucker. You need to get *gone*."

Axel and the Blade exchanged glances. Axel tried not to shift his eyes toward the covered cache of weapons against the alley wall, so as not to direct their attention to it. The bearded man took another step toward them.

Then, where Randy was supposed to be stationed at the

mouth of the alley, came a shout: "Seattle PD. What's going on back there?"

Axel felt himself get lit up by the cop's powerful flashlight. He couldn't yet see the cop because of the bright light, but he could hear static coming from the man's radio. Axel's eyes adjusted and he could make out the form of the policeman coming straight down the middle of the alley. The man had his hand on the grip of his sidearm.

Axel had been the leader of his unit because he could adjust on the fly to changing situations on the ground. His men valued him for the ability and trusted his leadership. Axel Soledad didn't panic. Instead, he adapted to the situation.

And this was a situation, he thought. But it was also an opportunity, given the players. Planets suddenly aligned.

If the homeless men were protesters on the street, it would be better. But this would do.

With one smooth motion, Axel raised his Glock and fired at the cop. He fired off three rounds low to hit the man in the front of his thighs and then he swung the gun up and put three more in his face and neck. Axel avoided firing center mass since it was likely the cop was wearing an armored vest.

The cop went down hard as the concussion from the shots echoed throughout the alley.

To the Blade, Axel said, "Bring me his gun."

For a second, the Blade was stunned by what he'd witnessed. Then, as he had in the field, he obeyed.

Axel swung around and bathed the two homeless men in the light of his flashlight. "You two—freeze where you are."

The men were frightened and confused. The bearded one hopped almost comically from foot to foot.

"We don't mean no trouble, man," the other one said. "Tell me you didn't just pop a cop."

The Blade appeared with the downed policeman's service weapon. Another .40 Glock 22 with fifteen rounds in the magazine.

Axel executed the two men with three shots each from the cop's gun, then handed the weapon back to the Blade.

"Wipe it down and put it in the cop's hand."

The Blade hesitated a moment, then a crooked grin formed on his mouth. "Oh, I get it," he said.

Axel tossed his own weapon toward the bodies of the two men. It clattered on the pavement and slid into the bearded victim, where he lay in a heap.

When the Blade reappeared, Axel said, "Let's load up the cache and get the hell out of here." Then: "Where in the hell did that weasel Randy go? I'll kill him if I find him for deserting his post."

Axel threw open the back of his van and the birds inside erupted. He didn't care. He and the Blade started stacking the middle aisle with guns.

RANDY PASSED the Asian bodega and glanced inside. The man was still behind the counter, but Randy didn't want to ask to use his phone.

No doubt the man had heard gunfire seconds before. No doubt gunfire at night wasn't all that unusual.

On the street, a large white van hissed by. Water sprayed out from beneath its tires and Randy sidestepped to avoid getting splashed. He looked up in anger and recognized the van from the trail cam photos he'd seen earlier. He could see two figures inside through the rain-smeared windshield. One Black, one white.

Painted on the side of the van was:

YARAK, INC.
We Make Your Problems Go Away

The van slowed and turned into the Gum Wall alleyway.

Randy froze where he stood.

A minute later, the night was ripped open by rapid gunfire punctuated by several heavy booms and the snapping staccato beat of semiautomatic rifle fire. Orange flashes from weapons lit up the dark walls.

Then the van reappeared, backing out of the alley at a speed too fast to be safe.

Randy began to run. As he did, he ripped away the plastic bag and left it behind him on the sidewalk.

RANDY RAN UNTIL his lungs ached. Two blocks at most. He heard an engine racing behind him in the street, coming his direction.

He didn't need to look over his shoulder to determine it was the Yarak van.

Randy ducked into the lit alcove of a FedEx Kinko's. Although there were two employees inside behind the counter, the front door was locked. Randy rattled it and pounded on the glass to get their attention. A young Asian employee in a FedEx polo glanced up and their eyes met. The employee shook his head.

"*Let me in!*" Randy hollered. His voice was hoarse from running.

He saw the FedEx staffer silently admonish his colleague to stay where he was and not open the door.

"Damn it," Randy said as he hit the glass hard with the heel of his hand. It did no good.

Randy tried another door of a darkened shoe store. Also locked.

Suddenly, the van raced up behind him and turned so its nose blocked the sidewalk. A beat later, the back doors blew open and there stood the huge Black man he'd seen earlier. The man hopped down to the pavement.

"Randy Daniels," the man said, his mass of dreads swinging from side to side as he approached.

"How do you—" Randy began to ask as the man reached out and grabbed him by his collar. He was strong, and Randy was tossed without effort into the back of the van.

With the doors slammed shut, Randy recovered to his hands and knees. He was in the middle of the vehicle surrounded on both sides by empty wire cages. Just like Axel's van—except without the live birds.

The Black man threw himself into the cab and roared away,

knocking Randy back against the back doors because of the momentum.

"How do you know me?" he called out at the driver.

The man didn't respond. He was driving fast, and Randy could feel the van fishtail as it took a corner.

That's when he realized he wasn't alone on the floor of the vehicle. A large body was propped into a sitting position against the back of the passenger seat, legs splayed. The victim was white with a blond ponytail cascading over his shoulder. He had a cruel face, Randy thought. The front of the man's jacket was black with blood, and Randy could smell it.

The man moaned. He was alive. Bleeding out, but alive.

The driver braked hard in front of a brightly lit storefront. Randy could see a glowing sign through the window of the side panel:

EMERGICARE

The driver turned in his seat and his eyes fixed on Randy.

"We're gonna carry him inside to get him patched up," he said. As the driver talked, he opened his parka and slid a stubby weapon of some kind into a sleeve under his arm.

"Then you and me are going to have a long talk. And don't try to run again or I'll light you up."

Reel shadows of the
indignant
desert birds.
The darkness drops again;
but now
I know
That twenty centuries of
stony sleep
Were vexed to nightmare by
a rocking cradle,
And what rough beast, its
hour come round at
last,
Slouches towards
Bethlehem to
be born?

—William
Butler
Yeats,
"The
Second
Coming"

CHAPTER TWENTY-FOUR

The Trap

By ten the next morning, the conference room of the Twelve Sleep County Library was set up to broadcast the press announcement regarding the discovery of the photo album and there was a palpable sense of urgency, tension, and confusion in the air. Joe tried to keep out of the way.

State-of-the-art video cameras, audio equipment, and lighting were set up in the room. The library's tech employee hovered from station to station in the background, frantically ticking items off a checklist. The gear had all been purchased early in the pandemic, when Marybeth had convinced the library foundation to obtain it so they could safely maintain book clubs and discussion groups. According to her, this would result in professional-looking events. The foundation agreed.

The singular focus of the lights, cameras, and microphones was on a lone table in the center of the space. On the surface of the table was the red leather-bound photo album that had once belonged to Julius Streicher.

JOE WAS CAREFUL not to trip over any of the cords or cables on the carpet as he crossed the room to greet Sheriff Tibbs, who had entered wearing a skeptical squint on his face. AnnaBelle Griffith, the new county prosecutor, was a few steps behind him.

The announcement was scheduled to go live at eleven a.m. mountain time.

"Hello, Sheriff. Hello, AnnaBelle."

The sheriff said, "Joe. I wish I had confidence in what we're doing here."

"I understand."

Joe had spent the morning going over with him what he and Marybeth suspected and why. Tibbs hadn't completely bought in on their theory, but Joe had been as persuasive as he could be. Griffith played her cards close to her vest, but she seemed to be more in favor of Joe's theory than the sheriff, who clearly had his doubts.

Griffith was young and professional, and she didn't waste words. The month before, she'd had lunch with Marybeth, and his wife had said the new prosecutor was, she thought, a "straight shooter." Griffith was obviously still trying to figure out where she fit within the male-dominated structure of Twelve Sleep County law enforcement.

"It's a gamble," Joe had said to them both. "But it's a gamble we have to take. Besides, what other ideas are there for smoking out and nailing these guys?"

Griffith had looked to Tibbs for an answer to the question. When there was none, she cautioned the both of them to be careful and to "go by the book." She said she'd be present to observe.

Tibbs had reluctantly agreed.

The library was usually closed on the Friday after Thanksgiving, so there was only a skeleton crew of staff whom Marybeth had pleaded with to come in. There were no patrons in the aisles. The timing was fortuitous, Joe knew, because they couldn't risk the safety of civilians who might have come in to browse the books or use the internet.

"Is everyone in position?" Joe asked Tibbs.

The sheriff eyed Joe coolly, as if prepared to dress him down. Apparently, he decided not to.

"Deputy Bass is watching the back door and Deputy Steck is set up in the front foyer," Tibbs said. "We're receiving assistance this morning from Chief Williamson and four of his uniforms to get the extra manpower. I had to make a deal with him."

"Let me guess," Joe said. "You agreed that he could commission his tank into use."

"You got it," Tibbs said with disdain. "So if this doesn't work out, you owe me big-time."

"Gotcha."

Chief Williamson of the Saddlestring Police Department had a well-deserved reputation for being overzealous and eager to use every tool at his disposal for any situation he could find. He believed in overwhelming force.

Williamson had been champing at the bit for years to roll out the MRAP—a mine-resistant ambush protected armored truck—the Pentagon had sent his department in the wake of the Iraq War. It weighed forty thousand pounds and the last time it had been used was for display in the Fourth of July parade downtown. Unfortunately, the MRAP was so heavy it had damaged the bridge over the river, and the incident had resulted in a recall election the chief had barely survived.

"The MRAP isn't conspicuous, is it?" Joe asked.

"No. He agreed to hide it in the alley behind the bank down the street. But how can a vehicle that size *not* be conspicuous?

"So," Tibbs said, "tell me your plan here again."

Joe glanced at his watch. "Marybeth will go live with the photo album in fifty minutes. The library will provide a video and audio feed to news outlets that have requested a live link and a video file to those who don't watch it in real time. She's also going to send the link all over social media."

"I hate social media."

"I do, too. But Marybeth knows what she's doing."

"Where is she now?"

"In her office going over her presentation," Joe said. "She's good at this kind of thing."

"And what do we expect will happen?"

"Like I told you, we don't know for sure. But based on what we've figured out, we're expecting the perps that murdered Bert

Kizer and Lola Lowry to show up. They don't want anyone to have the album or see what's inside of it."

"That sounds far-fetched."

"Our bad guys are desperate," Joe said. He didn't know if he sounded convincing. Or if he was convinced of it entirely himself.

"This whole thing is crazy," Tibbs said. "We're talking about Nazi memorabilia showing up at our little Podunk library. I hope we aren't embarrassing ourselves."

"Don't let Marybeth hear you say that," Joe warned.

"Who in the hell will tune in, or whatever?" Tibbs asked.

Behind him, Joe heard Marybeth clear her throat. When she spoke, her tone was icy, and the sheriff blanched when he heard it. Joe noted that Griffith turned away so the sheriff wouldn't see her grin.

"In addition to going live on Facebook, Twitter, and ConFab to millions of users, Sheriff Tibbs, our receptionist has been fielding calls and requests all morning. So far, we've got the *Casper Star-Tribune*, Wyoming Public Radio, the *Billings Gazette*, four television stations and five radio stations in Wyoming and Montana. All receiving the feed from our *Podunk* library."

Tibbs's face flushed.

"Oh," she continued, "we've also got the *New York Post*, CNN, Fox News, the Associated Press, *Library Journal*, and the *Wall Street Journal*. That's domestic press. Internationally, we've got *Die Zeit* and *Süddeutsche Zeitung* from Germany, the *Daily Mail* and the *Sunday Times* from the UK. Oh, and two Hungarian newspapers."

"Hungarian newspapers?" Tibbs repeated.

She paused and Joe turned to see she was reading off a handwritten list.

"*Blikk* and *Magyar Nemzet*," she said. "I don't know anything about them, but I find it interesting."

Her social media strategy had worked beyond her wildest dreams, she'd said earlier. News of the announcement had gone everywhere. And Steve-2 Price had come through on ConFab for Joe. Millions of ConFab followers were signed up for the live event.

"My God," Tibbs said. "What if nothing happens? What if these bad guys decide not to show up?"

Marybeth gave Tibbs her most withering glare. Joe was happy it wasn't directed at *him*.

"These news outlets aren't signing up to witness an arrest," she said. "They know nothing about our two homicides. All they know is that we are suddenly in possession of a photo album compiled by a notorious Nazi war criminal. A vicious monster of a man. It's *news*, Sherriff Tibbs. And we're generating it from our own little *Podunk* library."

"I *told* you not to say that," Joe whispered to him.

Tibbs raised his hands up and backed away. "Forgive my language," he said to Marybeth.

"Please clear the center of the room," she said. "We've got to get set up and I don't want either of you two in the shot."

Joe happily moved to a corner. Tibbs slinked to another, and Griffith joined the tech behind the camera to get out of the way.

LIKE THE SHERIFF, Joe listened to the outside mutual aid law enforcement radio channel through an earbud while Marybeth silently read over her presentation at the table. He noted that she'd attached sticky notes to particular pages of photos within the album that she planned to display to the cameras. There was a second stationary camera on a tripod over her shoulder to focus in on the particular images when she opened it.

Over the radio, the deputies and town uniforms identified themselves and their locations to each other on their handhelds. Three local police officers were seated in individual cruisers on the streets outside the library. Another uniform and Chief Williamson were in the MRAP behind the bank. Tibbs spoke to all of them in a low tone.

"Look, fellas, we don't know what exactly to expect, but be on the lookout for the two suspects in the green SUV that we've been searching for all night. Colorado plates. If you see something, report it immediately. They might arrive in another vehicle, so be alert. Also keep an eye out for anyone on foot.

"No one is to enter the library. If someone tries, detain them for questioning. And remember, our suspects are armed and dangerous. We want to take them without any drama and we don't want anybody hurt."

The officers all mumbled their assent to the sheriff. Joe gave him a thumbs-up.

———

A FEW MINUTES LATER, Deputy Bass broke in.

"Hey, Sheriff, I've got a sheriff's deputy from the next county here. He wants to talk to you."

Tibbs and Joe exchanged a confused look, and Tibbs said into the radio, "Who is he and what does he want?"

Bass: "He says his name is Deputy Tucker Schuster, Campbell County Sheriff's Department. He says he had a run-in with those suspects you mentioned earlier today and he has some information about them."

"What information?"

"He says he needs to talk to you."

Tibbs lowered his radio and searched the ceiling tiles as if looking for an answer.

Joe checked his watch again and signaled *fifteen minutes before airtime* by opening and closing the fingers on his free hand three times.

"Send him in through the back, but tell him to hurry," Tibbs said.

Marybeth looked up at the sheriff. She was annoyed by the distraction.

"I'll talk to him outside," Tibbs said to her. He left the room.

"That man," Marybeth said to Joe. "As if this wasn't stressful enough."

"You'll do great," Joe said.

She met his eyes. "Joe, no offense, but I think I'll be more nervous if I know you're standing there watching me."

"Say no more," he said, following Tibbs out of the conference room into the circulation room. Then: "Knock 'em dead, kiddo."

"AnnaBelle, feel free to stay," Marybeth said to the prosecutor.

"Thank you, I will."

"Fourteen minutes," the library tech announced.

JOE HOVERED OUTSIDE the plate-glass window of the conference room while Tibbs went off to talk to the deputy from Gillette. The interior of the original Carnegie library had been refurbished several times, but the bones were still there. It was dark with high ceilings, and the shelves were high and packed closely together.

He could hear the sheriff's boot steps recede on the stone floor toward the back door. Then a *clunk* as Tibbs pushed on the bar on the metal door to open it.

Joe was curious to find out what the deputy had to say, so he moved into the nearest aisle. He was in the fiction section, *L* through *O*. Through the gaps on top of the collection of Patrick O'Brian's Aubrey-Maturin series, he could periodically see the form of the sheriff four shelves away. Then the appearance of a man who flashed by the openings to approach Tibbs. The sheriff stood with his back to the last bookshelf and to Joe's position.

He got a brief glimpse of the deputy as the man moved through a narrow opening, and his appearance struck Joe as off. The deputy was older than most deputies, likely late thirties, and he had dark hair and black plastic glasses. No mustache or facial hair. Something about him seemed foreign, Joe thought. Something about the way he carried himself.

"I'm Sheriff Scott Tibbs. What's so urgent?"

"I'm sorry to bother you. Is this the place where the photo album is located?"

Joe caught the hint of an Eastern European accent.

"I thought this was about our suspects?" Tibbs said.

Joe could hear them clearly through gaps in the bookshelves. He hoped their voices wouldn't carry into the conference room and be picked up by the microphones.

Then there was a flurry of motion in front of the sheriff and a breathy *"Oooof"* as Schuster violently shoved Tibbs into the stack of books behind him. Joe caught a glimpse of the sheriff's flailing arms.

Tibbs fell back heavily enough into the bookshelf that it rocked back. Books on the other side crashed to the floor. The unbalanced shelf tipped and started a chain reaction as it fell into the next shelf, causing it to tip over as well.

Joe could see what was coming, but he couldn't prevent it or get out of the way in time. The second shelf crashed into the third and the third into the fourth and suddenly Joe was buried under the deadweight of hundreds of pounds of hardcover books and the shelves themselves. He went down to his knees as the books piled up on top of him and he knew what it must be like to be caught in an avalanche.

"Marybeth, look out!" he yelled.

He didn't know if his voice carried from the mountain of

books he was trapped under and he couldn't see anything for a moment. The distinctive smell of musty pages filled his nose and throat.

Joe found himself thrashing, not sure which end was up. He could hear yelling, then a scream. Then Marybeth cursing, which was unusual in itself.

He made himself stop moving for a few seconds so he could get his bearings. He realized that his knees were solid on the floor, so at least he knew which direction up was.

Then he started swimming, in effect. He worked his arms free and windmilled his hands, using the mass of the books themselves for purchase. A few seconds later, he pushed his head free and gasped for air. He could feel the hot burn from a dozen abrasions all over his body, but he didn't think he had broken bones or other serious injuries.

Before he could pull and kick the books aside so he could emerge, he saw Deputy Schuster run from the conference room. He could see him clearly because all of the shelves in that wing of the library had fallen over.

The deputy had the red-bound album under his arm and he was headed toward the back door. Marybeth and Griffith appeared on the other side of the glass in the conference room, gesturing frantically. Schuster had obviously snatched the book right in front of them. Joe was relieved they were both safe.

As the deputy reached for the door bar to exit, he was greeted by Bass, who entered with a *What's going on in here?* expression on his face, which changed into a horrified grimace when he was shot point-blank in the chest by Schuster and he fell away.

The shot was incredibly loud inside the closed environment of the library and it bounced down from the high ceilings.

Joe scrambled to get free. He pointed to Marybeth and Griffith and said, "*Stay in there. Don't move.*" Then he keyed his handheld.

"This is Joe Pickett from inside the library. Watch for a Campbell County deputy either on foot or in a cruiser. He's got the album."

Joe ran around the ocean of books via the center aisle. As he reached the back door, he caught a glimpse of Sheriff Tibbs's legs sticking out from under a large pile of books. Bass had fallen into the building and he writhed on the floor in a fetal position. Joe noted that Bass had been wearing body armor, and he hoped the bullet from Schuster's weapon hadn't penetrated it.

He drew his Glock and threw open the back door in time to see a Campbell County Sheriff's Department SUV scream down the alley and exit onto the side street. The passenger door closed as the vehicle drove away, meaning Schuster had a driver waiting.

"There he goes!" Joe hollered into the radio. "We've got two officers down inside. Call an ambulance."

"I've got him," one of the town uniforms replied. "He's going south on First."

Toward downtown and the bank, Joe knew.

"We see him coming," Chief Williamson cried out with undisguised glee. "We've got the son of a bitch."

The MRAP!

Joe exited the library through the foyer, ignoring Deputy Steck's pleas to stop and tell him what was happening. He ran across the lawn toward his pickup in the employee lot on the side of the building.

As he did, he could see the Gillette SUV racing away on First Street. Then the huge squared-off snout of the MRAP emerged from the alley behind the bank onto the street itself.

The driver of the SUV hit the brakes, and tires squealed as he did so. A town cruiser following the SUV nearly rear-ended it because of the sudden stop, but it veered away at the last second and careened into the parking lot of a saddle and tack shop.

Joe climbed into his truck and started the engine, but he kept his eye on the SUV, which was now doing a three-point turn in the middle of the street. The driver reversed course and was going to come back toward the library. Right *at* him. Joe quickly fastened his seat belt.

The SUV accelerated and roared closer right down the middle of the street.

As Joe pulled out of the lot, he could see two men inside the SUV, but he couldn't yet see their faces. Joe turned toward them and floored it.

The SUV closed fast, the MRAP looming behind it but losing ground.

Joe realized he didn't really have a plan. He'd been operating on adrenaline alone. All he knew was that he was roaring toward a head-on collision unless the SUV turned sharply in either direction. Or *he* did.

At the last possible second, Joe wrenched his pickup hard left. Unfortunately, the driver of the SUV turned hard right.

The crash rocked his pickup and threw him toward the passenger window, but the seat belt bit and prevented him from flying through the glass.

Both his vehicle and the SUV were motionless. A green-tinted cloud of radiator steam rolled from the SUV and into Joe's cab through the broken windshield and he could hear a loud hiss.

Joe found the seat belt buckle and unlatched it. His Glock was on the floorboard of the passenger side and he grabbed it and opened his door and his boot heel missed the running board and he tumbled out onto the pavement in a heap. He gathered himself to his hands and knees.

Through a groggy haze, he watched what happened next from his vantage point beneath his truck.

There were the big feet and boots of the driver of the SUV on the ground. He'd emerged from the damaged vehicle and was shouting in a language Joe didn't understand. Then the distinctive *BOOM* of a shotgun blast. Followed by a cacophony of *pop-pop-pop*s from at least three different directions.

A second later, the driver was down and his shotgun skittered across the blacktop. Joe could see him clearly because he was a big man and they were eye to eye at the same level.

The gargoyle.

The same man Joe had seen behind the wheel of the green SUV.

The gargoyle saw Joe and for a moment they locked eyes. Then the gargoyle closed his.

Forever.

The next thing Joe saw was Schuster striding out of the SUV in the ill-fitting uniform with his hands up, shouting, "I surrender! I give up! I surrender! Don't shoot me, please."

A few seconds later, a very skinny white man wearing only boxer briefs emerged from the back seat of the cruiser. The man hopped up and down in a clumsy kind of end zone dance, hooting, "Damned right! Damned straight! Good shooting, boys!"

CHAPTER TWENTY-FIVE

Kovács Family Secrets

LATER THAT DAY, JOE GRIMACED IN PAIN AS HE SHIFTED HIS weight on the examination table in a room in the emergency wing of the medical clinic. He wore a paper gown over his underwear and his naked feet dangled near the floor. His skin was mottled with bruises in their original shade of blue (they'd bloom into Technicolor in the days to come), but he'd been correct to assess earlier in the library that he had no broken bones or internal injuries. The slivers of glass in his scalp from the smashed pickup windows had been removed by an intern with tweezers. He was waiting for the doctor to release him so he could go home, and he eyed his uniform, which had been hung up in the small closet.

There was a series of sharp knocks on the door and he looked up, anticipating the doctor.

Instead, Marybeth poked her head in and smiled. Her face was flushed and she looked, well, *happy*.

"I found you," she said.

"You found me."

"They weren't very helpful at the front desk. So, how are you doing?"

"Dandy," he said. "Just cuts and bruises. I'm ready to get out of here."

"I told the girls to stay away. They've seen you in hospital rooms way too many times."

"True."

"I brought a guest," she said with a lopsided grin.

"A guest?"

"AnnaBelle is with me, so you might want to get decent."

From behind his wife, Joe heard AnnaBelle say, "I've seen half-naked men before, you know." Like Marybeth, she sounded almost giddy.

"Not this one," Joe grumbled. He stepped down from the table and quickly shed the gown. Climbing back into his uniform hurt more than he thought it would. He pulled on his boots but didn't tuck the cuffs into the top of the shafts because bending over that far made him wince.

"Have you two gotten into the wine?" he asked them as they came in.

"We should have," AnnaBelle said. "We have plenty to celebrate."

"Don't be grumpy," Marybeth said to him. "We've come with all sorts of interesting news."

Joe climbed back up on the table and gestured for her to continue.

"This is going to sound kind of convoluted at first," Marybeth said, "but hang with us. We've spent the entire morning getting enlightened. First, the guy who surrendered to the cops is named Viktór Kovács, and he's singing like a bird. We think we know everything now."

"I'm interested," Joe said.

"I sat in on Viktór's statement to the sheriff," AnnaBelle said. "I took notes. I was surprised he was so forthcoming, but he seemed to be getting a lot off his mind. We still have to verify everything he told us, of course. But he basically confessed to everything."

So it wasn't wine, Joe thought. It was *resolution*.

"I had a long talk after the event with a reporter from the *Magyar Nemzet* newspaper in Hungary," Marybeth said. "She watched our presentation and stayed online afterward. She really opened my eyes on what led to this and she answered a lot of questions."

Joe arched his eyebrows. "You're saying you did the broadcast? With all that happened?"

"The show must go on," Marybeth said. "AnnaBelle found the album in the wrecked car and got it to me with two minutes to spare. The media who participated had no idea what was going on outside the room. To them, it was all about the discovery of the album. We all think it went very well."

"Wow."

"And you're a hero, Joe," she said as she reached out and stroked his cheek. "You stopped them."

"I had help."

AnnaBelle dismissed his show of being humble, even though it wasn't an act. She said, "If you hadn't crashed into them like that, who knows how many citizens and law enforcement personnel could have gotten hurt?"

Joe shrugged. "And another pickup destroyed in the process."

Left unsaid was that Joe had the dubious honor of being responsible for the most damage to property than any other employee of the state of Wyoming. This would add to the list.

"Forget that," AnnaBelle said. "I'll vouch for you if you have a problem. The fact is, those brothers were desperate and they had a hostage."

"And they're killers," Marybeth added. "You stopped them."

"Brothers?" Joe asked. He assumed the hostage was the dancing underwear man.

"Yes," Marybeth said. "Here's where it starts to get weird. Believe me, I just had a crash course in Hungarian politics."

"VIKTÓR AND LÁSZLÓ KOVÁCS are brothers," she said. "They were going under assumed names and passports, but Viktór admitted it and the reporter from the newspaper confirmed who they were when AnnaBelle sent over their photo IDs. They are well known in Hungary, and they're part of a very prominent political family."

"Hungary?" Joe said, recalling the Eastern European accent he'd heard from the deputy. "How did they get hold of a Campbell County Sheriff's vehicle and the uniform?"

"They jumped Deputy Schuster in Gillette and took him

hostage," AnnaBelle said. "He told us all about it. They took his uniform, his gun, and his car. The uniform fit Viktór, so that's what he wore to get in the library. László was the driver. Schuster's okay, by the way. Like you: cuts and bruises. And a little embarrassed to go back to Gillette."

"I understand," Joe said. He did.

"Here's what the reporter told me for background," Marybeth said. "Apparently, the Kovács family has been involved in politics in Hungary at a very high level for a long period of time. They're controversial. She called them right-wing populists, for what that's worth. Anyway, she said there's a big election coming up that has completely divided the country. Their father, Zoltan Kovács, could very well be the next prime minister."

Joe sat back, taking that in.

"Viktór and László could be thought of as the Eric and Donald Trump Jr. of Hungary," AnnaBelle injected. "They're that well known."

"This is nuts," Joe said.

"It gets better," Marybeth said. "Their father, Zoltan, is leading in the polls, but there are allegations against him and the entire Kovács family that, if proved true, could cause him to lose. It sounds very heated. And the election is next month."

"What allegations?" Joe asked.

"Apparently, Zoltan's opponent says that the Kovácses are tainted by totalitarianism—that it's in their blood. They claim that if Zoltan was elected, he'd turn into a dictator because it's in his genes. The phrase used against him, in Hungarian, of course, is that 'He has extremism running in his veins.'"

"Based on what?" Joe asked.

"Based on rumors, most of all," Marybeth said. "The reporter said it's well known that Zoltan was a teenage communist while the country was occupied, but he's kind of been given a pass on that because a lot of Hungarians joined the party during those years just to get along. He denounced communism after the Hungarian Revolution, apparently. If that was all it was, the whole 'extremism runs in his veins' thing wouldn't be very persuasive to voters.

"But there's more," she said. "And that's where we come in. This is where it all starts to connect."

Joe was more than intrigued.

"There have been rumors for years about the grandfather, also named László," she said. "That he was not just sympathetic to Hitler, but that he was loyal and devoted to him. This wasn't that unusual, the reporter told me. There were a number of Hungarians who were out-and-out Nazis at the time. But when the rumors came up later, the Kovács family vehemently denied them. They sued newspapers that printed it, and they went after citizens as well, and there's never been any proof that the allegations were true."

Joe said, "The album."

"The album," Marybeth said. "I must have seen the photos a dozen times when I went through it, but they meant nothing to me. They're the shots of the Hungarian Youth greeting Julius Streicher with Nazi salutes. A bunch of little Nazi boys wearing uniforms with swastika armbands."

"I remember," Joe said.

"Well, the little troop leader for the Hungarian Youth in the photos is László himself. The grandfather. He's apparently still alive at ninety-five years of age and he's always denied his involvement. The photo in the album is what Zoltan's opponents have been looking for all along to prove that the Kovács family has a history of extremism. And all these years it's been sitting right here in Wyoming. Bert Kizer had something even he couldn't understand. When the Kovács family found out that these photos existed, they had to find them and destroy them. Viktór and László were sent over here to do just that."

Joe nodded. "They found out that the album existed when Bert asked John and Connie Sheftic to put the word out. They found out the album itself wasn't of that much value to collectors, but it *was* valuable to a certain family in Hungary."

Marybeth was excited. "The Kovácses would do anything to destroy those photos."

"Crazy," Joe said. "But why go to such ridiculous extremes? Why use false identities and come over here in person to take the photo back? Why didn't they just contact Bert and try to buy it? They didn't have to torture and kill him for it."

"I asked Viktór that exact question," AnnaBelle said. "The family was afraid of raising any red flags that the photo existed. Viktór said that they were afraid the photo might be posted to the internet to start a bidding war with them and that their enemies would see it. They used a private detective to track down the IP address for the Sheftics to here, and then they came up with a plan to arrive in person and take the album any way they could. Viktór said they didn't expect that Bert would refuse to sell it to them or give it to them. And things just got out of hand from there."

"Either that, or they didn't want to leave a single witness," Joe said.

Marybeth asked AnnaBelle, "Did we forget anything?"

"The sister."

"Oh yes," Marybeth said. "From what Viktór said, it was their sister, Hanna, who found out about the album and put the scheme in motion. Hanna is the keeper of the family legacy, and apparently she has political ambitions herself. She's the one who learned about the press conference online and ordered her brothers to stop it."

"Did Victór say who actually committed the murders?" Joe asked.

AnnaBelle took over. "He was cagey about that, but he pretty much put all the blame on László. He said his brother was crazy and violent, and that Viktór himself did everything he could not to hurt anyone. That all may be true, but I think Viktór was more involved than he claims to be. Unfortunately, we may never find out for sure, since László is dead."

"So are Bert Kizer and Lola Lowry," Joe said.

Marybeth and AnnaBelle Griffith nodded in agreement.

"We'll be able to convict Viktór on so many charges he'll never see Hungary again," AnnaBelle said. "He'll be spending the rest of his adult life in beautiful Rawlins, Wyoming, which is probably okay with him. I got the impression that returning to Hungary and facing the wrath of Hanna was the last thing he wanted to do. Plus, with this evidence, the Kovács family will be thoroughly disgraced. He wants no part of that."

"Good," Joe said. "What about the sheriff and Bass? How are they?"

AnnaBelle stifled a smile. "They're both okay. Bass has a bruise on his chest, but his body armor saved him from the bullet. The sheriff received a slight concussion when he was pushed into those books and he's threatening to resign. I think we should just let him."

"Agreed," Joe and Marybeth said in unison. Joe thought: Another sheriff. How many would he have to train in his career?

"Another thing," Marybeth said. "I think we found a good home for the album. The Hoover Institution at Stanford has an archive for these kinds of things. They reached out this morning and we're going to make arrangements to get it to them. I can't say I'll miss it at all."

At that moment, he felt his phone burr in the breast pocket of his uniform shirt. He dug it out, read the message, and hopped down from the table.

Marybeth watched him with practiced alarm. "Who was that?" she asked.

"Nate," Joe said.

Her mood changed abruptly. "Nate?"

"He says he needs my help. He's never asked for it before. I owe him, as you know." Then: "My pickup is shot. Marybeth, can you drive me to the airport?"

"Joe," she asked, her eyes widening in alarm, "where are you going?"

CHAPTER TWENTY-SIX

Portland, the Rose City

NATE OPENED HIS EYES AND ASSESSED WHERE HE WAS BECAUSE he'd just had a fitful dream that he was in an ocean-bound vessel being rocked by the waves. The ship was empty of crewmen, for some reason. On shore, barely within sight, were Liv and Kestrel. They were standing on the beach, waiting for him to arrive.

He wandered the boat, trying to find someone who could show him where the engine room was located. All of the rooms and ship's quarters were empty, as if everyone aboard had simply left in an emergency.

The ship was drifting slowly away from land and he couldn't figure out how to fire up the engines and take it to shore. Liv and Kestrel were silent and stoic, a trait he admired.

Nate determined that no, he wasn't in a boat, but a van. *His* van. But rather than driving, he was lying on his back on blankets. In his right hand was his phone. And there was something wrong with the upper right side of his body. He couldn't feel it.

And although Liv and Kestrel might be waiting for him, they weren't standing on a beach.

He plucked the phone out of his right hand with his left and raised it in the dark to bump it on. The call log revealed that his last call had been to Joe.

Then it all came back to him as his head cleared.

NATE HAD TURNED down the alley entrance in Seattle and everything had happened at once and too quickly for him to respond or adjust.

A police officer lay on the ground next to the right-side brick wall. The front of a black transit van was parked straight in front of him, clogging up easy passage.

Axel Soledad and a ghoulish, lean man were in the act of loading long guns into the back of the vehicle when the headlights hit them and everything went pear-shaped. Axel swung an AR-15 or similar semiautomatic rifle up and Nate saw the orange starbursts flash from the muzzle and the windshield imploded.

The shock of the rifle rounds hitting him were like blows from a baseball bat. His right shoulder, his right clavicle, his right ear.

Nate didn't have the chance to draw his weapon and fire back and he couldn't locate his entire right arm.

He recalled Geronimo clearing smashed glass from the windshield frame with the barrels of his shotgun, then thrusting it out the opening. He pointed it toward the two men just as Axel stepped behind his open driver's-side door for cover. The other man wasn't as fast. The blast was tremendous and he went down like a wet rag.

The next few seconds were hazy, but somehow Geronimo had pulled Nate out from behind the wheel and taken control. They flew backward toward the street as rifle rounds thumped against the grille of the Yarak van and screamed through the open windshield and out the back doors.

Then everything had gone black.

Nate winced as he slowly pulled himself into a seated position. His upper torso and neck were numb and he couldn't feel anything. He looked down to see that his right shoulder and neck were bound tight in bandages. When he reached up with his left hand, he felt the tape and gauze covering his right ear.

He attempted to flex his right hand, but it was unresponsive.

Geronimo was driving, but there was someone else in the passenger seat. A twenty-something male with spiked hair and pale white skin.

"Who's this guy?" Nate asked. His voice was a croak.

"Well, hello," Geronimo said cheerfully. "I'm glad you're back with us."

"Where are we?"

"Forty minutes out of Portland on I-5."

"I can't feel my arm or shoulder."

"They pumped you up with painkillers pretty good," Geronimo said. "You'll definitely start feeling it when the drugs wear off."

Nate asked, "How were you able to get me medical attention? Aren't gunshot wounds supposed to be reported to the police?"

"In normal circumstances, yes," Geronimo said. "But these aren't normal circumstances, I guess. The EMTs just wanted to get you patched up and out of there. They said the rifle rounds didn't hit anything vital, although you probably would have bled out if we hadn't gotten you there within minutes, which we did. It was like they were working in a war zone. They even gave me morphine for when the drugs wear off."

The man in the passenger seat said, "I could use some of those."

"No, Randy," Geronimo said with a dismissive laugh.

Nate turned his head toward the windshield. It had stopped raining, but fine mist hung in the air. Rivulets of water snaked up the glass. The odd high-pitched sound he heard inside the van was from wind whistling through open bullet holes in the skin of the vehicle and from the back doors.

The *windshield*, Nate thought.

"When did you get new glass? I thought it got blown to bits."

"While they were patching you up, I called one of those out-fits that will show up on the spot and put in a new windshield. Ain't America great?"

Nate grunted.

"Ain't it great, Randy?" Geronimo said to the passenger.

The man called Randy looked away.

———

GERONIMO SAID, "Randy and I have had quite an interesting conversation while you were back there dozing. Haven't we, Randy?"

"Yeah."

To Nate, Randy sounded dejected.

"Nate, meet Randy Daniels from Denver. He's been assisting Axel all the way to the shootout in Seattle. He was with Axel in Wingville just before us and he helped him load up the arsenal.

"But Randy witnessed Axel's true colors last night and now he's quite disillusioned with the man. Right, Randy?"

"Fuck, yeah," Randy spat.

"He's on our side now," Geronimo said. "Not all antifas are incorrigible. Right, Randy?"

"I guess."

"Go ahead," Geronimo said to Randy. "Tell him what you told me."

Randy sighed. He said, "I'm just rethinking everything right now. My mind is fucked up.

"I think we're all being turned into subjects by the big banks, big tech, and big government and their cops. They want to control us. We have *no* future. Day by day, they're taking our souls and turning us into drones. I thought this was a way to get our voices heard. We're *not* fucking drones. I thought maybe we had to tear everything down before we could start again."

"I get it," Nate said.

Geronimo's eyes filled the rearview mirror and Nate looked up at him. "So do I," Geronimo said. "But Axel is playing a whole different game, just like I suspected. He's using guys like Randy. You remember my conspiracy theory?"

"Yes."

"Well, Randy confirmed it. He overheard Axel telling his Special Forces buddy all kinds of things.

"As we speak," Geronimo said, "the word's out on social media that a cop in Seattle shot two Black men. Nobody knows much more than that, but folks are plenty upset. Cities are going to burn before the facts get out on what happened."

"What did happen?" Nate asked.

"I think Axel shot the cop and then the two poor homeless guys. He planted weapons so it would look like a bad shooting to whoever first showed up at the scene. I don't know if the cop had a body camera to show what really happened, or it was too dark, or what. But by the time they get it sorted out—if they ever do—it'll be too late.

"This is what I was afraid of all along," Geronimo said. "This is what I thought Axel might be up to. He was supplying more and more dangerous weapons in the caches he was leaving, knowing that young men with their blood up would likely use what they found. Axel is using his antifa ties to start a war where nobody wins and everybody loses. He stole your birds to raise money to help ingratiate himself with the antifa types like Randy here. He did it so he could whip up my more emotional brothers and sisters into a rage. He's been working this con for a while now, and it's all coming to a head. Go ahead, Randy, show Nate what you just found on Tristan's phone."

Randy turned in his seat and thrust out the phone. The screen was opened to a communications app where someone had posted a call to arms that read:

NORTH PARK
Bloc Up!
There's Been Murder in Seattle
Gather: Midnight
Move: 1:00 a.m.

Nate read it twice. "North Park is in Portland, I take it?"

"Yes," Geronimo said. "I've been there. It's five or six city blocks right downtown."

"Do you figure Axel is ahead of us?"

"Yes, I do, unless he stopped to get medical attention for his friend. He's got probably an hour or ninety-minute jump on us."

Nate nodded.

Randy said, "I overhead Axel telling the Blade that he was going to transfer your birds tomorrow to his buyer. He said there was a private jet waiting at the airport to take them to Saudi Arabia. I thought it was just bullshit at first, but I think it's real."

Geronimo added, "So it's tonight or never."

Nate looked down at his right hand and willed his fingers to flex. They didn't. "There's no way I can shoot."

"I don't have that problem," Geronimo said.

———

THIRTY MINUTES LATER, Nate looked up as they passed a logging truck. He'd never seen logs so thick or cut trees as long. The truck reminded him he was in a different world from the Mountain West. A place where trees grew to massive size, the underbrush was thick with ferns and moss, and everything just felt extreme to what he was used to.

Randy sat in the passenger seat, having a monologue with himself. He was more than disillusioned with Axel Soledad. He was disillusioned with his antifa brethren. Hearing Axel go on about the tenets of the movement—abolish the police, abolish capitalism, return all lands to the indigenous people—made him question how realistic any of it was.

"I gotta get my head straight," he confessed to himself.

Then Nate saw the highway sign for Portland International Airport.

"Take that exit," he said to Geronimo.

CHAPTER TWENTY-SEVEN

The Reckoning

JOE WAITED IN BAGGAGE CLAIM AT THE PORTLAND AIRPORT FOR his single piece of luggage to arrive. He loosened up his arms and legs from the stiffness that had set in from the flight. His injuries at the library had been minor, but he had the distinct impression that if he stopped moving for too long, he'd freeze up like a mummy.

It had been the last flight of the night on United Airlines, and most of the passengers from the aircraft had apparently used carry-ons, because there were only two other people at the carousel. One was a seventyish man with long silver hair and small round glasses who wore a tweed jacket. Joe thought of him as "old Portland." The other was a young woman about Sheridan's age with blue hair and elongated earlobe gauges that stretched nearly to her jawbone. She was clutching an overlarge teddy bear and she wore pajama pants and black combat boots. Young Portland.

"Are you from here?" she asked Joe. He could tell by the way she pursed her lips that she already knew the answer.

"Nope. Are you?"

"What do you think?"

"I think you're from here."

The woman smirked and turned toward the luggage belt that had jerked and roared to life.

Joe's piece came out first. It was a long black plastic case with a handle on top. It was obvious what it was: a battered rifle case.

The woman gave him a look of disdain. "What? Are you going bear hunting?"

"*Teddy* bear hunting," he said.

"Very funny."

"Don't worry. Bears aren't in season in Oregon," he said.

"How do you know that?"

"I'm a game warden."

She rolled her eyes and apparently decided to end the exchange. That was fine with Joe. He grasped his case as it came by and turned toward the arrivals area.

As he limped down a long hallway covered with garish green-and-blue carpeting that hurt his eyes, Joe drew out his phone. He sent a quick text to Marybeth telling her he'd arrived in Portland, and another to Nate asking where to meet him.

After a beat, Nate replied: Outside.

Joe felt the cool humid air the second he pushed through the double doors. The air, he observed, was a salty mixture of pine, the Pacific, and engine exhaust. The pickup area was covered by a massive portico to keep visitors dry from the rain.

While he waited, Joe squatted down on the curb and unlocked the fasteners of the gun case. He felt like a backcountry hit man venturing for the first time into the big city. It was unnerving.

He looked up to see Nate's Yarak van approaching and crossing over three empty lanes to pull up next to him. It was obvious that the vehicle had been through some adventures. Joe was well acquainted with bullet holes in cars, because every wreck in Twelve Sleep County was peppered with them.

He was suspicious when he didn't recognize either the driver or the passenger. The man behind the wheel wasn't Nate, but instead a big Black man with a mass of hair. The passenger was a pale, thin guy with ginger hair and a feral look.

The van stopped and the passenger window powered down.

"Joe Pickett?" the driver asked.

"Yup."

"I'm Geronimo Jones. Your buddy Nate is in the back."

He gestured toward Joe's rifle case. "What did you bring with you?"

"My shotgun," Joe said.

From the dark of the back of the van, Nate said, "That's good. He can't hit anything with his pistol, anyway."

Joe rolled his eyes and the driver laughed. It was good to hear Nate's voice.

"Excuse me," the passenger said as he opened his door. "This is as far as I go."

Joe stepped back so the ginger-haired man could exit the vehicle.

"Take care now, Randy," the driver called out after him. "Go home. Get on the straight and narrow. Get a job. Maybe I'll see you around in Denver."

"Maybe," Randy said. He passed by Joe with a furtive glance on his way into the terminal.

The driver patted the passenger seat, indicating for Joe to get in.

Joe did. He grimaced when he saw Nate sitting behind the seats with his back propped against the interior wall.

"How are you doing?" he asked him.

"Oh, just dandy. You?"

"Busy. We took down some Nazis."

"*Damn*," Geronimo said.

Nate grinned his cruel smile. "I wish I could have been there."

"Ah, we didn't need you," Joe lied.

As they crossed the Columbia River into Portland on the six-lane Interstate Bridge, Joe looked out his window. There was more water in view than existed in the whole of Twelve Sleep County, and possibly in the state of Wyoming. The buildings of downtown Portland glistened across the river to his left.

Geronimo briefed him as they drove.

". . . So we've got to find him tonight and get those birds back. By tomorrow they'll be in a jet on the way to the Middle East."

"Are we sure he's here?" Joe asked.

Geronimo brandished Tristan's phone. "We think so. We hope so. We're kind of running on fumes and wishes at this point."

"He's here," Nate stated from the back. His tone held no doubt. Joe believed him. Nate had that ability. His friend knew when bears, wolves, or mountain lions were around. It was uncanny. Axel Soledad fit into that category of predatory beast.

"He's got a guy with him," Geronimo said. "Randy told us the guy is named the Blade and he served with Axel in Special Forces. Axel picked him up outside a prison and they loaded a bunch of guns into their van. I think I shot the motherfucker back in Seattle, but I don't know how badly he's hurt."

Joe nodded. "Have you considered calling the police? Alerting them about Axel's transit van?"

Geronimo chuckled. "What do you think?"

"You're just like Nate," Joe said.

"I take that as a compliment."

Joe tried to track where they were headed, but most of the standard green highway signs were defaced by graffiti. So were the sides of the buildings and fences that flanked the highway. As they descended into the city, he noted tents and crude shelters wherever there was bare ground.

Geronimo took the I-405 South exit onto Couch Street and Burnside. He took a left on Burnside.

Joe couldn't help but marvel at what he saw. Every bank and most businesses were boarded up with plywood. Trash covered the sidewalks and gathered in the corners of buildings. Homeless people slept on the sidewalks and only some of them had sleeping bags.

"Where are we going?" he asked Geronimo.

"North Park Blocks."

AXEL DROVE TWO CIRCUITS around the Benson Hotel on Broadway until he found what he was looking for. Behind the boarded-up hotel was a small square bordered by Burnside, Ankeny, and Southwest Eighth Avenue. The square was open except for two old squat structures set inside it. There was so much graffiti on the walls of the buildings that it was hard to tell they were made of red brick.

A seven-foot chain-link fence had been erected around the square, but it had been mostly ripped down. Piles of trash littered the gravel inside.

Axel backed into the square over the top of the downed fence so the windshield of the van afforded a panoramic view of North Park across Burnside Street. He backed in slowly, aware of the possibility that he might roll over a sleeping homeless man. But he didn't feel the thump of a body beneath his tires.

When the transit van was wedged in the shadows between the two brick buildings, he turned the motor off and killed the lights.

People were starting to gather in the park, just like he'd hoped. There were fewer than thirty of them at the moment, but he could tell by their profiles under the streetlights that they were geared up in black bloc and ready to rumble. Most had backpacks and carried skateboards. They were masked or their faces were hidden by motorcycle helmets.

He said to the Blade, "Looks like there's just a few antifa assholes out at this point, but at least they aren't like those Seattle pussies. Now all we have to do is wait for BLM and the cops to show up."

The Blade responded with a moan. He was bent over double in the passenger seat with his arms wrapped tightly around his belly. Axel could smell blood and viscera. It had been like that all the way from Seattle.

"Hang in there," Axel said. "I'm going to need your help unloading the cache."

"I need a hospital, man. I'm dying."

Axel looked away, disgusted. He firmly believed that only the weak got themselves injured. He'd always thought the Blade had more integrity.

"This is your fight, not mine," the Blade said through clenched teeth.

"Hey, it's *our* fight," Axel said. He reached over and squeezed the Blade's shoulder. "We made this promise to each other, remember? Now it's all coming together."

Axel had looked at his phone as they drove south. The murders in Seattle were blowing up. People were angry that a cop had killed two Black men. Some reports said it was *four* Black men, and they'd been shot execution-style. It was crazy and it was perfect.

"Can you help me unload the guns?" he asked.

The Blade simply moaned.

"Fine," Axel said. "I'll do it myself."

As he climbed out of the van, he thought of four rivers coming together: antifa, BLM, cops, and a cache of loaded firearms located right in the middle of them. All he'd need to do was unload the weapons and announce the geocache location via his Signal app.

He'd headline the post:

FIGHT BACK!

Then he'd drive to the airport so he could be there when his buyers showed up first thing in the morning.

"THERE IT IS," Geronimo said, holding up Tristan's phone as they turned onto Broadway. He turned the screen of the phone toward Joe so Joe could read it.

FIGHT BACK!

Along with a Google Maps graphic that showed the exact location.

"How close are we?" Nate asked from the back.

"Close," Geronimo said.

Joe sat with his shotgun muzzle down on the floorboard between his feet. His stomach roiled and he felt way out of his league. This was an unfamiliar urban hellscape and he'd lost track of directions. Where was north?

He said, "Nate, I'm going to call 911. We need to get the local cops involved."

Nate said to Geronimo, "I told you he was Dudley Do-Right."

"I'm not participating in an ambush," Joe said. "I don't have any authority here. You guys need to think real hard about this. We're just three out-of-state dudes armed to the teeth driving around downtown. I'm not sure we could talk our way out of charges."

Nate said to Joe, "Forget for an hour that you're law enforcement. You're a stranger in a strange land. Roll with it."

"We don't want to blow it when we're so close," Geronimo said.

"Think of the cops as backup," Joe said. "We might need their firepower."

Geronimo shook his head. He wasn't convinced.

"Do what you have to do," Nate said. "But don't screw this up. It's our only chance."

Joe was well aware of that as he punched in 911 on his phone and raised it to his ear. Although he didn't know his way around downtown Portland, and all of the one-way streets they took confused him, he knew they were minutes away from the cache location and Axel Soledad.

"This is the 911 emergency network," said the woman on the other end of the line. "What is your emergency?"

Her tone wasn't as serious or urgent as Joe had expected. She had a distinctive nasally voice.

"I want to report a couple of suspicious men driving an out-of-state van downtown. Colorado plates. We think they're supplying weapons to potential rioters."

"What is your location?"

Joe peered out the window and saw a street sign. It was covered with stickers, but he could make it out.

"Burnside Street," he said.

"We're well aware of the situation developing," the dispatcher said wearily. "There have been many calls."

"It's not just the protesters," Joe said. "Maybe you didn't hear me. We think the men in the van are here to escalate the situation by giving the protesters guns and live ammunition. You've got to send units to stop them now."

"Units are on standby, sir. Order of the mayor."

Joe was poleaxed. "On *standby*?"

"Yes, sir. Welcome to Portland. But thank you for your call, sir. We're carefully monitoring the situation near North Park."

"Then *do* something about it."

"We get these calls every night and—well, it's about manpower. It's frustrating, to say the least."

"People may get hurt, ma'am," Joe said.

"Thank you for calling 911 emergency dispatch."

The call dropped and Joe lowered his phone to his lap.

"You tried," Nate said from the back.

Joe turned to his window with despair as Geronimo cornered the van on a side street. As he did, Joe got a glimpse down an opening between two boarded-up buildings and he saw it: the nose of a black transit van poking out between two brick structures.

"Did you see that?" he asked Geronimo.

"See what?"

"Axel's van. He's right on the other side of these buildings in some kind of alley."

Geronimo turned immediately and raced the wrong way down Burnside.

Joe looked to his left to see knots of antifa gathering under the lights of an open park. He looked to his right to see the small square behind the hotel.

The headlights of the Yarak van swept the square as Geronimo turned in to reveal Axel standing next to it with an armful of long rifles and shotguns.

"That's him," Geronimo bellowed. "You ready?"

Joe nodded, but he wasn't sure he was ready. Ready for what? His mouth was too dry to speak.

Geronimo steered with his left hand while he grasped his shotgun from the console between the seats. Joe reached down to assure himself where the safety was located behind the trigger guard of his Remington Wingmaster, even though he'd been familiar with it for a dozen years.

"Don't hit the van or shoot up my birds," Nate said from the back.

The Yarak van's front tires bounced over the curb into the

square and Joe held on. Geronimo positioned the van to block Axel's vehicle from the front, then slammed on the brakes.

"Go," Geronimo said as he opened his door and jumped out.

Joe looked up to see Axel frozen in place in the headlights, his eyes wide and his mouth slightly parted. He'd been caught by surprise.

Joe bailed out of the passenger side, racking his shotgun as his boots hit the pavement.

Axel still stood there. His eyes narrowed.

Joe said, "Lower the weapons and put your hands behind your head."

In his peripheral vision, Joe saw Geronimo to his left with his triple-barrel shotgun trained on Axel. Geronimo said softly to Joe, "Aim low. He might be wearing body armor."

Axel said, "You don't know who you're messing with."

"Oh, I know."

"Here's your one chance to get back in your vehicle and drive away."

"Where's your friend?" Geronimo asked Axel. Joe was glad he did. He'd forgotten that Axel wasn't alone.

Axel chinned toward his van. "Inside. Dying." He said it with contempt, and Joe felt a chill wash over him.

"Lower the weapons," Joe said.

Axel sighed theatrically. "Oh, all right."

Instead of placing the guns on the pavement, Axel dropped them and they clattered at his feet. In his right hand was a large revolver. He raised it quickly.

There was a massive *BOOM* from behind Joe that made him

duck instinctively. The slug from Nate's .454 caught Axel in his left shoulder and spun him around 360 degrees. Somehow, Axel managed to stay on his feet.

Simultaneously, Joe and Geronimo pulled their triggers. Both had aimed low and the combined blasts blew Axel's knees back the wrong way. He screamed and dropped, his revolver falling from his hand.

Joe ran forward and kicked the gun away. Axel's legs were folded under him in such grotesque angles that Joe had to look away.

Axel starting moaning and his eyes were clenched tight.

Joe looked over his shoulder.

Nate had pulled himself up so he could fire between the frame of the van and the open door.

"Not bad for left-handed," Nate said with a grimace.

Geronimo ran up along the passenger side of the transit van while reloading. He kept low until he reached the door and then rose up with the muzzle pointing inside the cab. After a beat, Geronimo lowered his shotgun.

"His buddy's gone," he said. "Axel let him die."

To THE DISCORDANT SOUNDTRACK of Axel's pitiful moans and the raucous exit of protesters from the park who wanted nothing to do with the firefight, Joe and Geronimo transferred Nate's falcons from the transit to the Yarak van.

While they did it, Joe expected the police to show up any second. It was a justified shooting, but still.

No one came.

Axel continued to moan and writhe on the pavement. Joe felt strangely unmoved, as if he were in the midst of an out-of-body experience. It had been that way since he'd landed.

When they were done, Joe punched up the most recent call on his phone.

"This is the 911 emergency network."

Remarkably, it was the same dispatcher Joe had talked to earlier. He recognized her distinctive voice.

"There are two shooting victims behind the Benson Hotel," he said. "One is dead and the other one will be if there isn't a quick medical response."

"Good," she said after a long pause. She disconnected the call.

GERONIMO ARRIVED at the Sea-Tac Airport in Washington State at three-thirty a.m. and cruised along the curb until he came to a stop outside the terminal entrance. There was very little traffic.

Nate and Joe were booked on the first morning flight to Denver, and then on to Saddlestring. They'd decided to avoid the Portland airport in case an alert had been issued about them.

Joe had booked the flights on his phone while they drove north. He'd used his credit card to purchase the two one-way tickets and he was grateful it had been accepted. Joe wasn't used to spending that kind of money in one place.

That didn't mean he was wealthy. But would he soon be? He didn't know. He'd figure that out when he got home.

"Let's get this guy back to his wife and daughter," Geronimo said to Joe. "I'll deliver the birds to you in Wyoming."

"Just get gone," Nate said to Geronimo through clenched teeth as they helped him out of the van. "Avoid Oregon if you can. They might be looking for this vehicle."

"Which is why we got a rental," Joe said. "Geronimo will exchange your van for a new one no one is looking for. He'll load up your birds and my shotgun and hit the road."

"You were sleeping when we figured out our escape," Geronimo added.

Joe was still coming down from the adrenaline rush of the shootout in Portland, even two and a half hours later. He didn't feel like a game warden. He felt like a criminal or a special operator. Geronimo had been much more lucid during the drive and they'd talked out how the three of them should split up to get away. Joe had the distinct impression Geronimo had done this kind of thing before. Geronimo was tactical and efficient in the mode of special operators like Nate. Had he been one? Joe wanted to know more about his background.

Nate put his arm around Joe's neck, and Joe steered him toward the entrance door, when Nate stopped. He turned toward Geronimo.

"Thank you," he said.

"My pleasure," Geronimo said while tipping an imaginary hat. "Maybe I'll pick up Jacinda on my way to your place in Wyoming."

"I'd like that," Nate said. "So would Liv."

"Who knows," Geronimo said, "maybe I can learn something about child-rearing *and* the bird abatement business."

Nate nodded.

They turned toward the brightly lit departure lobby.

Joe said, "I think I can make it home before the girls all have to hit the road. And I bet you can't wait to see Liv and Kestrel."

"I missed our second Thanksgiving together," Nate said through gritted teeth. "I don't plan to ever miss another one."

"We've got plenty of food left over," Joe said. "Come by with them and have turkey sandwiches. Turkey sandwiches are the best part of Thanksgiving, in my opinion . . ."

"That, my friend, is a good idea."

Supporting each other, Nate and Joe limped toward the glass doors in the early-morning mist.

Acknowledgments

I would like to thank the people who provided help, expertise, and information for this novel.

The Julius Streicher photo album from 1937 Nazi Germany is real. It was handed over to a former local Wyoming library director who asked not to be named here. Nevertheless, to his credit, he wisely found a home for the relic at the Hoover Institution. An online version of it exists here: https://digitalcollections.hoover.org/objects/56022.

Alton More, who allegedly returned home to Wyoming from World War II with Hitler's photo albums, is also real. My thanks to the library director for sharing this intriguing mystery.

Other sources included *Band of Brothers* by Stephen E. Ambrose, *Beyond Band of Brothers* by Major Dick Winters and Colonel Cole C. Kingseed, and *Antifa: The Anti-Fascist Handbook* by Mark Bray.

ACKNOWLEDGMENTS

I also sourced "Nazi Family Values" by David Jacobs at the *Hoover Digest*, "Antifa's American Insurgency" by Andy Ngo in *The Spectator*, and "Roots of Antifa" by Mark Hemingway in RealClear Investigations.

Special kudos to my first readers, Laurie Box, Molly Box, and Roxanne Woods.

A tip of the hat to Molly Box and Prairie Sage Creative for cjbox.net, merchandise design, and social media assistance.

It's a sincere pleasure to work with professionals at Putnam, including the legendary Neil Nyren, Mark Tavani, Ivan Held, Alexis Welby, Ashley McClay, and Katie Grinch.

And thanks once again to my terrific agent and friend, Ann Rittenberg.